A Symphony of Cicadas

A NOVEL

Crissi Langwell

CRISSI LANGWELL

The characters and events in this book are fictitious.
Any similarity to real persons, living or dead, is
coincidental and not intended by the author.

Copyright © 2013 Crissi Langwell

2nd Edition

Image Copyright Oleg Gekman, 2013.
Used under license from Shutterstock.com

ISBN-10: 0989066061
ISBN-13: 978-0-9890660-6-8

This book is also available as an e-book.

Please visit the author's website to find out where it
can be purchased.

www.crissilangwell.com

DEDICATION

To my Grandma Estelle, who is probably watching
over all her grandkids from Heaven

Table of Contents

CRISSI LANGWELL

Prelude

When a moment is so tremendous it knocks the familiar part of the world off balance, you'd think there would be some sort of clue before it happened. Maybe just a hint, or even a premonition that would have allowed me to at least hold my breath until the moment had passed and I could find my footing once again.

But life doesn't work that way.

Life is often unfair. Sometimes things have to hurt, sometimes they're even unbearable, and sometimes the pain is necessary.

I learned this lesson the hard way.

This is my story.

CRISSI LANGWELL

One

I could feel the sunlight against the back of my eyelids trying to ease me out of sleep, but I wasn't ready yet. I was still trying to hang on to the last few strands of a dream where John and I were past the point of planning our wedding and enjoying wedded bliss on our honeymoon. I could almost taste the salt in the air, feel the spray from the ocean, and hear the plaintive questions from seagulls soaring overhead. Opening my eyes would only succeed in ripping me from the light grasp of tropical serenity, throwing me headfirst into the reality that I had only a few weeks until the big day and so much left to do. And I just wasn't ready.

But my valiant efforts to stay embraced in the warmth of my dream were already starting to fail, the details becoming more skeletal by the minute. Reality tapped at my resolve, scattering the seagulls from my ears and replacing them with the sounds of traffic outside our San Francisco apartment. I breathed in the familiar scent of laundry detergent and sweat, the salty sea smell a mere memory as real life glared through the sunrays that streamed through the window of our bedroom.

John moved next to me, murmuring as he rolled over and settled under the blankets once again. I eased my eyes open to get a glimpse of him before it was time to face the day. The pillow had left light lines on his face, standing out against the mostly pepper scruff that left a shadow against his upper lip and cheeks. He moved his jaw while pursing his lips. It had been a year since he had placed an engagement ring on my finger and I had moved in with him, waking up to his face every morning since. It amazed me that it still felt so brand new. I was certain that even after a million mornings had passed us by, when we were in the twilight of our years, this very first vision of the day would continue to feel like a fresh experience.

He was still asleep, but I couldn't help scooting over and positioning my body so that I fit against him like a puzzle piece. He gave a deep sigh of contentment as he woke, wrapping his arm around my shoulders and drawing me closer to him. I nestled happily into his arms.

"Mmm, good morning, Rachel," he said against my ear before brushing his lips against it. The morning stubble of his face grazed my skin, sending shivers through my body.

"Good morning, darling," I whispered. I rested under the weight of his arm, even as my skin grew damp with heat from the closeness of our bodies. Although it was my tendency to prefer a mountain of blankets all year round, the briefest amount of cuddling reduced my body to a melting puddle of sweat. In response to my skin's reaction, John pulled away and traced his finger along my damp skin, making a solitary trail down my spine. I felt him pause at the scar from a suspicious mole I had removed years ago, touching it with curiosity before continuing his explorative journey.

"You're hot," he chuckled. He started to roll away a little more, but I moved with him so that we stayed connected in a spooning position. He laughed, drawing me closer.

"I don't want to get up yet," I complained, pushing my list of things to do out of my head just a little longer in my deliberate procrastination.

"I can see that," John murmured. He proceeded to move again, this time to maneuver on top of me.

"I haven't brushed my teeth yet!" I objected with a laugh. In spite of my halfhearted pleas, the danger of dragon breath didn't stop him from placing light kisses on my lips while positioning inside of me as our bodies woke up together with the gentle movement. I ran my hands across his back, feeling his muscles ripple with each motion. He left a flurry of kisses on my neck, my ears, and my cheeks before settling against my mouth once again. Any lingering worries over morning breath disappeared as our tongues mingled against each other in a sensual promenade of passion. I pulled his hips even closer and felt him groan against me.

Moments like these were a rare occurrence. Most mornings he was awake before I was, out the door to his construction job before I'd even had my first sip of coffee. Two weeks before, he had started a project on the outskirts of the city, building an elaborate home that made our modest apartment look miniscule in comparison. His free time was filled with painstaking work on the house he was building for us across the bridge in San Anselmo. It wouldn't be finished for close to a year, but I could already picture the greenness of the garden in the backyard and the stone path that would lead to our front door.

5

The urgency in John's movements intensified, and I clutched him against me. My breathing mirrored his, moving my belly against him before he pushed back against mine. We didn't hear the first knock on the door. But the second knock was unmistakable, vibrating the pictures that hung on the wall.

"I know you're awake," the muffled voice called from the hallway. "I'm trying to sleep, and between your racket and Joey talking in his headset, it's kind of hard."

John groaned in frustration. The moment was gone as fast as it had come, neither one of us getting to the point of completion before it was over. He rolled away from me and rubbed his eyes.

"You might as well stay up, Sam," John called back to his fourteen year old son. "We have a ton to do in the yard today while Rachel and Joey are shopping."

"Whatever, Dude," Sam replied. "I'm going back to bed. Don't wake me up."

Sam had just come back from his mother's house the night before after two days away. The house was always calmer in those days he was gone, especially for me. While Sam had never claimed he didn't like me or my son, Joey, I was unsure how he felt about our presence in this home, a place that used to hold just him and his dad. I often felt like I was walking on eggshells around him, trying not to offend him in any way. But in truth, I was unsure of what he would deem offensive. He was at a stage in his life when everyone around him was unclear on the concept, and his sole purpose in life was to set them straight. This meant he was often correcting me in a tone that was reminiscent of a parent exasperated with their child. Soon I stopped fighting him on his attitude altogether, keeping my mouth shut and stuffing my growing resentment towards him. But still, I was exhausted by always being in the wrong.

John stood up and pulled on his pants, smiling at me in apology.

"What's your plan for today?" he asked.

"First, to get Joey off his videogames," I said, giving in to the morning as I searched for my robe that lay on the floor beside the bed. "And after breakfast, we're heading out to the bridal shop so I can get him fitted for the wedding. I might take him out to lunch after that, depending on our timing. You?"

"I'll probably let lazy bones sleep for another hour or so, but I have to get the yard at Sara's house prepared for the rehearsal dinner. I'm thinking mums and marigolds would go well in that corner by the birch tree, but you're the expert. What do you think?"

I nodded my head and hummed in agreement, but my mind was already a million miles away. Just the mention of gardening reminded me that I needed to check if my sister had ordered the flowers we needed for a few extra arrangements. Being that Sara and I owned our own flower shop, the indoor wedding would have the feel of being inside a fragrant garden, yet without the San Francisco chill casting its icy breath on us. But if we didn't order them soon, we would be stuck adding carnations and baby's breath in between the lavender and white ranunculus.

I looked at the clock. It was almost eight, proving it wasn't as early as I thought it was. My appointment was at

10:30, and the shop was at least forty-five minutes away from our apartment.

"I better get a move on!" I exclaimed, jumping up while tying the sash on my robe.

I left the bedroom and padded down the hall to Joey's room. From outside the closed door I could hear him loud and clear as he chatted away with whoever else was up at this hour on a Saturday morning to play video games. Even though Sam's door to the right of me was closed, I was sure he could hear every word as well. I knocked on Joey's door. The talking paused for a moment before starting up again. Not wanting to further bother Sam, I chose to just open the door rather than knock again. The door clicked but refused to budge.

"Josiah, open up," I called in a muffled tone against the door. I heard him get up from his bed to open the door. "Since when did you start locking your door?" I asked him, moving past him into the room so I wasn't talking in the hallway.

"Since everyone likes to barge into my room," he pointed out.

He was only a year younger than Sam, but at times his seriousness made him seem years older. If it weren't for his lack of height or his youthful face, it would be hard to tell who was the older of the stepbrothers.

Joey still stood an inch or two shorter than my five foot four, although his shoe size had passed me up years earlier. He looked somewhat like me with his light brown hair and wide amber eyes. But the similarities stopped there. Beyond that, he looked just like his father, a man I hadn't seen in many years, and didn't plan to ever see again.

Tony had stepped out on me when I was still pregnant, visiting just a few times after Joey was born before disappearing altogether. It seems he decided that fatherhood just wasn't for him, something he stated in a letter he sent me weeks after his last visit, explaining that he couldn't handle the responsibility of parenting. At the time, I was grateful for even just a note. That feeling of gratefulness was later traded in for rage at a man who left me to shoulder the responsibility all by myself. However, time proved that things happen for a reason. Had I stayed with Tony, life would have been very different for Joey and me. Because he was out of our lives, I was free to raise Joey in a healthy environment, allowing my family's values to be the primary influence on my son's young life. And, of course, my new path in life led me to John, a man who showed me what love was supposed to feel like.

I began to view Tony for who he was: the man who was meant to create Joey, and nothing more. For that, I would always be thankful for his part in my life.

"Sorry for barging in," I apologized to Joey. "But you didn't answer. Besides, you know you're not supposed to be on the headset until after eight o'clock," I reminded him, citing the rule we had agreed upon to ensure he wasn't waking the house with his early morning videogame play.

"It's after eight now," Joey pointed out, nodding toward the clock that lay on the floor beside his bed. Even upside down I could tell it was only two minutes past eight o'clock.

"Fine, it's eight now. But I know you started playing much earlier than you were supposed to. Sam has already knocked on our door to complain."

"Well, I figured since you guys were already awake, no one would mind," he said. I blushed, ducking my head. Was everyone aware of what John and I had been doing that morning? I was embarrassed that Joey would be scarred by images of his mom in an intimate moment. But when I looked back, his attention was once again diverted by the images on the screen.

"What are you playing, anyway?" I asked him, settling on the edge of the bed. Joey's face lightened at my sudden curiosity in his game, and he moved so we were sitting next to each other.

"It's a game where a bunch of friends and I have to create a world and all that we want in it. Do you want me to show you what we have so far?" he asked. I nodded, amused by his enthusiasm. He went on to take me through the various neighborhoods he'd created in the town, complete with homes that were similar, holding only slight differences to set each home apart from the others. The roads were all in line, embellished along the sides with bushes and trees. Some held a seasonal theme, and I smiled when I saw one street dedicated to Christmas, his favorite holiday. A large lake stood off in the distance, and the screen traveled towards it at lightning speed, revealing the wildlife that surrounded the body of water and a small cabin he had placed next to it.

"This is where I live," he explained, and he opened the door to the home. The inside was bigger than the outside had indicated. The walls were lined with bookshelves, and

I marveled at the detail that included favorite titles of books we had in our real-life home. A large kitchen stood off to the right. From the black and white checkered floors to the kitchen island with copper pans hanging overhead, it appeared similar to the type of kitchen I had always dreamed of having. There was even a picture window overlooking the lake. I glanced at him sideways and he gave me a sly wink. "Hey, I hear things too."

"You'll have to show this to John before he starts working on the kitchen in our new home in San Anselmo," I said in all seriousness.

The center of the house held a large spiral staircase, and Joey led us up to the second floor. We passed through a large room with a fireplace and a huge bathtub behind glass walls before we continued our ascent to the third floor from the staircase. At last we reached the top floor. The outer walls were all glass, allowing a panoramic view of the whole world he and his friends had created in its entire expanse. Close by was the lake, rippling under the electronic sun while mirroring the green of the surrounding hills. The entire town stood off in the distance beyond the serene country. I could almost imagine all the activity that existed in the industrious city he had created. But I was puzzled as to why Joey chose to keep his home separate from the town, placing his house far away instead of in the midst of all the excitement.

"When you're inside the world, you can only see what's right in front of you. But on the edge of the world, you can see everything that's going on in it," he explained.

He began to get lost in tinkering with a few improvements in his virtual home until I reminded him that we had an appointment for him to try on his suit that morning. Joey groaned, ready to give a fight, but I stopped him before he even spoke.

"I'm not going to argue with you. We set this date weeks ago and I let you know about it then. There's only so much time before the wedding, and I'd appreciate it if you would just go along with all these plans instead of fighting me on them. Can you just start getting ready?" He closed his mouth and nodded, placing his game controller on the bed. I snatched it up at once.

"But, Mom! Come on!" he protested.

"I'm not taking it away." I headed out the door to go get myself ready, and called over my shoulder, "I'm just holding on to it as motivation for you to get ready. You can have the controller back when we get home."

With just a few weeks left until the wedding, I was feeling crunched for time. I had snatched up the controllers and high-tailed it away from Joey—now sulking in his room—in an effort to avoid a long and drawn-out argument, and to manipulate him into moving fast. It wasn't the first time I'd resorted to such measures. It seemed as though every one of my thoughts and actions needed to be rushed, to the point where I felt like a million jumbled ideas were electrocuting my brain in tiny shock waves. I just didn't possess the patience for hesitation.

Yet, in the midst of the stress over how much was still left to do in such a short amount of time, I was also aware of my excitement about being married to John in just a few short weeks.

The dress lay hidden in my closet, a size four ivory lace gown with a slender fit past my waist, hugging my hips while flaring out towards the bottom. I had been afraid to try it on when I first saw it at the bridal shop, certain that I needed something to hide the natural curves of motherhood no amount of exercise or diet could reduce. But the gown complimented the curves of my body, reminding me of one of those brides in the magazines who were airbrushed into perfection.

That is, if they used more mature brides to model their wedding gowns.

Being in my mid-thirties, I'd developed a sense of reality about my looks. I wasn't getting any younger. While time had been kind to me, I could still see where gravity was starting to rear its ugly head and how my younger years of sun worship were appearing in fine lines around my eyes. Even a few sparklers were manifesting in my tawny brown hair, resulting in monthly treatments of hair color to hide what I considered premature signs of aging.

But I had accepted that I wasn't going to be one of those child-like brides that showcased their doe-eyed innocence under a veil of white. This was a second marriage for both of us, and we were trading in the naivety we'd possessed the first go-around for a union of equality and mutual respect—and love. I'd take my slightly older appearance any day if it meant I could marry a man who loved me like John did.

And he did love me, caring for me in a way I had never been treated before. From the moment I first laid eyes on him, I knew he was different.

* * * *

He had walked into my flower shop, lost among the cases of roses and lilies behind the glass.

"Can I help you?" I asked him. He stood with his back to me, and I ignored the distinct broadness of his shoulders that tapered down to a slim waist with a shirt tucked into his jeans. Most of my walk-in customers were men, searching for flowers because they were brand new in a relationship and wanted to impress their girl, or because they had messed up and were looking for the quickest way out of the dog house. Working in a profession that catered to already-attached men would have been rather depressing for most single mothers. But I had sworn off men and all their complications years before, and I was more than happy to help a few guys out in the love department. Because of this, I could cater to the most attractive man without stammering under his smoldering gaze.

But I wasn't prepared when John turned around and looked me straight in the eye.

I had never been a believer of love at first sight. Having been burned by Joey's father, I was left jaded and pessimistic that I would ever feel romantic about another man again. Each failed attempt in the dating world only solidified this feeling. But when my eyes met John's, I felt a jolt run through me and had to look away. This was new, this feeling of electricity that traveled from his eyes to mine. My ears felt hot as my cheeks flamed red. For the first time, I felt my tongue twist up in my mouth so that words became an effort in a moment that seemed to last longer than it did in reality. But if he noticed, he was too kind to say so, only continuing his search for whatever blossom arrangement brought him into the store in the first place.

"I'm not really sure what the procedure is," he apologized. He had an inviting face, enhanced by the helplessness in his smile as his gaze darted around the store. His dark chestnut hair held a slight wave in a style just long enough to allow his hands to run though it in frustration. I couldn't help but find this habitual motion of his endearing. At last, his chocolate eyes rested on me with a silent plea for help.

"Well, the first step is to think of the colors she likes to wear," I prompted. "Is she more into light pink hues? Or does she prefer colors that are a bit bolder?" I managed to get the words out breezily, even though they sounded like a squeak inside my head. He shook his head in haste, a pained look on his face.

"No, no," he said. "I'm not getting these for a bouquet. I actually need these for a wedding, the boutonnières for the groomsmen."

"Oh!" I exclaimed, feeling foolish. I wasn't sure why I was letting this get to me, but hearing that the flowers were for his wedding was a shock, as if the distance between having a girlfriend and planning a wedding should make a difference to me. "Congratulations!" I told him, forcing myself back into business-mode, and the reason we were even talking in the first place. "When's the big date?"

"It's this afternoon," he said with nervousness.

"You're getting married today and are just now looking for a boutonnière?" I asked him, my voice rising in disbelief.

"No, I'm not getting married," he said. "My best friend is. And he forgot all about this until now and sent me to pick something out for him." I shook my head, in part from the sheer relief that it wasn't his wedding, but also at the absurdity of finding the right flowers with what I had on hand in the store.

"Why didn't he come in here to get them himself?" I asked him as I took a quick glance at the flowers that lined the walls, searching for some miracle of inspiration. The grim look on his face was washed away with a humorous smirk, revealing the crease in his cheek. I forced myself not to look away this time, even as the heat rose once again to my ears.

"He doesn't want to get in trouble with his fiancée," he grinned. "Apparently he told her it was already taken care of. And then he sent me out to do his dirty work." He took another look around before adding, "The colors are purple and white, if that helps."

The selection I held was rather slim since most of my flowers were ordered ahead of time and spoken for. However, I did have a bouquet of white ranunculus that had just arrived that morning to be used as an inspirational display of alternative wedding bouquets. With nimble fingers, I went to work by clipping one of the large tissued blossoms down to size, adding a sprig of lilac and a few loose leaves, binding it all together and adding a pin to the back.

"Will something like this work?" I asked him, holding the flower up for inspection. The look on his face revealed his approval before he even spoke.

16

"You did that so fast!" he said in amazement, and this time I allowed myself to blush.

"They say it's my job," I teased, placing the flower on the counter and starting on the other boutonnières, giving the groomsmen a simpler white flower in matching contrast to the more elaborate boutonnière of the groom. I gave him a few basic instructions on the care of the flowers so that they'd keep until the ceremony, and then completed the paperwork with the final price.

"I can't thank you enough," he said. "I'd love to repay you in some way." His eyes brightened. "I know! What are you doing tonight? I mean, if you're free. And you're not married," he added quickly. This time it was his turn to be embarrassed, his face taking on the slight shade of peony pink.

"I'm not married," I assured him. "And I'm not doing anything tonight. But are you actually asking me to be your date to *a wedding*?"

"I wouldn't have it any other way. I'm John Hanlon, by the way."

"I'm Rachel Ashby," I said, extending my hand into his.

* * * *

Three years later, I was getting ready to put the finishing touches on our own wedding. That is, if I ever got out of the house on time.

"Joey!" I called. "It's time to leave!"

Two

"I don't even want to go," Joey said, looking toward the line of tall redwoods whipping past us from the passenger window. I sighed, already frustrated with the whole ordeal before it had even started. Just before I thought we could leave the house, Joey had managed to squeeze into the shower at the last second, taking at least 30 minutes until the water was turned off. Then he needed to make his breakfast and decided that slow-cooked oatmeal made a much better meal than a quick bowl of cereal. Now it was past 10:30, the time we were supposed to be there, and I hated to be late.

Just like Joey, I didn't want to go to the bridal shop either. On my list of things to do that day, this was the most dreaded of all of them – especially since it required crossing the bridge to a town I had only visited a handful of times. Despite the fact that the city held hundreds of suit shops that would have been fine, my sister had insisted we go to the same shop she had used for her wedding. The shop was located in rural Fairfax, a small town on the other side of the bridge known more for its bohemian roots than being forward-thinking. It seemed strange to find something as serious as wedding tuxedos in a town that held so much whimsy. But the memory of

Sara's elegant wedding years earlier helped the decision along. I had been impressed with the tailored look of her groomsmen, taking note of the material and sleek lines that made each man look polished and elegant. So I had no reason to disagree when Sara suggested we go through the same shop she'd gone to for the tuxedos. But after weeks of coordinating each groomsman toward the sleepy town rather than a location convenient to all of us, I was beginning to question this decision.

"I'm not thrilled about this taking up our day either, Josiah," I snapped at him, out of patience with his reluctance.

"Then why do we have to go?" he asked, never once looking in my direction. I let out a deep sigh in irritation.

"Sometimes we have to do things we don't want to do. Besides, what big plans did you have for today? It's not like the video games won't be there when you get back." His silence served as his response to my dig. Another day, I would have been bothered by his deliberate quiet, and kept talking until I could get him to agree that this was a much better way to spend his time instead of holed up in his room staring at flashing images across a screen. But I didn't have it in me to further the conversation downhill.

I wasn't quite sure where the shop was, even though I'd already been there several times in the past few months. I had printed out a map before we left this morning, and I fumbled with the pages of directions as we drove the curvy roads.

"Mom, watch out!" Joey suddenly cried, and my attention jerked back up just as a deer was starting across the road. I slammed on the brakes and out of the corner of my eye saw my purse fly forward against the dash and fall at Joey's feet, along with the map that had been lying in my lap. We both lurched forward, and he leaned his hands against the dash to break his fall. I did a quick glance in the rearview mirror and was relieved to see there was no one behind me who might have slammed into the back of my car and pushed us toward the edge of a steep hill. The deer took one look at us and sprinted off into the forest below the windy road, disappearing into the trees that surrounded the tiny road we were on.

"Are you okay?" I asked Joey, giving a slow breath of relief. He nodded, smiling in a gesture of peace. The earlier argument was forgotten, carried away with the wayward deer.

"I'm fine. Want me to hold the map and tell you when to turn?" he asked.

"That would be great," I told him, grateful for his help, as well as the distraction from his earlier resistance. Joey took the map off the floor and turned it right-side in front of him. He traced his finger on it and sighed in frustration.

"Can't we just use the GPS on your cell phone?" he asked as he tried to locate where we were.

"We can't," I sympathized. "There's no cell service this far out in the country. Here, this is where we're at right now." I kept one eye on the road as I pointed toward our general location on the map. Joey peered at where my finger was pointing, and relaxed when he figured out where this road was taking us.

"Ok, go straight," he told me, and I smirked.

"No shit, Sherlock," I said. I could feel him grin next to me as we drove the rest of the way to the shop.

20

The trees began to give way, revealing a small town beyond the forest. Modest, colorful buildings hugged up against each other with little or no space between them. They appeared to be homes remodeled into businesses, complete with front walkways surrounded by lawns. The only thing that set them apart from being living quarters were the whimsical wooden signs that served as enticing sirens meant to draw in customers with their charm. Twirling kites and flags adorned many storefronts, a prelude to storytelling window displays that ranged from vintage to modern scenes. I forgot to hurry as I drove past the shops, struck yet again by the charm of this town, and glad I'd decided to step out of San Francisco for the suits. The shops of Fairfax would have been swallowed up where I lived, their sweet dispositions crushed by the gruffness of a hardened city. As I passed the merchants and the bohemian townspeople walking past in an unrushed manner, I took a mental picture and promised myself that I'd make it back here again someday when I wasn't on a mission with a tight schedule.

The pink bridal shop lay at the end of a cul-de-sac, mannequin brides in powder puff dresses looking out at us with a knowing glance as they stood next to faceless groomsmen. A large cream sign trimmed in pink screamed out 'Darcy's Designs' in a rosy hue, adorned with whimsical butterflies balancing on the letters. Joey looked at me with disdain.

"Really, Mom?" he asked, nodding his head towards the store.

"Really," I told him without apology. "Grin and bear it, kid. It's not like this is going to take forever. She just needs to measure you for the tux."

We both stepped out of the car and into the feminine shop. While I could feel Joey slump down even further from being surrounded by so much lace and frill, I couldn't help but feel a little giddy by our surroundings. Gone was the whimsy of the shop's sign, replaced by a sophisticated air. Bridal gowns, bridesmaid dresses and tuxedos, displayed in colorful themes, gave sketches of all the possibilities that could be put in motion. With brides planning their wedding months in advance, the store's current décor had a summery feel that stood in stark contrast to the wintery weather outside. I felt a pang of regret that we were planning a November wedding instead of getting married on a beach in July. The regret deepened when I saw the delicate lightweight bridal dresses, perfect for walking barefoot across warm sand.

I shook off the moment of disappointment. Our wedding was going to be gorgeous, even if it wasn't underneath a flawless sky on a warm beach. Besides, even in the summer months, San Francisco is not the place for a beach wedding.

"Rachel! How are you!" a blonde woman bubbled as she appeared from the back. Darcy came forward and greeted me with a hug as if we were old friends, even though I never would have remembered her name if it weren't plastered on the front of her store.

"Hi, Darcy!" I said, returning the hug before pulling away. "I'm so sorry we're this late. We were running behind. This is my son, Joey."

"Well, aren't you handsome?" Darcy exclaimed, and I could sense Joey longing to roll his eyes all the way up into his head. Refraining from that was as far as his good manners went, however; in response to Darcy, he just grunted a greeting that didn't include any words. "Don't worry about the timing. It's been a quiet week, and I don't have another appointment until later this afternoon," she told me. "So, how's the wedding planning going?" She beamed with sheer excitement as if she were going to be there, too.

"It's going well, actually," I answered, surprised to realize it was true. "I mean, we're down to those little details that need to be checked off, but I'm surprised that it's not as daunting as I thought it was going to be."

"It's amazing how those long to-do lists in the wedding books look so huge at first, but when you get there it's not so bad, right? You just have to take it a step at a time," she mused. Sensing Joey's discomfort in a store full of frills and lace, she turned towards him and beamed. "Let's get you fitted, shall we?"

Darcy pulled out her measuring tape and went to work. With quick movements, she stretched it out against various areas of Joey's body, taking rapid notes on a notebook that lay at her feet. In just a few moments she was already finished.

"Is that it?" Joey asked, looking at me as if I knew more than Darcy would. I nodded and smiled.

"Thank you, Darcy," I said, turning toward her and extending my hand. She brushed it aside and gave me another warm embrace before turning and doing the same with Joey.

"We'll see you in a couple of weeks!" she exclaimed, and smiled at me. "I bet you can't wait to be standing up there next to all your handsome men!" I was about to respond, but Joey must have sensed another gushing conversation was about to begin, because he pulled at my arm to lead me out of the store.

"Come on Mom, I'm hungry," he said. I glanced at my watch and saw that it was almost noon. My stomach rumbled to remind me that while Joey had enjoyed a full breakfast, I still needed to eat something. I smiled an apology at Darcy, but she shooed us out with a smile.

"Enjoy your lunch! Bye!" she called out as we left. Beside me, Joey gave a sigh of relief.

"That wasn't that bad, now was it?" I asked him. He turned to me in disbelief as we got into the car.

"Are you serious?" he asked. "That was horrible! Please say I don't need to do that ever again."

"Honestly, Josiah. What was so awful about that?" I kept my eyes on the road as we pulled out of the driveway and back through the quaint town. He mumbled something out of the side of his mouth in response that I couldn't quite understand. "What?" His sigh was deep as he shifted in his seat.

"She touched the 'd,'" he mumbled again.

"What? The 'dee'? What the heck are you talking about?" I asked him, confused.

"The 'd,' Mom. The boys. When she was measuring my leg, her hand brushed against it." It suddenly clicked as to what he was talking about. She had touched his penis during her measurements. And while the measurements had taken only a few moments, it must have lasted a lifetime for my teenage son. Judging by the way Joey slumped even lower in his seat, it may even have been an eternity. As I grasped what Joey was telling me, the laughter started bubbling up from deep inside me. I tried my hardest not to laugh, but I was almost crying by the time I gave up and burst out laughing.

"Mom! It's not funny!" he protested.

"I'm sorry," I chuckled, wiping my eyes. "It's totally not." I glanced over at him, and the wide look in his eyes almost sent me over the top. I bit my lip and shook with silent laughter. He couldn't help but smile as I laughed, breaking into a sheepish grin.

"Did you like it?" I couldn't help but ask, and he groaned in response.

"I totally got wood," he said, to which I caved to the hilarity of the situation and burst out into a full-on fit of giggles. Even Joey, despite his red face, grinned as we moved further away from the store.

"See?" I said. "Going to a wedding shop isn't so bad. I mean, you might get felt up by the staff."

"Ugh, Mom. You're so gross. She was like fifty."

"Watch it, buddy. She was younger than I am," I shot back, taking my hand off the wheel to nudge him. He laughed as he ducked out of the way.

"Mom, watch out!" he cried, the terror in his voice breaking the moment without warning.

I jerked my head forward as a semi-truck straddled the yellow line on the windy road, coming straight at us. With no shoulder on the road, there wasn't anywhere to pull over on my right. Instead, the right hand side was bordered by a sheer hill that crowded the road. On the other side of the road was a steep drop carpeted with thousands of trees. I had nowhere to move as the truck barreled towards us, and I weighed out my best chance of survival in a flurry of thoughts that lived within a second. My foot hovered over the brake, but I then saw my chance in the widening space on the other side of the truck. My only hope of survival was if the truck driver understood what I was doing, and moved over to the wrong side of the road to allow me to drive on the left.

I jammed my foot onto the accelerator and gunned it forward, driving over the yellow line and onto the left side of the road. The truck driver blasted his horn as I passed his truck, my tiny car teetering on the edge of the sloped roadway. I breathed a sigh of relief as I sensed the truck making room for me. However, I didn't anticipate the cars behind the truck. An older red car appeared out of nowhere, and I only caught a glimpse of the driver's terrified face before I swerved left to avoid hitting them. All my efforts of staying on the road were for naught as our car sailed over the edge of the roadway, floating towards the sea of green that lay in the forest below.

We were going down.

In between the chaos we'd just left on the road above us and the impact we were headed for on the ground far below, there existed a few silent seconds that became little lifetimes wrapped up in the shifting of tides. As memories and thoughts of John and Sam, my parents and sister, and everything I held close to me fluttered in scattered images behind my vision, I looked at Joey's silent and terrified face. He never made a sound as his eyes met mine. We both knew that this wouldn't have a good outcome. I reached out for him and he took my hand, squeezing it as if my hold would keep him safe. And it felt like I held his hand for years as we waited in the silence for what was going to come next.

"I'm sorry," I mouthed to him, unable to break the silence. He only nodded and squeezed my hand tighter.

There was a loud bang as his hand ripped from mine, and a searing pain electrocuted my body. I could hear a piercing scream inside my head as it rattled through my chest. The wail that escaped my lips drowned out the muffled crunching sounds of the trees colliding with the metal of our car. I grabbed blindly for Joey, no longer able to see anything. But I couldn't find him. The world thundered around me, making up for my loss of sight by flooding my ears with an undecipherable static. My voice was silenced by the eruption of sound, and by the gurgling liquid that invaded my lungs and left a copper vapor in my mouth.

The deafening noises around me began to fade into the distance, and I felt relief at the silence. There was peace within the absence of chaotic sound. The car seemed to have stopped falling, teetering upon what I guessed was a branch or the top of a tree. I couldn't feel my legs, and my hands were starting to go numb as well. It was like they were sleeping, inviting me to go with them as I faded in and out of consciousness.

Somewhere far away, a bird tested out the startled quiet with a soft song. It was soon joined by other calls in the forest. Sensing how alone I was, I focused on the cries that surrounded me, letting them become my faltering heartbeat, my labored breathing, the heaviness in my head.

Their song wove in and out of my senses, echoing in a dance of sounds. They, too, began to fade away. I yearned for the sound to remain in my ears, knowing that once they disappeared I would be on my own. But the sense of peace grew, wrapping my cold body in its layers of warmth. I felt my head grow even heavier against the car seat, the pain in my body evaporating with the sounds. When the last bird had sung, the whole world became quiet.

And I was cast into a sea of nothing.

Three

I sat up with a start in a room bathed with light. I blinked to allow my eyes to adjust to the images around me. I was in a bed, wrapped in a tangle of blankets. The pattern of the cover was familiar, the same loose weaving of lavender flowers and green leaves I had talked John into buying when we first began living with each other.

I was in my own room.

John was sleeping next to me, his back toward me under the heavy mass of blankets. I could only see the top of his head, but felt him stir a little. I unwound myself from the blankets and moved closer to him, spooning him from behind with my arms wrapped around him. I began to place my hand in his, touching my fingertips into the palm of his hand. But he moved his hand just out of my reach.

"I had the strangest dream," I told him. "I dreamed that Joey and I died in a car accident. It was so vivid…it was disturbing." I moved closer to him and brushed my face against his back.

"How are you doing?" he asked, shifting his body to lift his head off the pillow. His back was still to me, but I sensed a deep concern in his voice.

"I'm okay," I answered. "It was just a dream. But it felt so real!" I moved my hand again to place it in his, but he moved his hand away once more. I was confused by this. He felt so far away, almost as if he weren't even there.

I sensed another presence in the room. I sat up again, looking over on John's side of the bed. Sam was next to him, his eyes puffy and red as he lay on his back close to John. He had been crying. I hadn't felt him come in while we slept, and was concerned to see him in tears; I wondered what could be bothering him.

John stroked his son's hair as if he were just a little boy and not a fourteen year old teenager almost as tall as his father, comforting him as Sam kept his eyes up on the ceiling, trying not to cry. His usual look of disdain was replaced by the innocent expression of a distraught child.

"I just," he began, and the tears ran down the sides of his cheeks onto the bed, "I just can't believe they're gone," he whispered.

My hands shook as I tried again and again to touch John's hand only to have him move it away each time. Neither one of them turned toward me, acting as if they were alone and I wasn't even there.

"Who's gone?" I asked, my voice wavering as I tried to remain gentle. Sam only buried his head in his father's chest, both of them shaking as they cried together. "Who's gone?" I demanded. They still didn't respond. I leapt out of bed and slammed my fist against the wall over the headboard, only to have it sink into the drywall as if it were a foamy meringue rather than a solid surface. No sound could be heard from the angry movement. I pulled my hand back and tried again. Nothing. I kicked at the bed and tore at the covers. But all I could grasp before now seemed to slip through my fingers with ease. It made no sense. I could stand on the floor. I wasn't just sinking through the earth or floating off into space. And yet, every motion I made in my panic proved fruitless in contact. I gave up and faced John and Sam.

"Who. Is. Gone," I demanded through clenched teeth, staring straight at them and willing them to answer me. John leaned away from Sam and looked down at him.

"I'm going to miss them, too," he told his son, his voice breaking in sorrow. His face looked about ten years older, the lines more pronounced in the dark circles around his eyes. He hadn't shaved in what looked like a couple of days, and appeared not to have slept either. I knelt down and peered into his face.

"Please look at me," I pleaded with him. "Please tell me what's going on." John sighed and moved onto his back, both of them now staring at the ceiling.

"I still can't believe this happened," he said, choking down a sob as he tried to get beyond the tears. "I keep thinking they're going to walk through the door at any moment, that the police officer was wrong." He fumbled with the covers, taking several deep breaths in and letting them out slowly.

"I never thought yesterday was the last time I'd ever see Rachel or Joey again."

I felt my heart drop in my chest as the room began to fade away. John's and Sam's faces took on an ashen color before they resembled an image off a black and white screen. I could feel a sense of being pulled, my stomach tumbling as if falling in a roller coaster car in a steep decline. I reached out to grab onto something, anything. The room was gone, and all I came up with was air. Looking up, I could see a million stars and galaxies planted above my head in an infinite universe. Floating with nothing to hold onto, I was suspended in this space for only a moment before I was cast back into the world with a flash.

Pine needles crunched below my feet as I crouched down on the forest floor. I could smell the dampness in the air from the morning dew and feel the fog mist against my skin. It calmed me, though a feeling of fear also remained as I tried to get a sense of what was real and what wasn't. My ears pricked at the sound of voices in the distance, and I turned my head towards the trees around me in a search for the source. Men shouted directions at each other, and I could hear the distinct sound of a chainsaw cutting through trees.

"That's it, a little more," a voice said, followed by a crash that echoed through my wooded surroundings. What I couldn't see before appeared right before me. The voices of the men now matched the scene unfolding in front of me as they worked to extract something from a broken car. I recognized my car immediately, even in its crumpled condition. The windows were just shards of glass underneath the crumpled hood of the vehicle, the tires bent in odd directions like broken limbs.

"Did you find the other body?" one of the men asked. I could see flashing lights on the road far above where we all stood, a hazy glow surrounding them through the light fog of the late hour. Several cops with flashlights were making their way down the hill, and I could hear dogs barking in the distance.

"Yeah, they called it in on the walkie about fifteen minutes ago," an older man said, patting the device clipped to his jacket. "Said he was a boy, about twelve or thirteen. I'm willing to bet that's his mother inside the car."

I was both curious and afraid to see who they were referring to inside the car. I stayed planted where I was, now just several yards away from where they worked to pry off the driver's side door; but I kept my eyes trained on the car.

"Were there any others out there?" the younger of the two asked.

"No, I think there were just the two of them."

An emergency team joined them, and I could see them lifting a body out of the vehicle and onto a gurney. I only saw the battered skin on the woman's arm as they zipped up the body bag, relieved that I couldn't see her face hidden under a mass of tangled hair. But before the bag was closed altogether, I caught the unmistakable glint of the ring on her finger, recognizing the modest diamond on a band John had presented to me almost exactly a year before the day I left the world.

As if in recognition, my own body responded to what I had seen, taking on the horrific reality of my earthly body. Wounds and shards of glass appeared on my arms, traveling up to my shoulders. I fell to the ground out of instinct as my legs splintered and twisted in different directions. I couldn't see my face, but I could feel the warm blood dripping from my matted hair down my forehead and the blood filling my lungs with a sickening taste of copper.

"Help me," I gurgled, and my body was healed in an instant. It was as if it had never happened. I lay there shaking, past the pain of being broken and afraid that it would happen once again. But my skin remained unblemished against the muddy ground of the forest. I wondered how Joey was doing, if he were as confused about all this as I was. And that's when it hit me.

Joey. Where was Joey?

Four

I leaned up on my elbow, a slow panic growing inside me. I turned my head to look around. The gnarled trunks of trees surrounded me in all directions. I was alone, trapped within my forested cell under a canopy of pine that reached up into the fog. I didn't know where to go or what to do. The workers and the broken car had vanished; it was unclear whether they had evaporated into the forest or had simply gone without my noticing. The only sounds were a few distant birds and the stirring in the creaking trees around me. Even the insects had ceased their buzzing where I sat. I was left with an eerie silence that covered me like a protective bubble, keeping me separate from the world I was no longer a part of.

"Joey!" I called out. The word hung in front of me, trembling in the air but traveling no further than the space around me. "Joey!" I tried again, only to have my voice swallowed by the thick atmosphere surrounding my presence. I took a deep breath and screamed his name once more, using all of my power to force his name to travel with the wind, hoping it would reach his ears.

"JOEY!"

I could sense a sudden release in pressure as my voice shattered whatever was separating me from the rest of the forest. I was joined by a thousand cicadas, casting their deafening mating call in the trees as they, too, screamed for someone they loved. A flurry of birds broke out of the trees, creating a dark cloud in the sky. With each gust of wind, the cloud of birds above the forest rippled and shifted in shape, soaring and dipping through the sky in an ebony wave. I watched as the mass swirled above me. It was like a ghostly presence, the haunting movements of the birds growing and shrinking, becoming small before expanding to a large fog. The cloud above the forest grew darker and darker, pulsing in a hypnotic beat as if part of a dance. The hum of the cicadas around me mirrored the movements, keeping time with an urgency that ebbed and flowed.

I got to my feet, moving with care not to disturb the dance going on around me. I wasn't sure what was happening. It was clear that I had affected the forest in some way, but I didn't know why or how. All I knew was that the increasing energy that surrounded me was mirrored within me. I could almost sense the thought of every living creature reliving the scene around me. I lifted my arms out to my sides, closing my eyes to feel the rhythm going straight through me. The vibrations only got more intense as I submitted myself to the energy. Could they understand me? Could they maybe help me find Joey?

"Where's Joey?" I whispered. The sound of my voice sent a murmuring surge through the hum, reaching the skies with a shiver that rippled outward and then inward again before being handed back to the singing cicadas that surrounded me.

My mind was flooded with a million images and sounds in one instant, a static electricity that blinked rapid visions of the forest, the sky, the sound - everything that was happening right in this moment from copious points of view. Every thought included a small glimmer of light that shone around where I stood, wavering with a comforting brilliance.

I gasped when Joey's body appeared on the forest floor, the thoughts around me zeroing in on him like a kaleidoscope before focusing on him as a single image in the exact spot I was standing. I reached my hand out to touch him, forgetting that he was just a thought and nothing more. His body was bruised and cut up beyond repair, though the peaceful expression on his battered face gave the impression that he was sleeping. The image of his broken body sent a shock of pain through my chest as I saw my child hurt beyond repair. To keep from unraveling, I focused on his halcyon expression, willing him to open his eyes and see me, too. Instead, a small spark of light, the same light that had been sent to me earlier, emerged from his forehead and hovered just above him. His body and the encompassing forest glowed under the small glimmer of light, the glow adding a haunting beauty to the entire scene. I held my breath. The light grew in intensity, showering the surrounding area in a bath of white, swallowing it all with its blinding brilliance. And just as sudden as it gained strength, the light dimmed again. Joey's body appeared once more under the weakened glow from the light, but my focus was on the dying ember hovering above him. It gradually faded altogether, evaporating into thin air, leaving Joey's body abandoned on the forest floor.

Peering into Joey's face, I was taken aback by how unrecognizable he was. Even though it was still the image of the boy I had raised with all my heart for thirteen years, he looked more like a stranger than my son. Tears streamed down my cheeks as this image also faded, the thoughts scattering like leaves in the wind.

"But where is he?" I pleaded in a whisper, afraid to amplify my voice any louder under the quiet murmur around me. There was no answer this time, only the steady hum of a symphony of cicadas, singing the same song that had been sung now for hours. "Please," I said, "just show me where I can find him." The cicadas continued to ignore me, their hum growing quieter as they went about their business. But I was desperate to get an answer, feeling wild in my resolve. "Was he the light?" I begged of them. "Is the light still here? Is that what you're trying to tell me?"

It was no use. The hum continued to waver, losing the amplified energy that we'd been drawing from each other before as the sounds of the forest began to take on a more natural resonance. Fearful this was the last chance I had of finding my son, I took a deep breath and threw my arms out wide.

"Where's Joey?!" I screamed at the birds, the insects, the forest. I used all my force, doing my damnedest to ensure I wasn't going to be left without an answer. A resonating crack thundered nearby, and I jumped at the sound. The trees were blown around by a violent wind that burst through the forest, whipping through my hair before crashing into the trees with great force. The crack sounded again, this time right above me. I moved just in time as a branch splintered from the tree, crashing through the branches below it before landing at my feet.

The birds burst away from the sky, the cloud they had formed now divided into a million pieces of vaporing ash. As they scattered, the afternoon clouds moved aside to offer a glimpse into the universe. I watched as the millions of stars within this window of space increased in brightness, revealing the planets and their moons, soaring meteors, and swirling galaxies billions of light years away. I stood mesmerized by this mystical image, for the moment forgetting the storm that was brewing around me. But the clouds moved back into place, concealing the heavens with their angry darkness.

A bolt of lightning crackled from the sky, landing its brilliant tip at my feet with an electrifying sizzle. It sent me to my knees in fear. Flames materialized upon the pine-needle-covered ground, licking at my skin without burning me. The fire grew larger and larger, surrounding me as it tore at the trees around me. I whipped off my sweater and swung at the fire, trying to keep it from spreading through the whole forest. If I didn't concentrate on the branch of the tree, my sweater sank through it without even touching the bark. But when I focused all my energy on making a connection with the tree, I managed to hit it with a satisfying blow. Unfortunately, the process of trial and error as I re-learned how to do simple tasks left my firefighting skills ineffective. Every time I managed to get one flame out, several more would start up around me.

Soon I was engulfed in flames. And while it didn't burn my body, I still felt the intense heat from the fire against my spiritual skin, and the sting of the heat in my ghostly lungs as I panted from the effort I was making. It felt like hours had passed when I fell to the ground and gave in as the fire closed around me and devoured the trees that once held thousands of humming cicadas.

In its final gesture, the sky broke, sending large drops of water from the black clouds above. It started out as gentle taps that landed with a sizzle on the fiery ground. And then it picked up with gradual speed until it was a torrential downpour. The water waged a war against the flames, coming in like white stallions that trampled the flames into a quivering death. Soon the forest was reduced to a blackened and soggy skeleton of smoldering stumps and ash. I lay in a protective ball in the middle of it all, curled up in a fetal position to protect myself from any further attack from the elements.

I couldn't understand what was going on. It was unclear how long I had been here, how long the forest had been raging against my presence. It seemed like time was more of a suggestion than a rule. It could have been hours, or even days.

And what of this place I was in? Was I the only one? Did we all have separate worlds to occupy when our human lives had passed and we found ourselves in the afterlife? Is that why my son wasn't anywhere to be seen in the place where we both died?

And what made the lightning bolt start the fire? Or the rain that put it out? Was it me? Was it God? It felt strange to wonder that, given I wasn't even sure there was a God. But with everything I had just been through, believing there might be a God seemed like the least complicated of all answers – an ironic revelation since the idea of God seemed so complicated while I was still alive.

The wind slowed to a cool breeze, the rain subsiding to a light mist that brushed against my skin. I held my hands at the base of my neck, the way we had been taught as children during earthquake drills - as if our tiny hands could withstand the crushing blow from a falling ceiling. My hair was matted from the rain and charred pine needles, my clothes full of dirt and ash. I moved my arms underneath me and hoisted myself into a seated position, hugging my knees against me. The clothes I was wearing were the same ones I had worn to the bridal shop; a time that felt like a thousand years before. They were the remains of a nice blouse over a pair of what used to be white pants; not the kind of clothes meant to withstand a car crash and wild fire. At this point I was no longer wearing shoes. I didn't know where I'd lost them, but it didn't seem to matter. The jagged rocks and pointed pine needles I walked on weren't noticed at all as if my feet were calloused from years of walking barefoot. Pain wasn't an easy thing to come by in this world, and yet I welcomed the way it made me feel somewhat human in those brief twinges. Even the terrifying heat from the fire had felt somewhat energizing.

But now I had nowhere to turn. I couldn't understand the point of this, why I was here, where my son was...I was tired of being stuck in this world hidden within the only one I had ever known. I no longer wanted to be alone. I wanted answers to all of the questions I had burning inside of me with no one to ask. But most of all, I missed the sound of someone speaking to me, and hearing me when I spoke back to them.

"Well, you've really created quite the spectacle," a voice said next to me, almost making me jump out of my skin. "Are you done with your tantrum yet?"

Five

I scrambled to my feet and whipped around to meet the face behind the voice.

"Aunt Rose?" I stammered.

I had been ten when she had passed away. She was my mother's aunt, and no longer young when she had succumbed to an illness that had made her weak and frail. But before that, she'd been a vibrant part of our family, encouraging my sister and me to take risks that our parents would never dream of. It was Rose who encouraged me to balance on top of the playground equipment blocks from her house, cheering me on as I shuffled with fear on the tiny beam that stood eight feet above the sand, and applauding when I was successful in making it to the other end. She let me roller skate across the wood floors of her house, ignoring the scuff marks I left behind with my clumsy feet. Her large smocks became the costume wardrobe for Sara and me when we performed plays and musicals in the front yard. We'd try on her large-brimmed Easter bonnets, giggle as we slipped on her large bras over our dresses, teeter along in her heels, and spin around in satin sleepwear that became the magnificent ball gown of a princess within our fantasy-fueled imaginations.

Rose would let us jump on her bed, a sharp contrast from our father's reaction, which would be a swift spanking across a bare bottom. At night, she'd let us sleep in the large bed cozy with quilts, giving us the best room of the house while she slept on the couch. Breakfasts were always feasts of waffles or pancakes, bacon and eggs, or the sugary cereals our parents denied us. She always listened to us with great interest, feeding off the stories we pulled from thin air over a slice of apple pie with blackened crust. We were never treated like little kids, even in our constant barrage of questions and tireless demands for entertainment. At her house, we were treated as honored guests.

One of her rooms held a vast array of paints and canvases. She'd often have a fresh canvas waiting for us, having painted over it with white to give us a clean start on a new creation. While Sara and I would mash the paintbrush against the canvas with hurried and messy strokes, Rose would apply color with delicate precision on her own board beside us. She would soon transform her blank canvas into a mountain against an endless sky, a mysterious cave with wonders unseen, or even a green and blue wave ready to curl out of the canvas and lick the floor at our feet. The colors melted into each other with unfailing detail, and we could almost hear the ocean's call if we looked deep enough into where the green faded into the reflection of an unseen setting sun. She'd paint clouds that rolled over waving fields of wheat, the movement from the wind coming to life with glints of gold and brown in the valley that expanded beyond the painting. Sometimes she'd even paint pictures of us, capturing our likeness on the board while we slapped paint on our own canvases. Those she never painted over, but kept in a room she called her office despite her retirement many years earlier.

Standing before me now, Aunt Rose was just as I remembered her. That is, before the sickness had taken hold and stolen the soft roundness of her features, and ultimately her life. Her long white hair was piled into a loose bun on top of her head. The creaminess of her fair skin was interrupted only by the rosiness of her cheeks and twinkling blueberry eyes. Her laugh lines and crow's feet still lit up the roadmap of her kind expression, yet her face appeared more vibrant and youthful under its mature appearance. Her short and plump body was clothed in her usual painting smock over a pair of flowing pants, and she held a paintbrush in her right hand. I was so relieved to see someone familiar that I rushed over to embrace her, almost knocking her off her feet. It surprised both of us when I burst into tears, and I buried my face into her neck to try and stop the watery flow of emotion.

"Oh, my dear," Rose crooned. "There, there. It's all going to be okay." She pet my hair as I shook, her compassion opening the floodgates. Free to let my guard down, I stopped fighting against my fear and sadness, and allowed myself a good, ugly cry on her shoulder. She didn't try to stop me, only murmured comforting words while I let out all that had been bottled up since the moment I found myself in this new existence.

When I was able to come up for halting breaths of air, I pulled away and swiped at the tears in my eyes. She offered me the hem of her smock as if I were a little child. I was grateful and wiped my face on it, rubbing at my nose with an embarrassed chuckle.

"Now then, feel better, darling? You've had a rough time of it, haven't you?" she asked. I nodded, my momentary good cheer replaced by sullenness as I fed off her maternal sympathy. "Well, let me get a look at you." She stepped back and nodded in approval. "Oh darling, you are a vision!" she exclaimed. "You've become quite the young lady, haven't you?" I looked down at my body, taking in the damage from the crash and the fire, touching my matted hair with my hand to try and smooth out the tangles.

"Oh, Aunt Rose, I'm a mess," I said. "And I'm not so young anymore, I'm thirty-five."

"Posh," she countered, taking my hand in hers to stop me from smoothing my hair. "You're only a baby. Thirty-five? Darling, you've hardly lived!"

She took her paintbrush and smoothed it at my hair, brushing it with gentle strokes before moving to my clothes. I touched my hair once again, surprised at its sudden softness, looking at the ends of the golden brown fullness it now possessed. I watched as she transformed my torn clothing into a light blue sundress that fit me snug just above my waist before falling around my hips. On my feet she painted a pair of gold-colored sandals that wrapped around my ankles and calves like those of a Roman goddess.

"I'll have to teach you how to do a better job of healing yourself," she said with sympathy as she stroked my skin with the brush, all the cuts and bruises disappearing under her touch. Then she stepped back to admire her work, letting out a low whistle. "Oh darling, you're what they'd call a knockout!" she exclaimed.

I giggled with both pride and shyness, checking out her handiwork. Holding my hands out and noticing all the details she'd created with a mere flick of her brush, I couldn't help but agree with her assessment. My skin glowed under the morning sun, glistening as if still damp from the rains. I could feel my hair brushing across my back, and I shook my head to feel the new fullness. My nails were shaped in pink and white half-moon crescents, a far cry from the blackened stubs they had been just moments earlier. My feet were no longer covered in mud, caressed now by the new sandals that protected them from the elements. I felt beautiful, appreciating my new form with vanity, admiring the perfection it had become.

"Oh, thank you, Aunt Rose," I said, throwing my arms around her once again. "You've made me beautiful." She laughed and shook her head.

"Darling, you did that on your own. I just revealed it for you," she told me, tapping her brush against my forehead.

"But the brush," I said. "You did something magic with it!"

"No darling, this brush has no magic in it at all." She handed it to me for proof, and I swiped at the air only to have nothing happen. "Rachel, the magic is nothing more than our spirit released from our earthly bodies. We've had this power all along, even when we were alive. But being human has its limitations. However, when our spirit is unleashed from our bodies, the power we possess becomes unharnessed. You are capable of so much, you don't even realize it." She looked around at the tree stumps and blackened ground. "Well, maybe you have a

47

hint," she laughed. She took back her paintbrush and began painting small strokes against the ground. Tiny blades of grass and fern emerged from her paintbrush, multiplying across the darkened area in a gradual wave of green. "There now, that's a start," she said. She looked at me with eyebrows raised, smiling a small, meaningful smile. "The end of life is really just a new beginning."

"I don't understand," I admitted, leaning down to touch the new growth peeking out of the ashes. "You say your brush isn't magic, and yet you use it as a wand."

"Oh sweetie, I forget how human your thoughts still are. First off, there's no such thing as magic. Nothing I'm doing is magical at all, but only a part of the spirit. My spirit, your spirit, the spirit in the trees, the ground, the sky, and even these blades of grass...we are all pieces of the same source of energy. The lightning was a result of the energy being pulled from your spirit. The rain, that was you, too. Cleaning you up was a result of my spirit talking with your spirit. And this new life," she said, gesturing to the greenery scattered around us, "it was there the whole time. I just helped it along by combining my energy with the energy of the forest."

"But the wand, er, paintbrush?" I asked again. "You keep using it, even though you claim it's not magic. Surely it's helping you with all this," I argued, waving my hand to indicate the greenery that peeked out from the ashes. Rose laughed, sticking the end of the brush through the bun on the top of her head to free her hands.

"The brush only makes me feel like all this is my canvas and I am but a painter," she said. To emphasize, she placed her hand in front of her and moved it across the

48

scene of the forest in one slow motion. The ash was soon covered by a thick blanket of green. Small buds pushed through the ground, unfurling to reveal leafy, vibrant ferns that reached out in all directions. The charred wood of the fallen trees was soon hidden under a spongy moss, as if the trees had fallen years before. The smell of smoke disappeared under the damp smell of rain; a carpet of baby's tears covering a fresh layer of dirt. Soon there was no sign that there had ever been a fire, the garden of green around me so plush I felt I could just lay in it forever.

"I still don't understand," I told her, running my hands over the ferns that surrounded us.

"Oh darling, I know. I don't expect you to yet. But it will all make sense soon," she promised.

I wanted to be satisfied with this answer. I tried to let it be at that, afraid that all of my questions would eat at her hospitality and cause her to lose her patience. Yet, I was burning inside with so much that still didn't add up.

"All this is lovely," I told her. "But what if a person had been close by while you were creating this? I know I never saw anything supernatural like this happen while I was alive. But it doesn't seem out of the realm of possibility for someone to have come upon us while you, or rather your spirit, was drawing all of this out. How do you keep anyone from seeing this happen?"

"I don't," she said. "Our vision and the vision of humans are completely different things. Basically, they're seeing things occur much slower than what we're seeing." Her eyes twinkled at my obvious bewilderment. "Time is a much different thing when you're alive than it is in the afterlife," she explained. "As a human, you exist on a string of time."

She took the paintbrush out of her hair and drew a thin line in the dirt. Using her brush as a pointer, she went on.

"There's a beginning, a middle, and an end. Everyone's string is a different length; some shorter, some longer. You can't move backwards or up and down. The only way to move is forward." She then drew a circle in the dirt around the line before filling it in so the line no longer existed. "When your spirit is free of your body, you are able to experience time much closer to how our source of energy experiences time. It still exists, but it's not on a string. Instead, we're able to go as fast or as slow as we want, jumping from moment to moment in the blink of an eye. You can move forward, backward, side to side. The possibilities are endless."

Rose reached over and picked a berry from a nearby bush and held it up.

"The reason is because all of this is happening at once, with no point of beginning or end, not even a middle. There is no yesterday or tomorrow. The past is now. The future is now."

She smiled and took my hand.

"But that's a pretty heavy concept that even we can't fully grasp until we are reunited with our source of energy. So for now, we can just hop from one moment to the next."

"So, can we control where we land?" I asked her. "I mean, would it be possible to say 'take me to 1953,' and then just end up there?"

"We're not time machines," she chuckled. "But yes and no. If you can feel it, you can be there."

"What if I envision a person? Can I be close to them?" I asked, not even trying to hide the hopefulness in the question. I was still troubled over where Joey might be, even more so after seeing the vision the cicadas had given me of his broken body and the hovering light that disappeared with as much mystery as it appeared. But a different urgency was building inside me as I grew more comfortable in my new existence. I could feel my heart torn at the thought that I'd never see John again, feel his embrace, or even just see myself through his eyes when he looked my way.

I could see Rose's eyes cloud over, a concerned look appearing on her face.

"Darling, I wouldn't get too attached to those who are still alive," she cautioned, as if she could read my mind. "It would be best if you just let them be and moved on. I know there are people you love and miss terribly. But staying for them will only keep you from the greatest happiness you could ever experience, and leave you stuck in an internal prison of unnatural pain, never letting up until you learn to let go."

She held my hands and squeezed them so tight it caught me off guard. Her hold loosened only when I tried to pull away. She looked away for a second, and then gave me an embarrassed smile. "Rachel, please just trust me on this."

"Why are you telling me this, Aunt Rose?" I asked her, irritated about this limitation she was placing on me. "I mean, you're here, aren't you? And you're fine, right?"

"Rachel, I would give anything to be free from this divide."

"But who are you waiting for?" I implored her. "What's causing you to be stuck here?"

"Don't you know, darling? I've stayed for you and Sara."

I was flooded with sudden emotion, the reality of how much Aunt Rose had loved us becoming apparent with her sacrifice of happiness for us. I thought of the past twenty-five years, when her memory had come to me out of nowhere, providing me with a sense of comfort in times when I felt the most alone. I wondered if it was in those times she had been near me, watching me from another reality while trapping herself in a world she couldn't escape. She'd had no children in her lifetime, showering Sara and me with a love she would probably have reserved for her own children had she become a mother. And just as she had in her life, Aunt Rose had spent the last two and a half decades loving my sister and me while watching over us. I realized that even though she had died, she'd never left at all. The comfort that she gave me only intensified my desire to be close to John, to make sure he was okay before I left him alone forever.

But the realization that Rose had given up her freedom in her watch over my sister and me hadn't escaped me. I turned to her and took her hand in mine.

"I'm here now," I told her. "You don't have to wait anymore. And Sara is fine too. She's married and has children, and she's living a wonderful life. You're free to move on."

"You don't understand," she responded, her voice faltering. "It's not that easy."

"But I don't get it, Aunt Rose. You even said time doesn't exist here. So couldn't you get to the time when both of us are past our human lives and then move on to wherever it is we're supposed to move on to?"

"Don't you think I've tried that?" she emphasized. "I've tried everything I could to..." She winced, stopping herself mid-sentence as she wiped her hand across her forehead. "Let's just say that I have to move past this on my own to be able to free myself. Wishing for anything else only results in tragedy."

"Tragedy? Just for wishing we could be with you?" I asked her.

And that's when it hit me. Aunt Rose had said the way to be close to someone or a certain time, we were to feel it in every fiber of our being. While Rose had wanted to move on and be free, she was unable to because she loved me too much. I looked at her in alarm, my eyes burning as they searched over her panicked face.

"I'm so sorry, Rachel. I didn't mean for this to happen," she pleaded. "I didn't know!"

"You killed me?" I whispered. "You killed me, and you killed my son?"

"I didn't know this would happen!" she pleaded. "You were so happy, planning your wedding and about to start a new life. I couldn't have wished for a better happiness for you."

"Then why, Aunt Rose? Why couldn't you just let me be? Why couldn't you let me marry John and be happy?"

"I was jealous!" she burst out, her voice rising in her desperation.

Clouds began to cover the sky once more, sending a light drizzle that moistened my hair and clothing. But I didn't even feel the rain on my heated skin, seething from anger and confusion that Rose had taken away everything I had ever loved because of her own selfish needs.

"I couldn't be there," she pressed on. "You were planning this lovely ceremony, marrying a man who was absolutely wonderful to you and to your son. And all I wanted was to be able to be there with you, to hug you and congratulate you on your marriage. I wanted to help you plan all the details and give you advice." Rose's expression was bleak. "You are like a daughter to me, and it pained me that I couldn't be there with you."

"You are not my mother!" I shot at her, finding a sense of satisfaction in the anguish on her face. "You had no right, no right at all. I was happy!"

"Darling, I didn't know," she whispered. "It was a moment of weakness I wish I could take back."

I sank to my knees, realizing that my entire life had ended on the wish of one spirit. I felt more powerless than ever.

"How did you do it?" I whispered.

Rose sat down next to me. She reached for my hand, but I pulled it away from her grasp. Sighing, she placed her hands in her lap.

"You had just finished getting Joey fitted in his suit for your wedding. I was there with you, laughing along with you over Joey's awkward moment." In spite of myself, I couldn't help but smile at the memory of Joey describing his horrendous measurement experience. "You both were so casual with each other, so open and honest. And I felt this pang of jealousy. I had never experienced that kind of joy, never having had children of my own. I mean, I had you and Sara. And you both became my whole world. But at the end of every visit, you went home with your parents, and I was left alone in my own house. When I died, I stayed by you and Sara, loving you as if you were my own children. But something happens to you in this existence. Feelings are more intense, more powerful than anything you have ever experienced in your human life. I became your protector, almost like your guardian angel. I was limited in my physical involvement in your life, but wherever I could place my guidance over you, I did."

She took a deep breath before continuing. I kept quiet, holding down my simmering anger, afraid that if I spoke I wouldn't find out the whole truth.

"But the reality is, Rachel, a barrier still existed between you and me. You were living, I was dead. You weren't my child. I am not God. No matter how I tried to get close to you, you were always just out of my reach."

I was reminded of my first glimpse of John right after I died, how I tried to take hold of his hand only to have him draw away, how much it hurt to look at him and have him not see me. Tears sprang to my eyes as I remembered pounding on the bed and the wall in desperation to get his attention only to be shut out.

"When you and your son were driving home, that feeling of longing intensified itself into something much deeper than I had ever experienced. When it's happened before, I've managed to walk away until it settled into something more tolerable. But this time, I just wanted to see what would happen if I allowed myself to experience it. It grew into something so big, I could no longer control it. The truck driver changed course, heading straight for you, and I tried to stop it from happening. But by then it was too late. The plan was set in motion and I had no power over it."

"But Joey," I whimpered. "He didn't have to die!" The tears streamed down my cheeks.

"I didn't know this would happen!" Rose pleaded with me. "I never wanted you to die. I certainly didn't want Joey's life to end so soon. If I could take it back—"

"But you can't!" I exclaimed, jumping to my feet. "As a result, my son will never experience human life beyond the age of thirteen. He'll never know what a first kiss feels like, or deep and true love, or what it's like to be a father. John is left to pick up all the pieces, to plan a funeral for both me and my son when we should be planning our wedding! You've stolen so much from so many people. How could you?!"

"Darling," she began, but I interrupted.

"I am not your darling!"

The muscles on her face twitched with the deep sorrow she was trying to control. "Rachel, I'm sorry."

"That doesn't make it better!" I shouted at her. "This is all your fault. I'm stuck here in this forest, my broken body in some morgue by now, and I can't even find my son. Where is he? Where is Joey?"

"I don't know," she admitted. "He's in his own reality. And he's safe, I assure you. We all are. But you won't see him until it's time."

56

"There's no such thing as time!" I shouted.

"It's complicated darl... Rachel," she said.

I was overwhelmed with rage in an instant. I was angrier than I had ever been in my life. But even more than that, I longed to see John again, to be comforted by his presence and to make sure he was okay. The surrounding forest began to fade, the colors turning to muted tones behind Rose as they all began to evaporate.

"Don't go," she begged me, her fear and sadness sending another chill of anger through me. "Stay with me, Rachel!" If she said anything else, I couldn't hear it. Rose, the forest, the cicadas and the drizzling rain all disappeared into a cloud of emptiness, leaving me suspended in space before tearing me with a lurch into a new reality.

Six

"It was a lovely service," my mother told my father through her tears, her hand resting on his arm. "They would have loved it."

I stood near them, hiding behind the doorway of my parents' kitchen even though they couldn't see me. My father looked older than his sixty-eight years, his eyes burning holes into the ground while my mother, the eternal hostess, checked in with him before flitting around the house once more to meet everyone's needs.

My parent's home was not known for holding so many at one time. Now it was brimming with dozens of people I had known at one point or another in my life. My son's teacher sat on the couch, dabbing her eyes every now and then in between bites of a sandwich made from a croissant. A few of Joey's classmates stood in the corner, looking out of place and uncomfortable in a room filled with grownups and few other teenagers. One girl sat bawling in a chair, her friend comforting her as best as she could. The boys, however, kept solemn looks on their face. They seemed afraid to do more than just stand there in silent and awkward observation lest they end up like the crying girl. I had a feeling that Joey would have been amused by the whole scene.

A few of my regular customers from the flower shop chatted among each other, reaching out to my sister from time to time to offer their condolences or a memory they had of me. I listened with amusement as a restaurant owner I had deemed difficult to work with described me to Sara as someone who understood the fine art of customer service and always went above and beyond to meet his needs.

"I still think you were a pain in the ass to work with," I said out loud, amused at how my voice carried over the din of conversation and no one could hear me. "And your food sucked, too."

Sara stayed silent for the most part, smiling as if on cue when someone would speak to her. But for the most part, she kept a quiet front. Her husband, Kevin, sat near their two daughters on the couch. My eyes welled up as I watched the young girls eating from a shared plate of fruit, both wearing the special dresses Sara had chosen for them to wear to the wedding. Megan, the older of the two at five years old, wore the flower girl dress we had picked out months ago. The only thing setting it apart from that of a wedding dress was the baby blue sash she now had tied around the waist of the white gown. Her two-year-old sister, Lily, wore a dress in the same color blue as Megan's sash, splayed out over a pair of ruffled underpants. I would never get to hold them again, hear them giggle as they called me 'Anchel,' a name that stuck as a family joke when Lily dubbed that much easier to say than 'Aunt Rachel.' I wouldn't be there as an escape from their parents in their teenage years, to offer them advice when they felt no one understood. I wiped away the tears from my eyes, realizing that there were many firsts they would experience, and I was no longer going to be a part of any of them.

"Oh, Rachel," Sara whispered. She was now across the room, sitting far away from everyone on a couch in the corner, hiding her head in her hands and trying to make herself invisible. "Why did this have to happen? And why Joey? He was so young. I just don't get it."

I wanted to comfort her, but felt so limited. I tried to put my arms around her, but was unable to get close to her body. An invisible barrier seemed to exist between us that repelled me when I tried to rest against her. So instead I sat as close to her as I could and tried to comfort her through my presence alone.

"How are you holding up?" I took a sharp breath inward at the sound of John's voice. I leapt up out of the way as John sat on the couch next to Sara.

The navy blue suit he wore hung a little loose around the edges, his face appearing thin under several days' worth of whiskers. The dark circles around his eyes only added to his gaunt appearance.

"I should ask you the same thing," Sara said. She gave a swift wipe to her tears, summoning a smile as she patted his knee. "You look terrible."

"Thanks," John replied, offering a wry smile before looking down. He raised his eyes for a moment to nod across the room at Sam who was pretending to sleep on the couch amid all the conversation surrounding him. "It's Sam I'm worried about. The day the police came and brought the news, he broke down. I'd never seen him so vulnerable. But it's like he turned off his emotions as soon as he could. Ever since then, he's been totally stoic, no emotion at all. He moves around like nothing happened."

"Give him time," Sara advised him. "He's always handled things much more internally than most. He's probably processing everything in his own way."

"I know. I'm trying to be more understanding. But it's hard. I mean, they're gone." He paused for a moment and looked at the ceiling. His eyes filled with tears, mirrored in my own eyes as I watched him struggle for words. "They're gone, and they're not coming back. The house feels empty now, void of life. It's as if everything died with them when they went down in that crash." John wiped at his eyes, embarrassed. "I'm sorry, I don't want to cry."

"I think everyone would understand," Sara pointed out. Still, she got a Kleenex out of her purse and handed it to him. "Did you eat anything?" she asked him. He shook his head.

"No. I'm not hungry."

"John, you need to eat something. Starving yourself isn't going to bring her back. Let me get you a plate of food, at least some of my mom's quiche or something." She didn't wait for his reply, leaving him on the couch while she went to put together a plate of food for him. He wasn't alone for long.

"How are you, John?" Edna, my parents' neighbor, took the liberty of seating herself next to him on the couch. He looked up, and did a double take when he saw her. Her dress looked to be something straight out of the 1970s, with neon pink and orange flowers against a vivid green and yellow background. Judging by the musty smell, it hadn't seen the light of day since the seventies either. Among the solemn hues and muted colors around her, the elderly woman stood out in her vivid dress. Even her wispy hair screamed for attention; more lilac than gray, it fluffed out like a purple dandelion in a fruitless attempt to conceal its sparse growth.

"I'm as well as can be expected, I guess," John replied. He looked uncomfortable, and shifted on the cushion next to her. I saw it was an attempt to restore some of the personal space she had invaded, and noted that she confused his movement with an invitation to move closer to him.

"I remember Rachel as a little girl," Edna gushed, waving her hands in the air to add emphasis. "She and her sister were always playing in the backyard, taking turns pushing each other on the swings. Whenever they'd see me in my own backyard tending to my garden, they'd beg me to let them come over and play with my kitties."

I snorted a laugh before I could stop myself, covering my mouth as if anyone could hear me. I remembered things a bit different.

****

As children, Sara and I would often play in the yard. Edna, who had never had any visitors for as long as I remembered living there, would often come out when she saw us playing, telling us tales of her little cats she kept in the house. They weren't allowed outside, so we were intrigued by the stories of these mysterious cats, letting our imaginations paint a picture of their softness and playful nature.

The first time we were old enough to come over when she invited us in, we followed her through the gate and into her home. On the outside, the house looked like every other house in the neighborhood, with a porch that expanded from the front steps and potted plants framing the entryway. But upon entering the house, the fresh air outside was replaced by an overwhelming stench. The flowery smell of air freshener fell short in its attempt to mask the soiled cat litter. The reek was only enhanced by the steady flow of hot air blowing from the heater vents, despite the warm spring day.

Older by two years, it was Sara who convinced me to forge on, taking my hand and pulling me forward. We entered a bright pink entryway, the walls a blinding hue of rose surrounding a tile floor covered with fuchsia throw rugs. It led to the rest of the house that shared the same color theme, layers of pink on pink that were so bright they made my head hurt.

"Muffin! Mr. Tinkles!" Edna cooed down the hall. She clicked her tongue against the top of her mouth, creating a quick sound that echoed around the house. From a back room we could hear a drop to the ground and a low meow.

Edna had described to us two balls of playful fluff when telling us about her cats. The way she talked about them, we were expecting adorable kittens that would chase string if we dangled it in front of them. What came out of the back room was the exact opposite of this image. Two emaciated cats emerged, hurrying over to Edna for food and affection. One of them had part of its ear missing, one of its eyes closed up tight, and an obvious limp as it walked. Its dark fur was brushed well, but missing in several patches as if it had been scratched bald. The other, appearing a bit younger than the first, had short black hair all over, except for an orange patch over its eye. Its tail stuck straight up, curved in a crooked hook at the end. While the first cat ignored us altogether, this second cat took turns swirling at our feet. I bent down to pet it and recoiled at the feel of its greasy hair.

"Look, Muffin likes you," Edna exclaimed, bringing her hands together in glee. Muffin rolled over on her back, arching up as she rubbed her fur on the carpet. I took this as an invitation to scratch her belly, reaching down to pet the exposed underside of the cat. Muffin didn't want any part of that, and she reached up in a sudden motion, leaving me with a bright red scratch on my arm. "Oooh, Muffin. Did the wittle girl scare you?" Edna chirped, scooping the cat into her arms. "That's a bad wittle kitty. Don't scwatch Wachel, she's our guest." Meanwhile, I rubbed at my arm to help the swelling go down, afraid to let on how much it hurt as I bit back the tears. "Sorry, Rachel, she just gets excited when we have company. Would you like a cookie?" I nodded, sure that a cookie would make the sting of the scratch less noticeable.

Edna dropped the cat to the floor and walked into the kitchen to get us each a cookie. Muffin sat where she landed, licking herself and eyeing me with a wary look as if she were the wounded one, and not me. Mr. Tinkles, on the other hand, was lying on his side in a patch of sun. He was either sleeping or dead. I was tempted to walk over and nudge him with my shoe to see which one was true, but decided too much of my foot was exposed in my saltwater sandals to risk another swipe at my skin.

"Here you two go," Edna said, placing a napkin with a single cookie on the countertop for each of us. She also poured us each a small glass of milk. I followed Sara to the chairs that lined the countertop and she helped me to get up on a tall barstool before climbing onto her own. I picked up the cookie with eager anticipation, taking a mental note how many chocolate chips there were in it. And then I bit down. Rather than a moist, delicious dessert, the cookie crumbled like sawdust in my mouth. It tasted just as bland as sawdust, as well.

"It's my mother's recipe," Edna boasted with pride.

"Did your mother make them?" I asked the elderly lady, receiving a sharp kick from Sara under the counter. But I really was curious, wondering if they had been made a long time ago to be this horrible. I had never tasted a bad cookie before, always spoiled by my mother's baking skills. In my mind, it just wasn't possible for a cookie to taste anything but delicious. While Sara placed her cookie on the countertop and took a delicate sip of her milk, I kept nibbling at the edges of my cookie, trying to find the one spot that would taste delicious. It was no use; I kept coming away with mouthfuls of sawdust.

"Oh dear, no. I made those months ago and just pulled them out of the freezer. That way they always taste fresh."

"I think my mother wants us to come home," Sara blurted out, taking my hand and pulling me to come off the barstool.

"So soon? Well then, the kitties and I will be here the next time you come to visit," Edna said, leading us through the pink entryway into the fresh air outside. Both of us took a deep breath in once the door had closed, replacing the stench of the house that filled our lungs with the smell of sunshine and fresh grass on the wind. Sara looked at me.

"Never again," she said in her seven-year-old wisdom. I nodded in solemn agreement.

****

Edna had just finished telling John her version of our childhood when Sara spotted them on the couch.

"Oh Edna," she gushed. "My mother has been eyeing your gladiolas and wondering how you got them to bloom so well. She says it's how much you water them, but I bet you do something special to make them so pretty. Do you mind sharing your secret with her?" Edna's eyes widened as she got up with determination.

"Everyone knows it's what you do with the fertilizer. Honestly Sara, I could teach you a thing or two in your little flower business." She made a beeline for my mother across the room. I watched with amusement as my mom, who had invited the old lady, looked like a deer caught in the headlights. Leave it to my mom to invite someone none of us cared for just to prove she was the perfect hostess. A few moments later, she shot Sara a dirty look across the room as Edna waved her arms while giving a rapid lesson to our mother.

"She's either describing how to compost the soil, or how to swim across the Pacific while being chased by rabid sharks," John said. Sara covered her mouth in silent laughter.

"That woman is bat-shit crazy. You know that she had her cats stuffed when they died?" Sara giggled. "They now stand at attention on her kitchen counter. Creepiest thing ever!" She handed John a plate that held the quiche my mother only made for company, along with various appetizers that threatened to cover it. "Sorry, I didn't know what you wanted so I got you one of everything." He nodded, putting a cracker with a small shrimp on it in his mouth. He took a long time to chew his food before swallowing, and then moved a few of the other pieces of food around on the plate before setting it on his lap.

"I don't really have much of an appetite these days," he apologized. "But maybe I'll want to eat this in a little bit."

"It's okay," Sara said. "What about Sam?" she asked. They both looked at him on the couch where he had been pretending to sleep. Sara's younger daughter, Lily, was trying to wake Sam up without actually telling him to. As she placed a few of her toys on his chest, he inhaled, raising his chest in deep exaggeration to knock them off and not give up the ruse. Again, she picked up all the toys and lined them up on his chest once more. Sara started to get up to lead her away, but John stopped her.

"He's a big boy," he whispered to her. "Besides, this is more interesting than anything else going on here, even more than Edna describing her cats." In a final act of frustration, Lily grabbed one of her tiny dolls and slammed it on Sam's chest. He sat up with a start at the action, glaring at John and Sara who were doing their very best to hide their laughter from the mourning room. Conceding defeat, he swung his feet over the side of the couch and listened as Lily garbled the rules of play to him, handing him a doll so they could have a tea party. He glanced sideways at his father, his face a determined expression of bitterness before he gave in to an amused smirk. He then turned back to Lily and followed her directions on how to drink tea from a plastic cup with proper etiquette.

"You know, he really is a good kid," Sara said in all seriousness. John nodded in agreement.

"He has a good heart. Your mom tells me it's just his age that makes him so hard to reach lately," he said. "But sometimes I don't think I know what I'm doing with him. He can be so cold and distant at times, and is almost more of a stranger than he is my son."

"I know I was a rotten kid to my parents around his age. That's about when I became serious in my discovery of boys. About the same time, my parents turned into rambling idiots. They didn't fully regain their intelligence until I moved away," Sara laughed.

"I think that gives me about four more years until I can claim to know anything about raising a kid, right?" John joked.

"Something like that," Sara said. "Has he found a girlfriend yet?"

"Not sure. At least, he won't tell me. I've heard him speaking to someone who I think is a girl when he's on his videogame headset. Normally he's loud and crass when he's on the system. But when he's speaking to her, he talks much kinder and has more patience. However, when I asked him about it he just shrugged me off."

"He'll come around," Sara promised. "After all, he's going to want to know what to do once things get serious."

"Maybe," John said, lacking conviction in his voice. "He acts like he has everything all figured out, and I'm just in his way. He's been like this since his mom and I split up. In fact, he didn't start breaking down the walls until I met Rachel. But now that she's..." he broke off as tears entered his eyes once again.

"It's okay," Sara whispered.

"It's not, though," John whispered back. "I don't know what I'm going to do without her, without *them*. It's like everything suddenly made sense when I met Rachel and Joey. Everything seemed to just fall into place. And now that they're gone, I'm not sure anything will ever make sense again." He rubbed at his eyes, feigning tiredness to conceal the tears he was wiping away. Sara remained silent, her hand resting on his knee in a gesture of compassion. "I mean, what if he never talks again? Rachel had this way of skirting around his stubborn ego, breaking through to reach the Sam no one else got to see. We became a real family, and she was the one who helped to bridge the gap that had been widening before she and Joey walked into our lives."

"But Rachel always described Sam as a kid she had difficulty getting to know," Sara noted, curiosity in her eyes.

It was as if she were mirroring my thoughts. When I had first moved in, Sam spent most of his days shut off in his room. Despite the fact that John and I had been dating for three years before I died, I didn't know the kid very well. It took some time and lots of patience before he began opening his door and joining in on the conversation with us. However, it always seemed like there was this invisible barrier he kept in place to bar me from getting too close. As a result, I felt like I had to walk on eggshells around him to keep from breaking the already thin layers of our complicated relationship. It was an exhausting song and dance we played, and I would try to hide my sense of relief whenever it was time for him to visit his mother, knowing that life would feel effortless without him in the house for a few days.

"She definitely felt at odds with Sam," John admitted. "But I don't think she understood just how unreachable he was before she moved in. We lived more like roommates than father and son. There were days he barely said two words to me. And many of those days, I decided it was easier to just let it be than to fight him to hold an actual conversation with me. But Rachel, she had this way of not taking his silence as an answer, showing him she cared through her consistent efforts to reach him. Maybe it was just because she wasn't jaded by the negativity he's held onto for years. But through her persistence, she managed to change his habits from isolating himself into becoming a real part of this new family we were creating." He paused, taking a deep breath in. "But now..." he trailed off, his voice wavering. "It's only been a few days since they died, but it seems like all the good Rachel did since she and Joey moved in with us a year ago left with them."

"I know," Sara murmured. "It's still so hard to believe they're both gone. The other night I missed Rachel so bad I actually listened to an old message she'd left on my voicemail at least a dozen times just to hear the sound of her voice. And Joey..." Sara wiped at her eyes, being careful to dab at the corners to ensure what was left of her eye makeup would remain in place. She looked up at John and smiled. "Did you know that I was there in the room when he was born?" John shook his head. I had never gone into much detail with him about those early days, pockets of the hurtful memories sometimes even hidden from me. "Tony had since taken off, and Rachel had moved in with our parents. She asked both me and our mom to be there with her when she went into labor with Joey. I got to see Joey's first breath of air in this world, hear his beautiful cry, see him open his eyes for the first time. I remember him looking right at me as the doctor held him up, and I instantly fell in love. I had never known that about children, that they have this ability to make you fall in love with them at first sight." She took in a deep breath, looking over at her kids playing across the room. "It was Joey who gave me the desire to be a mother. Before him, I didn't think I ever wanted children. But seeing him for the first time, and then being there with Rachel as he took his first steps, said his first words, loved me as Auntie Sara…He was just such an amazing kid."

John put his arm around her. She smiled up at him and patted his knee.

"I'm sorry. If I'm having such a hard time coping with losing both of them, I can't even imagine what you're going through," she sympathized.

"Oh, I think you can," he said, placing his hand on hers and squeezing. "How about the flower shop? Is business going to be okay?" he asked her.

"I closed up shop for the next week. I had to transfer some of our orders to our competition, which just kills me. But there's been a lot of understanding from our clients about the situation. It's going to be really strange doing this without Rachel, though. I know I'm eventually going to have to hire another body for the floor, and I'm really dreading it. No one can replace my sister." She was having a hard time fighting the tears, a few escaping before she could catch them with her tissue.

"Sweetie," Kevin interrupted, "I think Lily has reached her breaking point. Think we can start heading home?" Across the room, Lily was sitting near her toys, rubbing her eyes. Sam had found interest in the food table and had abandoned her in favor of piling his plate with whatever was within his reach. Lily, in the meantime, was trying to conduct her tea party on her own. We all watched as Megan came over to try and help, only to be shouted at by Lily for touching her toys.

"Mine, Megan!" Lily squealed, pulling her dolls out of reach and spilling the whole tea party to the floor. Her face began to contort, twisting into a silent scream of protest before letting out the siren's howl.

"Uh, yeah. I think it's time," Sara chuckled, sniffing as she shifted from mourning and went into mom-mode. She went over and scooped up Lily from the floor while Kevin picked up all the toys that had spread out across the room. Right on cue, Lily stopped crying, stuck her thumb in her mouth, and rested her head on Sara's shoulder. She let out a little shudder of a hiccup from her crying spell, and kept her eyes wide open as she surveyed the room and everyone in it from the comfort of her mother's arms.

"John, if you need anything man, we're here for you," Kevin said, extending his hand. John shook it before ending with a semi-embrace.

I giggled from the sidelines, remembering John's explanation of a Man Hug, the handshake that transitions into an embrace meant to last only a second or two. "There are rules to these things," he'd told me.

Many of the guests took Sara's and Kevin's departure as their invitation to leave as well. My mother stood close to the door, ever the hostess, as she greeted the guests one last time and thanked them for stopping by.

John put on his game face as he was approached by guests before they departed. I could sense how much he didn't want to be there as he gave a distant smile towards anyone who wanted to tell him how sorry they were.

"Are you going to be all right driving home?" my mother asked after the last guest had left. "We have a guest room if you would rather stay the night."

"No, I'll be okay. It's only a forty-five minute drive. Besides, I think Sam would rather sleep in his own bed," John said as he gave my mother a hug goodbye.

"John, you know you're family," my father said as he extended his hand. "I know you didn't get a chance to marry my daughter, but in my book..." he trailed off. "You two are welcome in our home anytime you'd like," my father told John as he tried to keep himself composed.

John had told me once that my parents felt a lot like they were his own parents. Both of his parents had died a decade earlier. His father had suffered a sudden heart attack in his early sixties. His mother followed soon after, her mental capacity going downhill fast before passing away in her sleep. But of the scattered details I'd learned about them, I knew they had never been prominent figures in John's adult life. So while I sometimes regarded my parents' active involvement in my life as intrusive, John regarded it with admiration, embracing it to fill the void his parents had left in his life.

John embraced my father, forgetting the rules to his Man Hug in what seemed like a final goodbye.

"Thank you, sir," he said. He walked out the door with Sam right behind. My mother pet Sam's hair and gave him a hug. Sam returned the embrace, but appeared awkward in the obligated gesture. I could see his body relax with relief when they parted ways, bounding down the steps to join his dad at the car. And the two of them drove away, leaving the little neighborhood in Sonoma, to head back to the loneliness of their overcrowded city.

Seven

With a steady hand, I drew a thin line of black above my upper lash. I did this on both sides before enhancing the widened look of my eyes with a layer of mascara. My golden hair was already curled, and I pinned it back from my face and neck in an elaborate series of flowers and sparkling clips. After I touched my lips with a bit of rose stain, I stepped back from the mirror over my bathroom sink and inspected my work. I couldn't help but smile with pride, seeing a vision in front of me that had never looked lovelier. My skin was radiant, the lines I used to hide nowhere to be found in the face that smiled back at me. My hair shone like never before. Even my teeth appeared whiter against the dusty rose color of my mouth.

On the bed was a large white garment bag, one that had been cinched up tight in my closet for months. Beside it lay a white bodice and slip. I stepped into the slip, pulling it up over my narrow hips and placing the slit in the front. I slipped the bodice over my head and leaned forward so I could pull the ribbons tight in the back. The motion was so awkward I wished my sister were there to help me. My fingers didn't reach as far as I would have liked, but somehow I was able to get it closed without any assistance. Another glance in the mirror revealed an image out of a boudoir photo, my close fitting undergarments tightening my physique, revealing a voluptuous version of what lay underneath.

I unzipped the garment bag with care, placing my hand inside to save the dress from catching on the zipper. Pulling the bag aside, the dress I had been waiting for so long to wear shone back at me. I ran my hand over the soft fabric, admiring the creamy white material layered with small roses and lace. Lifting it off the bed, I stepped into the top of the gown and gathered it up to my breast. I pulled the ribbon tight in the back, taking the time to tighten each strand one by one until there was no more give.

Stepping into a pair of delicate white shoes that rested beside the bed, I took one last glimpse of my reflection in the mirror, and was taken aback by the vision of perfection that stared back at me. In all my months of detailing every aspect of our celebration, I had been sure I'd never achieve the classic look of a young bride often associated with weddings. And here she was, her innocence staring at me from the full-length mirror of my closet door, ready to be given away.

"Is this really helping?" a voice asked behind me.

"Does it matter?" I answered, not even flinching at the unexpected presence that had joined me. I turned around to see Jane, a girl I once knew in my college years, sitting on the bed next to the empty garment bag.

I met Jane in our freshman year of college. She lived a few doors down from my dorm room. Her roommate was best friends with my roommate, Lisa, which meant Jane would sometimes hang around with us. I didn't mind the girl, except that she had a little bit of a wild streak to her. This both captivated me and scared the shit out of me. Having grown up in a small town, I had been raised to keep a low profile and never do anything that would end up in the community's gossip mill. Jane seemed to have grown up in a much different environment, as she sought attention from anyone willing to be her audience. And when it came to seeking thrills, she had no fear whatsoever. She was not only a willing participant in a lifestyle of hard partying and risk taking, she was also known to push limits beyond the comfort zone of those around her.

* * * *

"Try this shit, it's fucking amazing," Jane said, shoving a pipe with some unknown substance in my face. The smell of burning plastic was so strong I had to push her hand away. "Come on Rachel, don't be such a prude," she laughed before bringing it to her lips and lighting a flame to it. I watched with both disgust and intrigue as the pipe took hold of the flame with her breath, burning into an orange ember before going out into a string of smoke. She leaned back, holding her breath before letting it out in front of her in a cloud of yellowed white. With a dazed look, she grinned over at me.

"I have no issues with being a prude," I told her. "I'm actually quite comfortable with it. That shit will kill you."

It was the night after our freshman finals and we were all blowing off some steam at a party a few seniors were throwing. Lisa was in the corner with a guy she had been trying to talk to for weeks and Jane's roommate had already disappeared into one of the bedrooms upstairs. Never being one to drink much, I nursed my red cup of beer, marveling at how I might be the only sober one in the room. The majority of the party was made up of freshmen, many of whom were taking advantage of the freedom they'd discovered this year by overindulging in anything illegal they could get their hands on. Next to us, a few girls giggled as they took turns snorting lines of cocaine off the glass coffee table. Marijuana joints glowed around the room, as casual as if they were regular cigarettes. Music played low on the sound system in the corner, allowing for a din of chatter to hum around the room while keeping a low profile from the cops. The party was a bit too wild for my taste, but I wasn't about to abandon Lisa by going back to the safety of my dorm. I figured if I just nursed the one beer, I could handle a bit of stupidity from my classmates.

Bored with me, Jane leapt up from the couch and made a beeline for the sound system in the corner of the room. She turned up the volume, eliciting cheers from those around her. The energy of the room transformed from the laid back atmosphere, filling with animated bodies who began to dance to a steady beat of music.

"Come on and dance!" a guy from my English class yelled at me over the music while holding out his hand. I grinned, taking his hand while still clutching my drink. I couldn't quite remember his name, but I had a feeling it didn't matter. Turns out I was right. Within moments of joining the crowd I lost him. More and more people migrated into the dancing room, coming together to create a shapeless entity that fed off the energy within. In the center of it all I could catch glimpses of Jane, her eyes closed as she danced to a beat all her own. She swirled in different directions as the high-energy dance moves around her clashed with her flowing movements. I could tell something wasn't quite right when she opened her eyes, and didn't seem to register all that was going on around her.

I did my best to maneuver through the crowd to her, a feat that proved difficult. As the song shifted to a trance beat, glistening bodies moved in suggestive motions against anyone who was close to them. Groping hands were everywhere, trying to caress whatever was within reach. The smell of sweat was pungent in the air, and my own clothes clung to me like a second skin. I sipped at my beer to cool off as I continued to make my way through the crowd, trying not to stare too long at the dancers around me. A girl with closed eyes continued to move while several of the guys around her took turns fondling her breasts. Another couple was entwined in a tangled embrace, their mouths exploring each other's lips as if no one were around them. All around me, the mood had shifted from a casual dance party to something much more risqué. And in the center of it all was Jane who had fallen to the floor and now lay there with her eyes wide open.

"Jane!" I screamed, leaping past the few people who stood between us and kneeling at her side. She turned towards me with a blank stare, her skin glistening with beads of sweat and reflecting the colors that flashed from lights around the room. I touched my hand to her cheek and it was burning up. "Turn off the music!" I yelled to those around me. "Someone get help!" No one heard me as the deafening beat continued to pound through the room. Jane lay there flat on her back, her arms and head exposed to the shuffling feet around her. I shielded her body with mine to help protect her from getting trampled, hitting at the legs closest to us. "Call for help!" I yelled again as I tried to get someone to notice what was going on.

"Right on sister," a guy yelled with approval, giving me a provocative look as I straddled Jane's body.

"No!" I shouted. "She's hurt! Get help!" His face took on a look of recognition when he saw the vacant stare in Jane's eyes. He tapped the guy next to him and pointed towards Jane.

"Someone's hurt, we need to make a path." The sea of people around us began to part as the guy helped me to hoist Jane up and move her toward the edge of the room.

"The cops!" someone shouted, and the crowd began to scatter in a chaotic frenzy. The guy helping to hold Jane up looked at me with an apology in his eyes.

"I'm sorry, but I can't get in trouble. My parents will kill me."

"Wait!" I said as he lowered his side of Jane's body to the floor. But in a moment he was gone with the rest of the crowd. I kneeled to the floor, resting Jane's head on my lap and running my hand over her damp forehead. I could tell she was trying to fall asleep to escape whatever it was that was haunting her, but every now and then her eyes would jerk open in terror. "It's going to be okay," I told her, even though I knew she couldn't hear me above the music still pounding around us in the darkened room.

The cops swarmed the room, pouncing on us without warning since we were the only two people left in the house. "She needs help!" I screamed as they pried us apart. A large officer had his arms around me, hugging me from behind as I struggled against him with my kicking legs. I could see the officers pulling Jane to her feet, catching her as she fell over and carrying her from the room. I had no choice but to stop fighting, my strength no match against the determination of the officer who was restraining me, knowing that soon I would have my own troubles to deal with when they called my parents. I never saw Jane again, as she didn't come back the next fall.

* * * *

"So what'd you die from? Overdose?" I asked Jane as she sat on the bed drinking in the image of me in my wedding gown with amusement.

"Naw, that shit was nothing compared to the cancer," she said with a casual wave of her hand.

"Wait, what? You had cancer? When?" I had heard rumors that Jane had passed away a few years after I'd last seen her, but no one knew anything for certain. I'd always assumed she had died as a result of her reckless lifestyle, so to hear that it was from something like cancer caught me off guard.

"I had it as a kid and beat it. But it came back in my twenties, and this time it was a bitch. Apparently if it attaches itself to enough organs it becomes inoperable." For a moment her body transformed to reveal the gaunt image of her former self, her bones pushing against skin that held no fat, her eyes hidden within the dark circles that surrounded them, her stark scalp shining white underneath a few patches of wispy brown hair. But it only lasted a few seconds. Within the blink of an eye, her emaciated appearance transformed back into the Jane I remembered. She wore her dark hair short, cut close to her head in a pixie haircut that would have looked masculine on anyone but Jane. But for her, the cropped style only enhanced her petite features, revealing the wideness of her coffee eyes and the dramatic bone structure of her flush cheeks. The heavy makeup she wore in our college days was now replaced by a more natural look. As in life, she had chosen a more punk style – a sharp contrast to the wedding gown I was wearing. Her tight jeans were ripped at the thighs, and she wore a cropped tank top underneath a black leather jacket that was adorned with small chains and buckles. Despite her rock-and-roll fashion, she had a captivating radiance I'd never seen on her before – a warm appearance that had once been hidden under a mask of constant intoxication and hard knocks.

"So what's the big occasion? Getting ready for prom?" she joked.

"Funny. Actually, it's my wedding day. At least I think it is. I just kind of appeared here when I was thinking about my wedding day, so I'm guessing this is the day. And since I couldn't wear my dress in actual life, I might as well get to wear it now, right?" I studied my image in the mirror, trying to ignore the look of disdain she was giving me.

"Are you for real?" Jane asked. "Okay, first of all you need to get a handle on your traveling technique," she sighed in exasperation. "You own the power to move where you want to go, not the other way around. You shouldn't just be showing up places and not knowing where you're at. Second, this is not your wedding day. You're dead. Third, the sooner you move on from your former life, the better. Trust me on this."

The memory of Aunt Rose in the forest burned through me, her warning ringing in my ears like a bell. I shook my head to rid myself of her image.

"I will," I promised. "Soon. But give me a little time. All this is still so fresh, and I just need to stick around a bit more for closure."

"Your closure, or theirs?" Jane asked. "Because last I checked, they've already lost you and are fully capable of coming to terms with your death without some ghost haunting them. And sticking around people you love who ignore your presence isn't exactly the recipe for getting over longing. I mean, isn't that what bad relationships are made of? Stalking someone who doesn't want you around?" It was hard to ignore her dripping sarcasm.

"That's not fair," I told her. "They don't know I'm here. But if they did, I think they'd want me to stay. I'm not haunting them, I'm just..." I paused, trying to come up with what I was doing. In all honesty, I didn't know. Was I doing this to provide them comfort? Was I being selfish by hanging around? Was I just being codependent on people I loved who had no idea I was even there? What was I trying to accomplish by dressing in my wedding gown on the day that was supposed to be the happiest of my life, a day that would never happen because I was dead?

"You're just being pathetic," Jane said, finishing my sentence. I whipped around and glared at her.

"Maybe I am. But don't I get that right? Everything in my life was finally perfect, and now it's all over before it even began. Can't I be pathetic about it for at least a little while? I just died, for Christ's sake. I think I should get at least a little bit of empathy from you. After all, you weren't exactly the most brilliant being in your former life." She smirked at my attempt to shoot her down, her eyes twinkling as the insult left her ego unscathed and sailed right past her.

"Fine. Wear the dumb dress. Let's go see what your family is up to. If it gets too dreary, maybe I can cause a few things to fly around the air and liven things up," she said laughing.

"You wouldn't, would you? Promise me you won't?" I pleaded. This made her laugh even more, and I realized she was only joking.

"Rachel, they wouldn't see anything even if I turned the room upside down. We're in a whole different kind of world."

I still didn't understand this, knowing she was referring to the same truth Aunt Rose had lit upon when we were in the forest. But I didn't want to distract her from accepting my need to hang on to my former life for just a bit longer. So I gathered up my skirt and started for the door.

"Let's go to the church," I said as I walked out.

"Whatever you say, corpse bride," she joked. I was ready to walk the whole way there, but she grabbed my elbow to stop me. "Honestly Rachel, you need to stop acting like you're human. Walking? Really?"

It was going to take a while for me to get used to my new reality. Feeling sheepish, I smiled at her, and then closed my eyes in deep concentration. In my mind, I visualized the tall ceilings of the church, picturing the dark wood support beams that were in contrast with the white of the walls. I could see the sunlight streaming through the colorful glass windows that showed the scenes leading up to the crucifixion and resurrection of Christ. In my mind the communion was all laid out on silver trays sitting on white sheets draped over the altar. I could almost smell the incense from the bronze thurible, the smoke wafting through the intricate design of the round metal censer.

And soon, I could.

I opened my eyes and we were there. The room was empty as Jane took a seat in the last pew and I made my way with thoughtful steps toward the front of the church. I couldn't help but pretend that today was real, that there was someone waiting for me at the end of the aisle. When I reached the front, I paused and then turned. No one stood between me and a large statue of the Virgin Mary at the side of the apse, holding up her hand as if to comfort those who looked upon her.

An audible snort could be heard from the back pew, and I turned and glared at Jane.

"If you are this amused by something that is so not funny, maybe you should just go," I spat out.

"No, no. Go on. I don't want to miss the part where no one says you may kiss the bride." She snorted again, not even covering her mouth as she burst into a fit of giggles. The look on my face must have shot daggers through her, because when she looked at me again she did her best to control her laughter. "I'm sorry. I'm being cruel. I'll try to be better."

Standing there at the front of an empty church with a dead addict judging my every move opened my eyes at the absurdity of the whole scene. Why was I here? To play one big game of pretend? Was I hoping that my death would turn out to be just a dream? Was I actually so deluded to think if I wished hard enough, John would appear and we could live happily ever after? I realized I was avoiding reality with silly lies.

I sat on the front pew in both embarrassment and a feeling of confusion. I didn't know where to go from here. The idea of moving on and letting my life go was terrifying to me. What would it say about my life if I just walked away from it? Did it mean I loved John less than I thought I did? Would it mean my life and Joey's life meant nothing?

With a start, I became aware that someone was making their way up the aisle. I turned to see who it was, holding my breath as John reached the front of the church and paused. In an awkward motion, he genuflected while facing the altar, and then sat on one of the pews opposite me.

"He's a looker," Jane called from the back of the church. I ignored her as she gave a low whistle.

John leaned forward and rested his head over his closed fists, and I could hear the murmur of his whispers while his eyes were closed. I realized with a start that he was praying, something I had never seen him do when I was alive. I leaned in to listen, afraid to get too close despite the reality that he wouldn't even know I was there. While anyone else in the room might have heard the shuffling of his lips without any words taking shape, I could hear his prayer as clear as if he were whispering it into my ear.

"Please, Lord, give me strength to make it through every day, especially today. I know I haven't been the man you created me to be, and I haven't really done that much for you or for others. I don't attend church anymore, and I can't remember the last time I donated anything to those less fortunate than me. Lord, I know I don't deserve your kindness, and maybe you're paying me back for not doing enough. But I can't do this without your help."

John sighed, whispering "Please Lord" over and over as his prayer. He stayed like that until the audible sound of the doors in the back opened, signaling that he was no longer alone. He ended his prayer with a flurry of hand movements from his head to his heart before touching each of his shoulders. Whispering "Amen," he turned to see who was coming in the room. My parents held hands as they walked down the aisle, followed by Sara and Kevin. I peered around them to see if Megan and Lily were following, but they weren't anywhere around. The four of them joined John where he sat, my mother resting her hand for a moment on his shoulder. By the way she pursed her lips, I could tell she wanted to say something. But instead, she squeezed his shoulder before sitting right next to him.

A few more people filed in, and took a seat. Looking around I could see that these were all people we had invited to our wedding, although they were not dressed for a celebration. Wearing different shades of navy, gray, and black were my cousins, a few aunts and uncles, some friends of my parents, and a few acquaintances, many of whom slid into a pew close to the back. The turnout seemed to be fewer than the affirmative RSVPs I had received in prior weeks. I sat in solitude on my pew in the front row, as did John and my family steps away from across the aisle.

The priest came from a doorway next to the front of the church wearing a long white cassock crested with a purple stole that wrapped around the back of his neck and hung long on the front of his robe. He walked to the altar and lifted the thurible. Swinging it to the right a few times, and then the left, he sang a low prayer in Latin before placing it back on its hook with care.

"In the name of the Father, the Son, and the Holy Spirit," he said, lifting his hands in the sign of the cross towards those now standing in front of the pews. "Please be seated." The pews creaked in complaint as everyone took their seat and waited for what would happen next.

"Hallelujah!" the priest exclaimed. The room jumped at his sudden proclamation, not expecting his voice to be so explosive. The priest held his hands out in a V. "It is said in the Book of Revelation nineteen, verses six through nine, 'Our Lord God Almighty reigns. Let us rejoice and be glad and give Him glory! For the wedding of the Lamb has come, and his bride has made herself ready.'" I held my breath at these words, afraid of how they might affect John as he sat next to my mother on what was supposed to be our wedding day. "'Blessed are those who are invited to the wedding supper of the Lamb,'" the priest continued, adding, "These are the true words of God." I peered over at John, but he held no emotion on his face as he listened with intent to what the priest had to say.

"Friends, today was expected to be a different kind of celebration, one with much joy and laughter over the beginning of a new life of unity for John and Rachel. But the Lord works in ways we cannot understand, sometimes changing the course we have set for ourselves and closing off the paths we expected to travel." He paused, letting these words echo off the stark walls, puncturing the silence among my friends and family. "I do not pretend to know why the Lord called Rachel home early, or the plans He has for you, John, in the wake of her death. But as a servant of the Lord, I can only determine that He has a purpose in all of this.

"The verse I just read is of the feast that awaits us in the second coming, when the world is no longer and we are reunited with the Son and our Creator. The bride is the church, the people who have spent every day of their earthly lives preparing for the moment they come face to face with our Lord and Savior to serve Him in all eternity." The priest took another dramatic pause against the quiet before continuing. "Rachel may not be here today for a wedding celebration. But friends, she is attending a wedding celebration of another kind. She is with our Father, our God in Heaven, reunited with our Lord for all eternity in a feast unmatched by what can be created on earth. Today, Rachel attends a wedding celebration more beautiful than anything we can imagine."

The priest continued to speak of life after death to the small crowd of mourners, but his voice became lost in the background as I tuned out. This afterlife he described seemed like the stuff of fairytales. My upbringing had included Sunday visits to church, and stories out of the Bible; I had been fed lines of hope, just like these people who gathered in memorial just weeks after my death, that there was something wonderful waiting for me on the other side of life. But I stopped attending church in my adult years and lived life with little thought of religion. Even so, I was at peace believing that those who passed before me were headed for Heaven. It seemed much easier to believe that there was life after death than to believe that our life on earth was all there was.

But now, here I was, continuing to exist despite the absence of my human body, and I had yet to see any pearly gates, angels singing in exaltation, or a God in Heaven who was welcoming me "home."

Anger overwhelmed me all at once. At a time when I needed help most of all, I felt abandoned and deceived by the stories fed to me in my youth. I wanted to create a scene, shake the room, do anything to get the attention of everyone who was there and reveal that all this religious talk was nothing but a lie to give them comfort – that in fact I was stuck on the other side of life with nothing but my overwhelming emotions and a loneliness like nothing I'd ever felt before.

I could see by John's face that he was finding peace in the priest's words, and my anger intensified. How dare this priest drag John into believing this bullshit!

"It's all a fucking lie!" I screamed, jumping from my seat and facing my family and friends who sat watching the priest from their pews. "Don't listen to him," I shouted at them. "There is no Heaven or Hell, there is no God welcoming us home or devil trying to snare our souls! When you die, you just exist forever in this nothing of a hellhole. There is no reason, no purpose, nothing!" The small crowd looked in my direction, their expressions peaceful as they peered right through me towards the priest as he spoke.

I marched over to John, pushing my billowing white skirts to the side and kneeling in front of him so that my eyes were at his level. "John, there is no magical reason for all this," I whispered inches from his face. "There is no higher purpose as to why I died. I was killed for no other reason than to serve a selfish need of someone on the other side of life. It wasn't to open your life up to better things or because God was calling me home. Our destiny was shaped by the whim of a lonely woman. That's all."

I was pained by the vacant look in John's eyes, even as I tried to catch his attention with my intense gaze. I missed the recognition that had lit up his expression whenever he saw me, how his eyes had smiled down upon me even when his mouth wasn't doing the same. Being near him now after death, I knew there would always be this invisible barrier between the two of us as long as he was alive and I was not. For a brief second I was able to understand the intensity Aunt Rose must have felt in my final moments of life, but I shook the feeling away as fast as it came. There was no way I would ever feel any kind of compassion for a woman who upended the lives of so many in favor of her own longing.

The energy in the room shifted as the priest gave his final thoughts on life after death. When he finished speaking, those in the pews filed out one by one. The last to leave were John and my family. They stayed just long enough to thank the priest before making their exit through the large wooden doors that led out of the church. Even though it had been my intention all along to follow them, I stayed behind in the almost vacant church. I watched as the priest bowed his head over the altar and moved his lips in a silent prayer. He then gathered up the tray of Communion and the thurible, and disappeared through the same door he came in at the beginning of the service. The church was now empty except for my spirit, as well as the spirit of Jane who still sat almost forgotten in the back of the room.

Eight

I could feel Jane come up to me in quiet kindness as I sank onto the pew in front.

"You know it isn't always going to be about you." She sat down next to me, folding her hands in her lap. We both faced forward, the statue of a dying man on a cross looking down at us. "They're going to move on, live life without you, forget certain details about you as their lives keep going."

"I know," I whispered. "Coming here was a mistake, wasn't it?"

"I don't know," she replied. Her sarcasm was gone, replaced with a seriousness I had never experienced from her. I sensed she would answer any questions I had in the moment, but I was so confused I didn't even know where to start. After a few moments of silence, I decided to begin with the most obvious.

"Is the idea of God a lie?" I asked, turning toward her. She smiled.

"I don't think so," she said.

"What do you mean?" I asked, more confused by her lack of a definitive answer. "How can you not know? You've been dead for years!"

"First, time is relative. To you it felt like years since our paths last crossed, but to me it varies from feeling like a mere moment to feeling like an eternity. Second, we still exist even though we're unattached to our bodies. The fact that we don't just evaporate into a vast nothing tells me that there must be a force greater than ours. Have I seen God? No. But I feel Him, and I believe in Him, and that gives me hope that there's a reason behind all of this."

"Like the hope those people were given about where I am in death, even though it's nothing like where we actually are," I muttered.

"You could see it that way," she said. "Or you can believe like I do, that this isn't our final destination. I can't help but think there's more to this, that we haven't seen all there is to come."

"But you've been dead for over a decade! I know to you it's 'all relative,' but in human time, almost fifteen years have passed since you were alive. And you still haven't seen God? You're going to tell me that, despite all that, you're still waiting for something more to happen? What if this is all there is?"

"Rachel, if every person who died had a spirit in the afterlife, wouldn't this place be crawling with them? And yet, how many spirits have you come across?"

"Two, including you," I admitted. I hadn't thought of that. "So where are they?" I asked her.

"That's the part I don't know. I can only assume there's a Heaven. I've felt the pull toward something unknown out there, a feeling that entices me to leave all this behind for something much bigger. But I'm not ready yet. I loved the world, and despite appearances, the world loved me. So I stick around just to see life unfold without me, and find my own sense of Heaven in that."

"Do you know where my son is?" I asked her.

"Maybe Heaven? Maybe a reality that differs from this one? I don't know. But I wouldn't worry about him. Nothing can happen to him if he's already dead," she said, not even trying to be gentle about the truth. Despite my own lack of life, the mere mention of his death made me wince.

"I can't help but worry about him. This is the first time I've ever been away from him. It kills me that I couldn't protect him in life and he died as a result. I don't know how he's handling death, if he's scared and alone like I was, or what. I want to find him, but I feel helpless because I don't know the first place to start."

I stopped there, even though there was more to it. The bigger truth was that I felt torn. The mother in me, the woman who loved her son more than life itself, wanted to race to the ends of the earth to find him and make sure he was safe. But a deeper feeling had taken root, overwhelming my maternal instincts, and it wanted me to stay where I was. My desire was to stay close to the people who were still alive and see how life went on without me. But that desire was being translated into a mess of jealousy, longing, sadness, anger, and frustration, a war of emotions as I viewed the people I loved—maybe even loved more in death than in life. And yet, as close as I got to them I still felt separated from them. Just remembering the way John looked through me while in the church filled me with an unquenchable thirst to be noticed. Even though I now had more power than I had even attempted to discover, I missed how it felt to be human, to feel emotions on a lesser scale and tethered to the earth in my body. I missed being in John's arms and how it felt when he breathed into my hair. I missed the sensations I took for granted in life, like being cold or hot, hungry or tired, and all the other feelings that I once dreaded.

Amidst the reality of my death was the somber awareness that being around those still alive was more important to me than knowing where my son was. I tried to tell myself it was because he was okay. After all, he was already dead. I ended up okay after death, so why shouldn't he? But truth be told, I had no idea if he was okay or not. And while I was worried, I was afraid to leave behind everyone I loved in life to go search for him. Besides, I didn't even know where to start.

"Let's get out of here," Jane said, interrupting my thoughts. "I know the perfect distraction for you. But first, you really need to get out of that dress." I looked down at my wedding gown, then gave Jane a sheepish grin. I closed my eyes and concentrated, envisioning myself in a different outfit. It took just a moment for the weight of my wedding dress to be replaced by the feel of a lighter fabric. I looked down and smiled at the filmy yellow material of a sundress, a color that had washed out my complexion in life whenever I had attempted to wear it. Now, my skin radiated a brilliant gold next to the sunshiny hue.

"Okay, ready. Where to?" I asked her.

"That, my dear girl, is a surprise," she smirked, grabbing me by the wrist and pulling me into a vortex of speed, darkness, and light. The dramatic lighting and silence of the church was left behind, soon replaced by the sounds of laughter and music, flashing lights, and the smell of cotton candy and popcorn. My eyes adjusted to my surroundings and I grinned at the scene around us.

"A carnival?" I squealed. "That's your distraction?"

"Can you think of anything better?" she asked. I shook my head with a smile as I surveyed the grounds. I recognized this place; we'd traveled to the boardwalk carnival in Santa Cruz. I hadn't been there since I was a child, and I flashed back to when my parents had packed up my sister and me for a weekend trip to the rides and roller coaster on the beach. I remembered how the three-hour car ride had felt like an eternity, though the soundtrack of Genesis singing 'Home by the Sea' and 'Illegal Alien' through the tape deck helped us to sing the time away. Years later, that album still transported me back to seven-years-old, when our only view was of the ocean as we went round and round on the Ferris wheel. And now seeing the same view, I felt seven-years-old again, the excitement inside me hard to contain. I watched the people traveling from booth to booth, trying their hand at shooting targets to knock down ducks, or throwing darts to pop balloons. The dings of the bells filled my ears as someone won a prize. A carnival worker handed a lady a bouquet of balloons and she thanked him with a hug. Then, without warning, she floated into the sky as if it were the most natural thing in the world.

"What?" I asked, unable to believe my eyes. "But I thought..." It was Jane's turn to be sheepish.

"Okay, so you know how I said I don't know where everyone goes when they die?" she asked with a grin. "It's not exactly a lie. I really don't know what comes after this. But I do know where some spirits go when they're not ready to leave the world. Usually it's places that are filled with happiness and lots of other people. When I died, that's all I wanted to find. That's how I discovered this place. Apparently I wasn't alone."

I looked around. Now that I knew what I was seeing, it was clear that there were more spirits here than just us. Among the carnies and the laughing families in the living world, I caught glimpses of those in my own world hitching a ride on the fun. A group of boys ran past us, joined by two more they couldn't see who wore cropped pants and button-up shirts from another era. Spirits joined the living on the colorful rides, nabbing untaken seats just before the ride began. As if they were a little brighter, I was soon able to spot the dead from the living. Some wore old-fashioned clothing, others wore the styles of today. They all seemed to be having fun.

"Come on!" Jane prompted, grabbing my hand and pulling me to follow her through the crowd. I laughed as I followed, getting wrapped up in the vibrant colors and delicious smells, the sounds of ringing bells and laughter becoming a part of us. Jane grabbed a tuft from the top of an unsuspecting child's cotton candy and placed it in her mouth. With only a slight hesitation, I copied her action and placed the stolen pink cloud in my mouth. I was surprised when the brightness of the sweet candy sparkled with flavor on my tongue, just as it had years ago as a child.

"We can still taste food?" I asked, and she laughed.

"Of course we can! Can't you hear, smell, and feel? Why can't you also taste?" I immediately grabbed another handful of cotton candy from a kid passing by, this time a baby blue, and stuffed it in my mouth. A hot dog lying on a cart became my next meal, and I savored the way the hot juices exploded in my mouth with each satisfying bite. All the foods I had resisted as I worried about calories and getting fat were now beckoning me to indulge in a feast of culinary abandon.

"I never thought anything could taste so good," I said in between bites of nacho-cheese-covered tortilla chips, popcorn, and chocolate-covered ice cream, inhaling the feast I had laid out in front of me.   Jane had her own spread of forbidden foods in front of her, gorging on pizza and a hamburger as if she hadn't eaten in weeks.

"I know!" she exclaimed with a full mouth, making it come out in a garbled answer. Holding her finger up, she chewed for a few more moments and then gave a hard swallow. "When I was a kid, I was totally fat," she told me. I blinked in disbelief.

"But you were so thin when I knew you!" I exclaimed. I'd only seen her with a lean frame, her appearance showing no hint that weight had ever been an issue for her. I had a hard time envisioning her as anything heavier than the healthy weight she now carried.

"Trust me, I knew how to pack on the pounds. I guess I just loved food so much I didn't know how to say no. The worst part was that my mom and sister were naturally thin. I took more after my dad who sported a gut almost all of my life. My mom was always on my case about food, comparing me to my sister. 'You'd be so pretty if you just lost the weight,' she'd tell me. 'Look at Tabitha; why can't you be more like her?' she'd ask, holding me up to an impossible goal. My mom would limit my foods and hide the sweets from me. But I knew where they were, and would constantly skim off the top, sneaking in bites of hidden candy and feeling guilty all the time. When she had me put the dinner leftovers in the refrigerator, I'd take advantage of the food in front of me and help myself to another serving. My favorite snack was a heaping spoonful of peanut butter and ice cream. Food was my addiction, and because of it I got up to two hundred pounds by the time I was fifteen years old."

"So how did you stop?" I asked her, picking at the nuts that covered my ice cream. I could relate to the love-hate relationship with food all too well. Like every woman I had ever known, I'd fed into the impulse to be thinner and more fit, especially as my wedding approached. Thing is, even when I'd lose the five pounds I had set my mind to, it never seemed enough. I'd end up losing and gaining the same five pounds over and over again, all the while certain that those few pounds were a screaming billboard on my thighs and waist. But even as I thought about my own struggles, I knew they were small compared to the struggle with obesity Jane was detailing.

"I guess I just became aware of the way people were looking at me and how I was being judged by my weight. When my mom did it, it was one thing. But eventually my friends started hanging out with me less, a swimsuit was the most terrifying contraption in the world, and I kept growing out of my pants before they were even broken in. I found the motivation to change when I realized that no one wanted to be around the fat kid, not even me." She smirked, popping a French fry in her mouth. "Of course, you got to see how that turned out."

"You mean the drugs?" I asked.

"Yup. I started out with the best of intentions, cutting my meals in half and avoiding all foods that made me want to binge. I began taking walks around my neighborhood and riding my bike everywhere. I even began to see some weight loss. But you know how the teenage years go. Someone introduced me to speed, and I realized I could lose weight even faster while also experiencing this incredible adrenaline rush. With that came my liquid diet of tequila. And soon I was on a constant high with whatever I could get my hands on. I traded one addiction for another." She took another bite of food, this time chewing much slower before she washed it down with a drink of soda. She then looked at me and grinned. "I guess that's one of the reasons I love it here so much, because of the food. It's my favorite part. I can eat whatever I want and never get sick or full, or even fat. And I can actually enjoy my food because there's no guilt. I think it makes it taste even better that way."

I looked off to the lights of the Ferris wheel as it turned its lazy rotation against the darkening sky. The blinking red, yellow, and blue held their own slow beat, beckoning me with a hypnotic pulse as they went around and around. I held Jane's hand and felt only the slightest pull as we left the feast of junk food and found ourselves sharing a seat at the top of the ride looking out across the whole of the carnival.

At the highest point, the park looked like glowing embers. We could hear the faint metal sound of the roller coaster whipping around the tracks, screams echoing in an ebb and flow of fear mixed with delight. Carnies called out from unseen games, their words not quite audible to us as they got lost in a sea of noise. The whole carnival was alive, filling us with that void in our afterlife, feeding us the heartbeat and pulse of blood we were missing as we pretended to be a part of it all. In the distance I could see the spirits of those who had passed, rising and falling into the night sky, plunging against the stars while holding dozens of balloons.

"I think I could stay here forever," she said, and I agreed.

We studied the view in silence on our slow journey around the wheel, catching our breath at the jump in our bellies as it picked up speed, and taking in the gusts of air that rushed past our cheeks and through our hair. I closed my eyes and leaned back, reveling in the moment of being off guard, out of control, and at the whim of the ride. But in the back of my mind was John, his unshaven face and sad eyes staring back at me in abandonment. Even further behind him was Joey, his evaporating image haunting me with the knowledge that I still hadn't found my son. I opened my eyes and looked at Jane. Her eyes were still closed as the wind whipped her short hair away from her face. A small trail of tears was traced from her eyes into her hairline, the constant rush of air pushing it back from her face instead of down her cheeks. I realized the Santa Cruz carnival was her escape, where she hid from all the demons that haunted her in life and followed her into death. It was here that she was able to leave them all behind, even for just the moment. But did we ever really get to leave behind these hurts that ate at our souls while we were living? Judging by the emotional stream on her face, I guessed not. I took her hand again, and she opened her eyes and smiled at me. The tears evaporated as if they never existed.

"I can't really stay here forever," I told her, and I saw the slightest quiver in her smile before she squeezed my hand.

"I know," she said.

"I have to find my son," I told her.

"He'll find you when it's time."

"I need to stay with John," I whispered. Her smile was wistful.

"I know," she repeated, whispering the words back to me. We let the weight of that statement hang between us in the moment. I knew I was willing myself to be weighted down in the afterlife by focusing on the living. I was beginning to understand even more what Aunt Rose had described to me, the addiction that takes place when surrounded with those we loved in life, and how much heavier it became with time. I knew that on this Ferris wheel I was being presented with a choice – to walk away or to run back into the addiction. I knew that I was making the wrong choice. But I didn't care. I realized that no heaven was truly perfect unless I could see John's face every moment of the day.

"What happens when he moves on?" she asked me, and I flinched.

"Then I'll be happy for him," I lied. "I only want him to be happy."

"Then let him live," she pleaded. "The longer you stay with him, the longer it will take him to recover from the loss of you."

And in that statement, my decision was sealed. I didn't want him to recover from me. I wanted him to miss me every day, just as I missed him. Jane sighed when she saw the shift in my face.

"You know where I'll be if you need me," she said, squeezing my hand again, this time in defeat. I smiled back at her, grateful for her understanding.

"I wish we had been better friends in life," I told her.

"We're friends now."

I looked away, peering past the carnival where the darkness of the mountains met up with a purple sky peppered with stars. I could feel the pull inside of me as my mind turned to John, but I realized I needed more time. I glanced back at Jane, but she had already left. I swung to my side, lifted up my feet, and stood up. Placing my foot on the metal bar that separated me from the open air below, I took a deep breath in and exhaled.

"Here goes nothing," I said to no one, then pushed off with a jump into the air.

Nine

To my surprise, flying proved to be effortless. I had thought for sure I would start out with a plunge to the earth and gain a few bumps and scrapes along the way. But instead it felt like the most natural thing in the world, as if I were made for flying. I held my hands out at first like Superman, looking down on the world that was streaming below my soaring body. But I soon realized it didn't matter which position I held myself in as I ascended through the air.

I passed birds at high velocities, their thoughts mingling with mine as I came close to them. They saw me as just a speck of light, I realized; the vision presented to me earlier in the forest making much more sense. With their direction, I knew when to move up or down to travel with the air current, and when to turn so I was on the right path. But getting lost didn't worry me. I had all the time in the world, or rather, the lack of time's existence. I didn't know how long I had stayed at the carnival. To me it felt like just a few hours had passed. But judging by the green tops of the trees and the fresh moisture in the air, I could tell the seasons had changed from a long and dreary winter to a hopeful spring.

Images of our familiar neighborhood flashed from the minds of the birds that flew around me, popping at me like the scattered pages of magazines. I descended from the air, passing the few trees that lined the streets before touching my feet to the sidewalk. I walked the last few steps left toward our apartment complex; its gray cement adorned with windows dressed in iron bars looking back at me in cold contempt.

I never liked this place. Inside we had made it a home, the photos and warm colors brightening up the tone from the busy world outside. But outside it was dirty and riddled with angst. Our neighborhood stood on the edge of the Tenderloin, the streets lined with those out of luck who carried their belongings with them at all times. It was a rare day in life when I didn't have to step over a sleeping body to climb the stairs or wasn't asked for a cigarette despite the fact I hadn't smoked a day in my life. Bags of trash overflowed into the streets, at times forgotten by the city waste management as the rats took turns tearing them open and grabbing what they could for their home. Blocks away were the adult bars where girls danced on stage for money, and patrons drank more than they should to drive home safe. They parked in our neighborhood, and I'd often see them stumbling back to their cars and groping for their keys, hitting the metal trash cans on the side of the road at ungodly hours of the night before driving off. Some were even too drunk to drive. I'd pretend to ignore their passed-out body at the steering wheel as I'd leave for work in the morning, hoping they were only sleeping and not, in fact, dead.

On this afternoon, one of our regular homeless inhabitants sat next to the stairs of our apartment, staring straight ahead as his dog slept at his feet. In life I had ignored him, so repulsed that I had to live near these people with their mental problems and affinity for booze. But this time his thoughts prodded at my mind despite the fact that his face looked blank.

So hungry, he repeated in his mind, and I felt the way his stomach churned inside of him. Beside him lay a wrapper that held a half-eaten sandwich that looked to be weeks old. He picked around the rotting parts with care and placed it in his mouth. On the outside, he didn't seem to mind eating the spoiled food. But I felt his disgust at the way it tasted, eating it only so his stomach didn't rip in half. I brushed away my repulsion as I experienced every ounce of his affliction, just as I brushed away my shame for my lack of compassion towards him during my life.

Sensing the old man's hunger and thoughts, it dawned on me that I could feel the thoughts of anyone. The only thoughts I had heard were those of the birds and cicadas – but only when they projected their thoughts to me. To actually feel what people were feeling, to see what was hiding behind their words… The possibilities in this tiny detail of the afterlife seemed to make up for everything else that was just outside my grasp in this existence.

I closed my eyes and imagined the inside of our apartment, feeling myself pulled within the cold walls and away from the starving man outside our steps. In an instant, I was surrounded by blaring music. I opened my eyes with a start.

The house was in total disarray. It looked as if the dishes hadn't been washed in weeks, maybe months, and they overflowed from the sink to the countertops and all across the dining room table. Clothes were slung over the back of the couch and on the floor, some of them clean and never folded and others still sporting the stains from a full day of construction work. I wrinkled my nose at the smell that wafted through the apartment, a mixture of garbage and air freshener creating an odd bouquet of odors.

I could sense that John wasn't in the apartment. But someone was there; probably Sam, judging by the awful noise coming from the stereo. I walked up the stairs and turned the corner. The closed door to Joey's room stared back at me, daring me to come inside. I was curious if they had kept the room the same, or if it was now being used for something else. I didn't want to know yet, and focused instead on the source of the loud music.

Sam's room was overflowing with clothes and papers, and he lay on the bed with some girl I had never seen before. They lay in an intimate embrace amidst the chaos that surrounded them.

"Come on, Lacey," he whispered between messy kisses while his hands searched out the buttons of her pants. "My dad isn't supposed to be home for a few more hours." She found his hands at her waist and pushed them away.

"Not yet, not now," she said, pulling away. "I can't." I could feel his frustration bubbling inside him, even as he tried to appear understanding. His thoughts groaned, pounding the walls of his brain as he saw another opportunity to lose his virginity wash down the drain.

"It's okay," he told her, stuffing his frustration in an effort to not ruin it for future attempts. He smoothed his hand through her hair to keep it from falling into her eyes. She smiled up at him as she moved to lie in the crook of his arm. They both closed their eyes, drifting into sleep despite the heavy beat of the music that screamed around them.

I left them like that, moving away from Sam's room to face Joey's door once again. Reaching forward, my hand moved through the door to a room I couldn't see. I took a deep breath and walked in.

His bed was still unmade, the video game controller I had taken from him now placed on his pillow. Almost everything lay as he had left it, right down to the dirty laundry that spilled out of his laundry basket and his backpack with papers falling out of the pockets. But along with Joey's mess were numerous boxes that took up much of the remaining space. I peered in one of them and my heart sank when I realized it was all of my things. Everything I had ever owned was now hidden away in a box of cardboard, locked up in a room so that the ghosts of memories would cease their haunting. I did a quick inventory of everything inside the rest of the boxes and saw my favorite coffee cup, the dress I had worn on our first date, the tattered blue robe I wore every morning before getting dressed... Even my wedding dress was in the room, though it hung from Joey's closet instead of being stuffed as a wrinkled mess into one of the boxes. I felt a pang of regret when I realized that John had to see the dress for the first time after I had died. It hung there now in innocent perfection, as if waiting to be slipped over the head of a girl with a mind full of hopes and promises. The only thing amiss was a small square of fabric, about three inches in length, missing from the hem of the skirt. I looked a little closer and could see the rough edges of a crude cutting job.

Despite the music that still blared from Sam's room, the click of the front door was unmistakable to my heightened sense of hearing. John was home. I was at his side in an instant as he walked into the house and grimaced at the mixture of mess and noise that greeted him.

"Sam!" he shouted. He tried to be loud enough to be heard over the music, but it was no use. He sighed and hung his jacket on the doorknob of the closet, unwilling to push aside the shoes and stacks of unopened mail blocking the closet door so he could open it and hang the jacket inside. He thumped up the stairs, his lack of energy adding cement to his weighted feet. "Sam, can you turn that down," he said as he neared the room, freezing when he saw that Sam wasn't alone. The two of them woke with a start. Lacey sat upright and pulled her sweater back over her bare arms. John started to say something, his face a mask against the thoughts reeling in his head. But he closed his mouth and turned towards his room, shutting the door behind him. I could hear every question he left unspoken. *How could they? How old is that girl? How would Rachel handle this? What am I supposed to do?*

In Sam's room, Lacey put her shoes back on and grabbed her backpack. "I really should go," she apologized, and Sam nodded in agreement. Inside he swore at his dad for ruining the slim chances he still had of getting in her pants. But he covered it up by giving her a brief hug and helping to carry her things to the front door.

"I'll talk to you tonight," he said, giving her a light kiss before closing the door behind her. Then he bounded the stairs by two and slammed his own door, locking himself in his room.

At his desk in his own close-off room, I saw John wince at the sound. I tuned into him, taking special efforts to sense everything he wasn't saying out loud.

He was aware of the irony, a whole apartment of space and this was how they spent their time. He was ashamed at how he'd let the apartment go, allowing the two of them to live like dogs in their own filth. He couldn't even remember the last time he had cooked dinner for the two of them, both of them left to fend for themselves when it came to mealtimes.

At least there was still food, he thought to himself. *At least I'm still going to the grocery store to make sure we have something to eat.*

It was as if a light went on inside him, and I wondered if it was because I was standing next to him with my hand as close as I could get to his body. He got up and opened the door to his room and went downstairs, gathering the clothes that lay on the stairs he passed. He created several piles in the room, separating the mail and the clothing, and gathering all the dishes into a consolidated mass of dishes and cups. Filling the sink with hot water, he worked at the glued-on food of each plate, rinsing them clean and placing them in the rack next to the sink. When it was too full to hold any more, he dried them and put them away, then started over on the diminishing pile next to him.

"What are you doing?" Sam asked behind him, startling John as he stood immersed in the hot, sudsy water.

"You scared me," he said, but Sam stood emotionless and unapologetic. "I'm tired of the filth. I'm just straightening up."

Sam watched him without speaking, his dad's back to him as he continued to wash dishes. I could see the wheels turning in his head, and I was cast into the feelings of a fifteen year old boy full of more anger than he knew what to do with. For months his dad had acted like he had died with me, choosing to be absent as a father even when he was physically in the apartment. This sudden act of waking up from wherever he had disappeared to confused the hell out of Sam. He didn't know whether to be angry or grateful to have this glimpse of his old dad. He wanted to confront him on it, ask him who the hell his father thought he was, say everything he wanted to say in the past six months about his dad having been a vacant vessel. But instead, he grabbed a towel off the counter and began drying the wet dishes John had placed into the rack.

John turned to him and smiled at Sam, grateful for the help. The two of them finished tackling the dishes together before moving on to the rest of the house and putting it back together. The music still blared upstairs, but it served as a beat to move to rather than a force to move against.

Later, they both sat down at the table, eating the first homemade dinner they'd enjoyed since before my death. John chewed on the words rolling around in his head, questions he didn't even know how to ask. I could hear Sam's thoughts as his dad figured out the right thing to say in a situation like this.

Please don't ask. Please don't ask. Please don't ask.

"So who is she?" John asked, and Sam slumped in his seat in defeat.

"No one," he mumbled, pushing at his food with his fork. "Just some chick."

"She seemed more than 'just some chick,' Sam. Is she your girlfriend?"

"No."

"Well, what's her name?" John prompted. He took another bite of food and waited, trying to appear casual even as the rest of his questions pushed to be first in line. I could sense that one opening in the conversation would cause them all to come spilling out to the floor, drowning John and Sam in the confusion of puberty, growing up, and experiences that could change a life forever. But Sam remained tightlipped, choosing now to remain silent as if the question had never been asked.

"Sam, I asked you a question," John said, the curiosities about Lacey now evaporating against the heat rising up inside of him. There was nothing that made him angrier than when Sam shut down like this, losing any outward displays of emotion as he ignored whoever was speaking to him. It was the game he played whenever John acted as someone with more authority than a roommate who fed Sam and paid all the bills. Instead of fighting his father, Sam would just keep his mouth shut and react as if no one were speaking to him at all.

****

113

"I don't think he can hear you," I said in bewilderment the first time it had happened. Sam remained tightlipped and calm while his father reddened in the face, repeating several times what he had said. It had been dinnertime then, too, the only time Sam was ever around us. Other than mealtimes, he would lock himself in his room with his videogames or hang out with his friends until moments before it was time to eat. I had been dating John for just a couple of months, but I was beginning to see that Sam was fighting against any kind of parental control. He wasn't a bad kid, and as far as I could tell he wasn't rebelling in any major way. He just didn't like to be told what to do.

On this particular occasion John was merely asking him what his plans were for the weekend. We all sat in silence as we waited for his answer, and I thought I saw just the hint of a smirk as he got up to put his plate in the sink. Beside me Joey ate his dinner as if nothing were amiss, though he watched in silent curiosity to see how things would unfold.

"Sam, your father is asking you what you are up to this weekend," I said to him. Sam looked at me with a calm demeanor, as if I were a child who didn't understand the way things worked.

"I heard him," he said.

"Then why aren't you answering him?" I asked. "Are you mad at him?"

"No, I just don't feel like talking," he said, and he turned to walk out of the room before anyone could say anything else.

****

"Sam, don't start this shit again," John said, setting his fork on the table and looking at his fifteen year old son as they sat alone at the table we had once shared as a mixed up family.

"I don't know what you're talking about," Sam mumbled. "I'm not doing anything."

"Then why aren't you speaking when I talk to you?" I could feel the heat of John's infuriation simmer inside of him, threatening to explode as he did his best to keep things under control.

"I don't have to talk just because you spoke to me, Dad. I can talk when I want," Sam said, sitting up out of his slouch and looking his dad straight in the eye.

"You see, that's where you're wrong, Sam. If you don't want to talk about something, I'll give you that. But tell me that. Tell me you'd rather not talk about her, or whatever it is you're feeling. But to blatantly disregard me is rude. And if we go down this road again, I'm just going to give you much of the same and forget to feed you or drive you wherever it is you need to go." John sat back in his chair and folded his arms in front of him, confident his last word would sink in with Sam. But Sam looked at him with blazing eyes, standing up and glaring down at John.

"What the fuck do you think has been going on the past couple of months?" he shouted. "Have you been feeding me, driving me anywhere, or even talking to me? You've been ignoring me ever since Rachel died. So don't tell me how to act around you when you can't even do the same shit for me!" With that he picked up his plate with food still on it and threw it into the sink with enough force that it split into three separate pieces. He started to go back up the stairs to his room, but realized that was expected of him. In a split-second decision he opened the front door to the apartment and slammed it behind him as he left.

John sat in silence at the table, numb as a flurry of emotions shot through him in a passionate fight to be center stage. Sam was right. He'd been absent as a father as he mourned the dead and forgot about the living. I danced in his swirling thoughts as he remembered that first week I was gone and how I was everywhere. I was in the smell of my hair that still lingered on my pillow. I was in the photographs that beamed out at him from every corner of the house. I was in the books stacked upon my dresser waiting to be read, whose resolutions I would never know.

He had spent that first week finding everything that reminded him of me and hiding it in Joey's room, shutting the door on the past several years that made up the best parts of his life. But he'd paused when he came to my wedding dress, hidden within an opaque garment bag. I peered into his memory as he unzipped the bag with halting fingers, letting the creamy silk spill out onto my side of the bed as he looked at the dress he'd never see me wear for him. He took in the way it ruffled at my imaginary waist, hugging my curves and flowing into a subtle bell where my feet would be. One of my stray hairs remained on the dress, and he lifted it off with care, touching the fabric with his calloused hands and remembering the softness of my skin. I sat in silence in the corner of this memory as he lifted the dress to his face and sobbed into it with muffled cries. I stood next to John at the dinner table as he relived this very first cry. It was the one that opened the floodgates, leading to weeks of staying in his room and sobbing in secret. So ashamed of this weakness that possessed him, he left Sam to fend for himself, a temporary solution that soon became a habitual practice. And I was everywhere, haunting the apartment in his memories despite the fact that every part of me was locked up tight in Joey's room.

In time, John tore himself away from the wedding dress, hanging it in Joey's closet after maneuvering around the piles of boxes that took up every inch of space. Seeing it hang there, shining its promise within the darkened room, he was stuck between closing the door on it forever and the fear of forgetting me once he abandoned the dress to the room of memories. The idea was still formulating in his mind when he walked back to his room and grabbed the pair of shears that sat up straight in the cup of pens on his desk. He hesitated for only a moment before he began cutting into the fabric, taking a square piece of material and putting it in his pocket before closing the door of the room for the last time.

Months later, the material remained hidden in his pocket. He rubbed it between two fingers as he sat in solitude at the empty dinner table, the slam of the front door echoing over and over through his head as if it were hitting against the vortex of hurts.

Bang. Rachel and Joey are gone.

Bang. You will never hear her laugh again.

Bang. You may even forget what her laugh sounded like.

Bang. You are losing your son.

Bang. Rachel was the glue that held this all together.

Bang. You are a horrible father.

Bang.

John stood up and threw his plate at the wall, another porcelain casualty of a war that couldn't be won. I shrunk down in the corner of the room at the violence in the action, ignoring the nagging thought that I was the cause of it. I couldn't be. He was still mourning. He'd been suffering without me here. Nothing had changed.

The plate was the last thing in the house to be broken that night, if I didn't count John's heart. He stopped himself at the climax of the action, his breath heavy as he stared at the food that stained the wall, and the pieces of white that were now scattered across the dining room floor. For several moments he stood like that, clenching and unclenching his hands, fighting the urge to grab something else and heave it with a satisfying smash into the wall. His breath came out in forced rushes of air as he worked to expel the anger and rage that was clawing to fight its way out of him. He wanted to shout, to scream at the unfairness of having to be a father even though his whole world had come crashing down around him and he wasn't sure how to pick up the pieces.

Six months after my death, and I was still both his waking breath and sweet suffocation.

We both stayed quiet in that room, his breath slowing to a calm rhythm in the heavy air around us. Without a word, he grabbed the broom and began sweeping up the shards of plate. Once the floor and sink were free of broken porcelain, the walls without evidence of the earlier actions, and the remaining dinner dishes cleaned and drying in the rack, John sat in a chair in the living room in silence, waiting for Sam to cool down and come home.

Ten

S am never did come home that night. I left John alone in the apartment and found Sam huddled in the poor lighting of a pier a dozen blocks from the apartment. He sat at the edge, tossing tiny rocks one by one into the still water below. They lay gathered in a pile near his crossed legs, collected on his walk towards the bay. It was a fascination he had carried with him from his childhood, gathering rocks in moments of his life, one for each experience to hold onto the memory a little longer. There were rocks in his room that looked to be just ordinary pebbles to the unknowing eye, but held secrets that only he knew every time he looked at them. He could tell where each rock was from and what he was doing in the moment, even years after collecting the insignificant pebble.

He never felt younger than he did as he sat alone on the pier away from his depressing home. In that moment he was five years old, lost and needing some guidance in the confusing reality of being fifteen. Trying to let go of the hurts that tore at him, he watched as each pebble dropped from his hand, taking its memory into the blackness of the water and disappearing. I was surprised to see my face among the images he included in his tally of life's unfairness. But at the front of the list was his father,

120

John's likeness making numerous appearances as the list grew longer and longer until everything disappeared except for him.

"I don't even care," Sam said out loud to no one, trying to convince himself that this was how he felt. He couldn't fool himself, however, and swiped at the tears that kept spilling from his eyes. He held onto one of the larger rocks and looked behind him to see if his dad was searching for him. No one was there, and the cell phone in his pocket remained unlit. He added that hurt to his rock and dropped it in. "He doesn't care enough to try and find me," he whispered as the water accepted the small stone. He picked up another one and thought about the past couple of months.

He had fended for himself when his dad went under the dark hood of depression. At first he kept up the cleaning, trying to help out his dad because John was so sad.

"He didn't even notice," he whispered as he dropped in another rock.

He made his own meals and always made sure there were leftovers for his dad to pick at. When his dad did eat from the food Sam prepared, he never thanked him, didn't even acknowledge how the food got there.

Another rock fell in.

He had to remind his dad when to go shopping, making lists so they had enough food. His schoolwork was growing in difficulty, and he was falling behind in several of his classes. His birthday came and went, and all John could muster in celebration was a card with fifty dollars in it, a gift that was gone before the weekend was over when Sam spent it on some experimental weed instead of the videogame he had been trying to save for. The housework was getting to be too much for him to keep up with. So he ceased helping out around the house, testing to see if his father would notice all Sam had been doing, or even start doing something on his own. Neither happened, and the house began to fall apart. A few more rocks tumbled from Sam's shaking hand.

And then my face showed up. He tried to push against it, but it became clear that he missed me. He wouldn't say it aloud, but I could hear it as if he were whispering it to me in my ear.

With just a simple thought, I saw the part of Sam he kept hidden from me.

When I was alive and first began to know Sam, he did everything he could to push me away. I was the intruder to a life he and his dad shared that, to him, didn't need fixing. Sam could come and go as he pleased, and never had to worry about spending too much time behind locked doors. He could do what he wanted and was never questioned. It didn't even occur to John to pry a little bit more into Sam's life. That had always been Wendy's department when they were married. But Sam stopped spending as much time at his mom's house soon after the divorce, limiting his time with her to only a couple days a month and spending the rest of his time in his *real home* with his dad. He was angry that she even left, giving up without even a fight. But more than that, he knew he had more independence in his dad's house than under the watchful eye of his mother.

When I came into the picture before the body of the broken marriage was even cold, Sam was angry. I stood in the way of his mom ever coming back home. With the anger he held against his mother, the conflicting hope for his parents to get back together confused him. But he didn't argue against it. He only knew he didn't want me around.

For the next several years Sam was wary around Joey and me, keeping himself closed off in the bedroom and ignoring my insistence to get to know him better. And then I moved in and wrecked everything all over again. I brought with me this other kid who now had to share his bathroom, his food, his space, and his dad's attention that was already overwhelmed by me. But even when Sam was at his most brilliant in teenage defiance, I never wavered.

When I was around, he wasn't invisible.

Neither one of us could pinpoint the exact moment when the change took place, when Sam accepted the fact that I was there to stay, that even a defiant teenage boy wouldn't change that. It took me longer to realize that Sam actually didn't mind that I was there. However, he still took the time to test me, checking to see if I, too, would get up and walk away like his mom did. He got away with less while I was around, but he stopped caring. In truth, he appreciated that I cared enough to notice, even if it limited his comings and goings.

****

"Where have you been?" I demanded of Sam one evening when he showed up long after dinner was over. I faced him in his bedroom, demanding an answer and getting nowhere as he remained silent, his expression blank.

Earlier in the evening, Sam's plate lay untouched as we ate our dinner. John had shrugged it off, though he called his son's cell phone several times to remind him that dinner was getting cold. I was angry that the meal I cooked lay untouched on Sam's plate at the table. I announced to John and Joey that someone who couldn't bother to make it home on time for dinner didn't deserve to eat, tossing the food down the garbage disposal. When the door slammed and heavy footsteps bounded the stairs, I looked at John.

"I'll talk with him," John said. I could hear them upstairs, Sam's voice loud against John's calm reasoning.

"I'm not even hungry!" I heard Sam yell, and the door slammed. John came down soon after, his face a mixture of fury and frustration.

"I don't know what to do," he said in defeat. "If I'm easy on him, he walks all over me. But when I come down hard, he's impossible. There's no winning with him!" He helped Joey clear the table, looking at me as if I knew what to say. I didn't. Joey hadn't yet reached an age of rebellion, finding it easier to just go along with the flow rather than fight against it. I liked to think that it was because I had raised him a certain way or that he was just a mellower child, but I knew it was more probable he just hadn't hit the years of testing boundaries and exercising the ability to go against society.

"I'll give him a few moments, and then I'll try my hand with him," I told him, cooling the urge to knock down his door and give him a piece of my mind in favor of being the anchor to John's mounting chagrin. John smiled at me in both apology and relief.

"I hate to have you do it. He's my kid, I should know how to handle him."

"He's my stepson," I told him. "And this is our family."

He raised his eyebrows at me, but didn't have to say anything for me to know what he was thinking.

When I had first moved in, I didn't even know what to say to Sam. I was terrified of the kid, sensing his anger over his parents' divorce and assuming he was placing the bulk of the blame on me for how messed up his world had become. I was the stranger in the equation, I was the easy target.

But I didn't actually know how Sam felt. While the kid would move sideways when we all moved up and down, he never directed his disdain at me. He'd yell at his dad, slam doors, and leave his belongings all over the place. But when it came to me, my newness to his world caused him to tread with careful steps.

It didn't occur to me until later that, in actuality, I had—and should have—authority over him. In the newness of the order of command, I gave him way more leeway than a then-fourteen year old boy should have. As a result, we both ended up moving around each other in an awkward dance of never quite saying what we meant and of choosing words with care.

I regretted telling John I'd try to get through to him that evening. In the moment I felt like anything was possible. But as the closed door came into view I realized that I had no idea what I was doing. I'd never done this before, and just the act of knocking on his door felt daunting. I raised my hand in hesitation, holding it frozen in front of the door for a few moments as I rehearsed what I was going to say.

You need to call if you're going to be late.

We thought you were dead when we couldn't reach you.

Do you have any idea how you're killing your father?

Why can't you just stop being difficult and start joining this family?

What the hell is wrong with you?

"What's wrong with you?" Joey asked as he rounded the corner. I dropped my hand from the door, my face reddening as I realized how much weight I was putting into Sam's reaction. "I don't get what the big deal is, Mom. He's being an asshole. Just knock on the door." And with that he banged on Sam's door and then slipped past me, closing the door of his own room before I could grab him.

"Joey!" I shouted in frustration, angry that I was now stuck. Sure enough, Sam opened his door and looked at me. His face changed in an instant from contempt to surprise, settling to his mask that hid anything he might be thinking.

"Yeah?" he asked.

"Can I come in?" I requested of him, all the demands I'd rehearsed leaving through the open window of his room. He moved aside and allowed me to walk past him. I cleared a spot on his bed among the clothes and piles of books that took residence along with the tangle of sheets and blankets. I sat down at the same time he did in a chair across the room, and we both looked at each other in this foreign act of socializing. I realized that, despite my fear, I needed to act more like a parent and less like a scared stranger.

"Where have you been?" I demanded. And that's when I saw. His eyes were rimmed with red, the whites of his eyes an unnatural pink that contrasted with his tan skin and blue irises. "Have you been smoking pot?" I asked him. He looked away in embarrassment, but didn't answer. "Seriously, Sam? You're fourteen years old! Why are you messing with drugs? What would your dad say?" I blurted out the last sentence without even thinking about it, giving away the fact that I didn't want to tell John. Sam relaxed when he realized this at the same time I did. He looked at me and shrugged. That's when I saw there was more to the story. While his eyes carried the giveaway-hue of rosiness, the reddened rims of his eyes were from something else. "Have you been crying?" I asked, this time with concern.

"No," he said, breaking his silence. But he swiped at his eyes to catch the small amount of moisture that still existed at the edges.

"What's going on?" I asked him.

"What do you mean?" he answered with his own question to evade the actual issue. I realized we were stuck back in the Sam game, going round and round instead of getting straight to the point. But I had my own theories about what was up. I decided that instead of trying to win an unbeatable game, I'd just run with what I figured was going on.

"Sam, I know you're upset about your mom being gone, and that I'm here instead of her. I promise you, I'm not here to take the place of your mom. But I know it's rough when you don't see her as much as you used to. And if you ever want to talk about it, I'm a great listener. But sweetie, the pot has to go." He tensed up across the room. I could see him struggling with his demeanor, trying to challenge me while also tiptoeing through a respectful stance.

"It's not like pot is bad," he argued with me in his fourteen-year-old logic. "It's only considered bad because the government wants you to think that. And it isn't any worse than you drinking a glass of wine," he countered.

"But it's illegal," I said, my tone weak as I tried to wrap my mind around a sound argument against marijuana. "I don't want it around you or Joey, and I definitely don't want it in this house."

"But you have wine in the house, and you drink that around us," he said with a smug air.

I was struggling in the moment, ill-prepared to give a talk on the war on drugs. If I had prepared I would have researched facts on the effects weed had on a young mind and the laziness it encourages at a time when he needed to be at his most ambitious. But all I could think of were the many times in my own youth when I had enjoyed getting high in the privacy of my bedroom before slipping on a pair of headphones and drowning in the music. The intense experience of having every note go straight through me as I sank into the bed I was laying on was a delicious feeling I never experienced any other way. And now in my thirties, I was neither dumb nor worse for having smoked out in my teens. But I had also grown past it; my last joint years ago with Joey's father in a life that felt like it belonged to someone else.

To argue against something I enjoyed in my own youth felt hypocritical. But more than that, I felt like I'd be a bad parent if I gave in, and worse if I condoned this. If Sam were my own son, I'd have a much clearer argument against drugs in his system, and I'd be confiscating the pot by now. I realized that even though he wasn't my son by blood, I still owed him the duty of being a parent to him. I needed to treat him as if he were my own son.

"Look, when you're out of this house and supporting yourself after eighteen, you are free to do what you want. But while in this house, you go by our rules. That includes not bringing drugs into our home. So hand it over." I held out my hand and waited.

"What? No! I'm not giving it to you!" he said, his voice raising. I could hear John starting to ascend the steps.

"Look," I whispered. "I don't want to get your dad involved, but I will if I have to. Either hand it over or I'll have your dad come in here and get it from you."

In that moment, we both knew I had won. But I couldn't help feeling like a tyrant when he groaned, stuffing the plastic bag of weed in my hand; I pocketed it just as John poked his head in the room.

"Everything okay?" he asked.

Sam looked at the floor, and nodded in silence. I looked at John and gave him a smile.

"Everything's fine," I said. I realized that I hadn't even addressed his lateness for dinner, but decided we'd covered enough ground for one night. "Sam understands that he needs to be a little better about letting us know where he's at if he's going to be out, and that he'll be home by six o'clock for dinner unless he tells us otherwise. Right, Sam?" I caught the faintest glimpse of a smile before he buried it in a blank stare at the floor and nodded in reluctant agreement. "Great. Are you hungry? The food's totally cold, and it's a crapshoot if there's enough left to make a full dinner plate. But there are a few leftovers if you want them."

"Thanks. I'll come down soon," he said.

****

Of course, I'd been wrong about what was bugging him. Sam smoothed his hand over another rock, ready to drop it into the water. On that day, he'd been rejected by the girl he liked. Worse, he'd seen the girl kissing one of his friends. It made him feel as if he were a loser, as if no one would ever think a pudgy kid like him could be cool. So he took off with a few other friends and smoked out. It wasn't his first time, as I had believed in the moment, but more like his third. He thought the weed would help him escape from the pain of rejection, but the pain only intensified as he sank under the weight of his own mind, grabbing onto the last thought he'd had before he went under to keep from falling too deep. That was the image of his friend and this girl. And it made him question the loyalty of the guys who now sat around him, his paranoia doing double time as they sat chattering and laughing while waiting for their turn with the joint. Soon he just slipped away, his absence unnoticed as he started walking home, letting the tears fall free as he felt friendless, weird, and ugly.

But when I had talked to him about his mom, it reminded him of another sadness he'd been stuffing deep down, and he added it to his list of faults and failures. In a strange sense, he was glad to add it to the pile of hurts. He was in a space of mourning and wasn't ready to leave it. And while his dad made careful efforts not to mention the fact that his mom wasn't calling so much and never even fought for him to stay with her, I had been bold in my acknowledgment. He didn't even mind that I called him out on his possession of weed, appreciating that I cared enough to set boundaries, despite how he argued with me.

Sam picked up the rocks that lay at his feet, holding the final pebbles in the palm of his hand and closing his fist over them. He missed me, wondering if anyone else would ever see through his defenses again. He even missed Joey, the little brother he felt like he never got to know. He ached over his dad, seeing him slip even further into being an absent parent than he was before he met me, despite the fact that they lived in the same house. He missed his mom, the way she used to smooth his hair on his head before kissing the top of it, and the pancakes she used to make every Saturday morning in celebration of another week successfully survived. He missed the mom she used to be before things got bad and she moved out, before she became too busy with life to care about a teenage boy who needed her to break through the barriers he put up.

And in one swift movement, he lifted his arm and flung the rest of the rocks out into the water with all of his force, hearing the satisfying sounds they made as they disturbed the smooth surface.

Except, not one of those rocks took away the pain he was carrying.

Eleven

"I brought some oatmeal bread," my sister said, standing on the other side of the apartment door facing John. "I just made it last night and thought you and Sam might want a loaf. You look terrible, by the way."

"Um, thanks," John said, giving a small laugh before moving aside to let her in. "How are Kevin and the kids?" he asked. He raced in front of her to grab the laundry that was starting to pile on the couch again and dump it into the laundry basket in the corner of the room. As he attempted to straighten up, Sara waved her hand to dismiss his efforts.

"Please don't worry about cleaning on my behalf. You've seen what the girls can do to my house in a matter of moments. I'm not afraid of a few clothes and papers lying around." She placed the bread on the counter and surveyed the dishes that filled the sink. Rolling up her sleeves, she turned the water on over them and let the sink fill with sudsy hot water. John made no efforts to stop her. "The family's doing fine. Kevin received a small promotion last month that gave us a little extra income in the household. But as a result, he's been working longer and longer hours at the office. The girls and I have been going at it alone much of the time, which isn't as fun as it sounds with two little kids."

"Must be hard to have him gone so much," John said, trying to sound sympathetic.

"It really is. I feel like a single mom! I don't know how Rachel did it for so many years." She paused then, realizing how all this sounded. "Oh god, John. I'm sorry. Here I am rambling on about being alone in the house, and..." She didn't know how to talk her way out, hesitating in the awkwardness that lay between them.

"It's okay, Sara. It's been six months. The emptiness of the apartment is starting to feel normal. I don't even see Sam that much these days." John grabbed a towel and began drying the dishes that Sara had washed.

"How's he doing?" she asked.

"Fine, I guess. He doesn't talk to me much, though I can't blame him. I wouldn't talk to me much either. He mentioned his mother the other day, talking about moving in with her for a little time." Sara set the dish she was washing back in the water and looked at him in alarm.

"And what did you say? Did you tell him no? Wendy doesn't seem to have much time to be raising a kid. Besides, you'd be left here all alone!"

"Well, it's his choice really."

"I guess, from a court's point of view. But he's your son! Surely you told him it wasn't a good idea!" she protested.

"Not really. And he's her son too. I mean, I wasn't happy about it, and I think he knew that. But I didn't fight him about it. Besides, it was more of a musing than anything else. I don't think he really wants to move in with his mom. He'd have to leave behind all his friends and his school," John reassured Sara, and himself.

He left the subject at that, not telling Sara the relief that also lay in the thought of his son moving in with his mother. He was failing Sam every day he slipped into his grief, unable to get out from underneath it and move on with his life. If Sam moved out, he could check off his parental duties and be free to fall headfirst into his sadness and pain. While it was true that Wendy lived far enough away that Sam couldn't continue at the same school, summer vacation was close enough that Sam could stay there for the summertime. John couldn't help but feel that this was a good answer for both of them.

"I guess you're right," Sara said. "And I get his natural curiosity about wanting to know about living with his mom. But it wasn't like Wendy was the most attentive parent when she was here. Has he talked with her about this? What does she say?"

"I'm not sure. If he's said anything to her, she hasn't told me. Hey, how's the flower shop doing these days?" John asked, changing the subject. Sara had a million more questions about Wendy, and what it would mean for Sam if he went to live there. But she caught John's cue that he was done talking about it. She wasn't sure why she was feeling so protective of Sam in that moment. Perhaps it was even John she was protecting. All she knew was that the idea of Sam moving in with his mother felt like a bad choice, and she was disturbed by how apathetic John was being in a decision that could mean losing his son. It made her think of her own daughters, and how she would fight tooth and nail to keep them with her if she were faced with a custody battle. She shuddered at the thought.

"The shop is doing really well. With summer approaching, we're at the peak of our game as orders have been flying in. Thank goodness for Hannah!" she breathed.

"Is that the new girl? How is she?" John asked.

"She's great! She came at such a difficult time, when we were all reeling from the loss of Rachel. But she holds such an air of grace and professionalism, the transition was almost seamless - from a business standpoint, of course," Sara noted in haste. "No one could ever take the place of my sister. But Hannah has really pulled through in understanding what needs to be done while also being sensitive to the fact that she has this job because Rachel passed away." Sara finished the last dish and set it in the rack on the counter, drying her hands on the towel while glancing at the clock. "Speaking of which, I need to be getting back to the shop. Do you need any other help around here before I go? I'm a whiz with a vacuum and a dust cloth, you know."

John looked around and gave a sheepish grimace when he realized how far he had let the place go once again. It was going to take some practice getting back in a routine of keeping things in order.

It was ironic since he had been the stickler for tidiness when I was still alive. He was often on Joey's case when he left tiny tornado paths in every room he visited, and shaking his head at the permanent pile of clothes and books I kept next to my bed with a promise that I'd clean it later. Now he was the one who had a hard time remembering to switch the clothes from the washer to the dryer, sometimes washing them three times to get the mildew scent out of them from sitting damp for so long.

"You're really kind, Sara. But I have a handle on it. I can't thank you enough for just washing the dishes. I'm embarrassed that you even had to do that, but it helps a lot," he said, giving her a hug. For a moment he smelled me in her hair, and he breathed deep, holding her a moment too long before letting her go. He blinked hard when he saw Sara's face in front of him, and he shook away his mistake in hopes that Sara hadn't noticed.

Sara had no idea that I was the thought that had passed through his head when he hugged her. She was too preoccupied with the feeling of intimacy that came from just a simple hug.

'What is wrong with you?' she asked herself. But she knew. It had been so long since she had been held with such care, making the distance that had been growing between her and Kevin that much wider. She pushed away the feelings of comfort the hug gave her, giving a vague smile to John as she picked up her purse.

"If you need anything – a friend, a home-cooked meal, a cheap maid – I'm here," she told him. He chuckled and led her to the door.

"I will," he promised.

When Sara was gone, John did another quick survey of the room. He began to pick up the various piles of clothes, and then stopped. He just wasn't in the cleaning mood. He knew that's what got him in this mess to begin with, but it just seemed like a waste of time at the moment.

"I'll do it later," he promised himself, taking a line from my book in a phrase I often used. He grabbed his keys and scribbled a quick note out to Sam.

"Went to San Anselmo, be back tonight. Don't wait up," it read. With thoughts leaning toward black and white checkered floors and a walkway lined with flowers, John headed out of the apartment and toward his car in the covered parking lot. He was going to the house he was building – our house. I clapped my hands in excitement, stowing a ride in his car as he crossed the bridge and headed toward the familiar road that led home.

I'd visited the abandoned project often in the past few weeks. I'd wandered the dusty hallways, the floors covered in sawdust below lights that swung from fixtures that still needed to be fastened to the ceiling. I ran my hands over the bare walls, imagining our family photos covering every square inch of the smooth plaster with our laughing faces. I'd stood in the center of our bedroom, remembering the last time we'd made love before we'd been interrupted, placing us in this bedroom instead of the one in our cramped apartment. I spun circles in the large kitchen with sunshine streaming through the picture window over the sink, brightening the room despite its unfinished state. I dug my hands in the soil outside, pretending I could feel the dirt form to my hands and travel underneath my fingernails.

I kept waiting for John to resume his work on the house, even though I knew that if I were in his position, I'd never set foot in the place again. But that didn't keep me from hoping he could overcome the temptation to scrap the project and move on. I'd taken to whispering images of the house into his ear while he slept. I was delighted whenever he dreamed of the two of us unpacking wedding gifts in the living room, lounging on the couch watching TV, making love in the grassy backyard... But always, when he woke up, the visions were forgotten at once, and he would be mistaken in his sadness about being unable to dream.

"You can only mess with the living so much," Jane had told me on one of her occasional visits as we jumped from dragonfly to dragonfly. "You may be able to see him, hear him, even smell him. But you're still worlds apart." It didn't stop me from trying, though.

As John pulled in front of the house, I settled into the reflection of his blue iris and looked at the house through his eyes. His carpenter's mind saw past the perfection in the wide porch with solid railings, the inviting red door, the friendly double-paned windows that let in the sunlight but kept out the sounds of the outside world. Instead, he saw the way the unfinished wood on the porch bowed in the middle. He saw the brown crabgrass that had choked out a once-plush lawn. He saw the minuscule chips in the red paint on the door, the way the bottom of it had too much of a gap to keep the house warm, the smears on the windows from months of neglect.

John walked up to the house and put his key in the door, opening it with slight hesitation as if something were behind it. The hinges complained under the movement, the creak echoing through the vacant house. John walked in, the sound of his footsteps on the wood floors ping-ponging off every surface in the house. He had turned off the electricity months ago, knowing it would be some time before he set foot in this house again. The sun was high in the sky outside, its rays spilling into each room through the large windows I'd insisted belonged on each modest wall. But despite the bright light it still felt dreary and dark in the empty house. John flipped the light switch in the living room once or twice, as if a little leftover charge could be pulled from the wires.

There was still a lot of work that needed to be done on the house, but when John peered past the walls that still needed painting and the naked electric sockets, he could also see how close he was to the end. He didn't know what he was going to do with the house. He wasn't sure he could live in it without me, but he was afraid to sell it and be done with it. Even renting it out seemed like a betrayal to me, allowing someone else to have a part of the dream we'd created together.

He concluded that no decision was necessary right now, but that leaving it to rot among the manicured lawns of the quiet neighborhood seemed a shame. Grabbing a broom, he put all his energy into cleaning up sawdust from the floors and swiping at the cobwebs that hung like drapes in the corners. He kept at it well into the evening, not noticing as the sun cast its rosy hue on the walls as it set in the late spring sky. It wasn't until the streetlights lit up outside the living room window when the late hour caught his attention. He picked up his cell phone, noting a missed call from Wendy on it with no voicemail message attached. He also noticed it was after nine o'clock at night, and Sam was probably wondering where he was. He pushed the guilt out of his mind that Sam was on his own for dinner, excusing it with all the times Sam hadn't shown up for dinner at all in the past couple of months.

John didn't arrive home until almost ten o'clock at night. The lights were off when he opened the door of the apartment and peered in. He figured Sam was in his room, seeing the note he'd written crumpled up on the counter next to a plate with the remnants of unknown leftovers. John picked the dish up and washed it along with the dirty pans abandoned on the clean stove. He was left with minor frustration at how they were just left behind in the sink despite the fact that the rest of the kitchen was sparkling clean.

He was even more irritated when he saw that half of Sara's oatmeal bread was missing before he could even cut into it. John dried his hands and cut himself a slice in a hurry, as if waiting any longer would result in the bread disappearing right from underneath him. While no longer warm, it still held the fragrance of just being baked. He bit into it and smiled as if sharing a private joke with someone in the empty room. Through him I could taste the dryness of the bread that was almost good. Sara had never been much of a baker, or anything that mothers were assumed to be good at. It was always a source of family amusement when she became a mom, as she had a difficult time boiling water without burning it. But she managed just fine with the girls and they were better for it, even if her bread-baking skills left something to be desired.

Not wanting to disturb Sam, John ascended the stairs with quiet footsteps. He paused at the top, looking over at Joey's room that held all of his belongings, my belongings, me. He diverted his attention to Sam's room, the light shining through the gap underneath the doorway. John tapped on his door and listened for movement to signal whether Sam was awake or not. No sound could be heard. He knocked a little louder and still no one answered or even stirred behind the closed door. He turned the doorknob and pushed against it, but something was blocking him from opening it more than an inch. John groaned when he saw that Sam had pushed a chair against the door to keep him from opening it. Ages ago, John had removed the lock from Sam's door, tired of being locked out while Sam ignored him from the inside. He had taken the lock off the door to give him a chance of reaching his son. This was Sam's habitual way of keeping the barrier in place.

"Sam, come on. Would you open the door?" He wasn't surprised when Sam still didn't answer him, so he struggled with the door to get it open. Little by little, the chair moved with the door until John could reach his hand through the space he'd created to push the chair over. Sam sat at his desk and regarded his dad with eyebrows raised, as if John was just an overreacting child.

I'd seen him give me the same look countless times when I'd try to reason with him. Rather than speak, he'd just let that look land on me for a few moments too long as if to size me up or see if I'd waver. On the outside I'd remain firm. But inside my blood would boil, just as John's was doing now under Sam's calm and amused gaze. And then Sam would do whatever it was I was asking him to do, whether it was to clean his own bathroom or stop acting as if all of us were in the wrong.

141

But he'd do it with an air of conceit, letting us know through his silent demeanor that he was only doing this to promote peace, and we should be thankful he was humoring us. It infuriated me then. But now I was beginning to understand why he acted this way, why he found pleasure in the figurative steam coming from his father's ears even as he climbed to the top of the power struggle by using his father's force against him.

"I am sick and tired of you wedging your chair against this door, Sam!" John yelled, his face red in his growing fury. "It wrecks the door and can break the chair." John breathed hard while looking at him, waiting for Sam to say something against it so they could have at it. Sam, knowing his dad was anticipating a challenge, kept quiet for a few moments, his stone cold demeanor standing firm before he gave his dad the reaction he wanted.

"It wouldn't wreck the door if you didn't try to push it aside all the time. Maybe if you just gave me my lock back, your precious door wouldn't get ruined." He said it in a calm voice, looking John in the eye as he spoke. John, in the meantime, was feeling crazy on the inside, flailing against the air of Sam's cool disposition.

"Damn it, Sam! You don't have a lock because then I'd never see you! Why can't you just do what I tell you to do?" he shouted.

I could see the sparks in the air as Sam broke, something snapping inside of him after months of walls upon walls being built up between them.

"Because you're never here! Even when you are here, you're not! You don't want to see me, you don't even talk to me. And tell me what to do? It's not like you've even been a parent to me at all since Rachel died. It's like you've locked yourself up in that room with all her stuff and have nothing left for me. But Dad, I'm not dead, I'm here!" Sam stormed, clenching and unclenching his fists as he yelled at his dad. It was the same argument from a few weeks earlier, the unresolved emotions flying up between them after having been pushed down and ignored for too long. "I'm sick and tired of this house, this city, YOU! I can't stand it here any longer!"

John held his breath at the words, realizing what was coming next. As much as he'd thought this eminent plan of action would bring him relief, he was suddenly faced with fear at the thought of his son moving out. At the forefront, he knew he'd miss his son. But underneath this fear was the knowledge that once his son was gone, John would be faced with my presence in every wall, on every surface, and in the air he breathed despite the fact that I and all my things were locked behind Joey's door.

"What are you saying, Sam?" John asked, his body rigid as he waited for what they both knew was coming.

"I'm moving in with Mom."

John let out a slow breath, sitting on the bed across the room as a wave of unexpected peace washed over both of them. The fight ended with those words. John wasn't going to forbid it, a fact proved obvious in the way he looked at the ground. And while Sam hoped his father would protest a little, he didn't expect him to. Besides, it wouldn't have made a difference even if he did.

"Does your mom know?" John asked.

"Yeah, I called her when I got home and saw your note. But I've been thinking about it for a while," he admitted.

"I know. I mean, I knew this was coming. It doesn't make it any easier though," John said. His eyes watered, though he held the tears at bay. But the sentiment wasn't lost on Sam who needed to see some kind of regret from his dad. The wall between them crumbled piece by piece as they stood at the crossroads, finding their truce at the most unlikely of places. "What does she say about it? Is she fine with this decision?"

"She was actually happy about it. She said she'd call you to hash out the details." John remembered the missed call from Wendy, realizing that was what she was calling him about. He was glad he hadn't heard his phone ring.

The move wasn't going to happen for a few more weeks, allowing Sam to finish his sophomore year at his current high school before summer vacation started, transferring to the school in Sebastopol in the fall. When it was settled, John embraced Sam for the first time in years. Sam leaned into John, just as he had when he was young, when life didn't mean death or the end of marriage, when families stayed intact and everyday life was predictable.

Twelve

The next several weeks, John made every effort to be present in the home. He knew he only had a few weeks left with Sam, and he wanted to make it right. It was during this time that I felt him distance himself from me. For him, this meant he pushed my image away whenever I entered his thoughts. For me, it meant there were a lot more barriers, a lot more hurdles to jump through just to get close to him. And when I did get close, I felt like I was fighting against the wind, struggling from being blown away as he repelled me away like the wrong side of a magnet. I couldn't touch him, hear his thoughts, or even be in the same room as him whenever he worked to push me away.

It was different when I listened in to those who didn't know me or even think to keep their minds closed to me. I could dance in their thoughts, sometimes even appearing to them as a flash of an image they were either aware of or not. Their inner dialogue was the stuff from which stories were made, and I would often sit for hours just listening to them talk within their heads.

Did I turn off the stove? I'm sure I turned off the stove. I picked up the pot of oatmeal before it burned, and then, oh yes, there it is. I turned off the stove. The cat is probably licking away the oatmeal left in the pot by now. That's going to be a glued on mess to clean up when I get home, I know it. Maybe the cat will be hungry enough to lick it clean. That damn cat. I wonder if Peter will know it was me if I leave that door open and let him accidentally run outside.

The physical effects of John's resistance caught me off guard. It surprised me that a connection like this existed where the living had an effect on the dead, even if it was keeping me away. My natural reaction was that of a jealous girlfriend, trying everything to keep myself in his thoughts in an exhausting array of tricks. I'd learned how to break through the barrier that separated his world from mine, allowing me the power to move objects that existed in the land of the living. Of course, such a feat took every amount of concentration I had. Thus far I had only succeeded in being able to knock things down, using gravity to help my cause along. But I knocked items down in front of him every chance I got – the one photo he kept of all four of us on the mantle, one of my books that was still in the room despite his sweep through in the first week of my death, and the most impressive of all – dropping the remote so that it turned to my favorite movie.

That one took immense planning. On a day when he was gone and I could move about without worrying about being repelled out of the house, I flipped through the TV listing book they published every Sunday in the newspaper. There it was in black and white, the title of my favorite movie, "Made in Heaven."

I had made him watch the movie with me often, forcing him to endure two hours of my laughing and

146

crying, sometimes at the same time, as the hearts of the characters on screen were broken over and over. If that movie appeared on the TV screen now, there was no way he'd be able to ignore me.

I memorized the time of when the movie was playing, and concentrated my hardest on staying within a human timeline rather than the non-existence of time in my own reality. And then I just prayed he'd be there at the right moment.

All the other schemes of opening him up to my memory – the photo, the book, and anything else of mine I could place in his path - only resulted in John picking up the wayward item and depositing it in Joey's room, keeping the thought of me at bay with impressive strength. But the remote control trick gave him pause, the memory of me filling the room as Elmo, the main character of the movie, filled the screen. John sank to the couch as Elmo sang to the radio in his car, the book "Mike and Me" flung next to him on the passenger seat.

Rachel, just give me time, he thought, as if he knew I could hear him. His resistance gone without warning, I found myself cast inside of him with a lurch. I should have known, having planned this little action with such deliberation. But still, it caught me off guard. I'd only expected a smile, a memory, only one brief moment of recognition for all the effort I put into this plan. Instead I could feel the way his hair moved across my forehead, his breath in my mouth, the beat of his heart in my chest. I was wrapped up in his smell, intoxicated on the familiar scent I adored.

I danced in the memories that flashed through his head, enticing him to keep me there with him as he let his imagination run wild. But then he thought of Sam and I felt the barrier rising up again. I screamed in pain as it fought against me.

I haven't forgotten you. I love you more than my own life. But I also love my son, and I need to be with him now.

With that final thought, I was flung from his body, from his home, from the city, at thousands of miles an hour. I was thrown with the force of a speck of dust flicked from an otherwise-flawless suit jacket. I found myself propelled through space with such velocity I was sure I was on fire.

My pride wounded, I realized there was no fighting back. I needed to stay away, at least for a little while. I'd sewn myself too deep into the fabric of John and Sam's life. I had become so involved, even from the stance of a mere fly on the wall, I sometimes forgot I was even dead.

The thought of walking away from them terrified me. Would John end up forgetting me? Would he learn to live without me? Would I become a memory from a past life and would he begin something new with - and the next thought almost paralyzed me - someone new?

But I knew staying away was the only answer. And out of respect for the man I loved and the relationship he had with his son, there was no other choice but to let go for now. So I fought every fiber in my being that ached to be near him. Instead, I spent a few days of human time in space, practicing my own form of meditation by closing my mind to John. I focused on the wonderment that existed in the pure nothingness that held me up; surrounded by stars and meteors, planets and black holes, experiencing the coppery taste that existed in the lack of atmosphere, and the siren's call of the heavens that bordered the delicious quiet of the universe and could only be heard if I didn't move at all.

And I thought of Joey.

Despite my disbelief in Heaven in those early days of my death, I had grown to believe that there really was something out there. I could sense a stirring within me at the faint trembling notes that existed in the corners of space, and I felt its pull whenever I let go of my hold on the living long enough to exist in the world of the dead. And I believed Joey was there.

"What do you want to be when you grow up?" I watched myself ask six-year-old Joey. We were at the breakfast table back then, and in a journey through time, I was watching now from the leaves of the ficus I had inherited from my Grandma Bonnie after she died.

"An astronaut!" he exclaimed. He grinned, revealing his two missing front teeth before diving into the Cheerios in front of him. I had forgotten how young his voice once was, how his hair had once been a sandy blonde before darkening to the milky caramel it was before he left the earth.

"Why an astronaut?" I asked him. "Is it because you want to see if the moon is made of cheese? Or maybe to see if the cow jumped over the moon?" I asked him in all seriousness, though a hint of a smile pulled at the corner of my mouth.

"No!" he giggled. "Those things aren't true; those are just jokes!" he informed me, and I feigned shock that I had been misinformed.

"I had no idea! What will you see if you travel to space?" I asked him. And in his young wisdom, he described to me a vast universe with giant planets that traveled around the same sun as us, moving in a silent journey at varying speeds with tiny spheres of moons that traveled around them like our cats that swirled around our ankles in the morning before I opened their cans of food. He told me of the meteors that enter our atmosphere, how they are smaller than the palms of our hands but fifty times faster than the speed of a bullet. And he talked of the more impressive comets, the dirty snowballs of the sky that orbit the solar system and hold glimpses of early life. I listened then in the kitchen, and now in the folds of the ficus, with amazement as my young kindergartener explained the secrets of the universe, giving me information I'd learned over the course of time as well as new insight to a mysterious horizon that existed beyond the minuscule earth we lived upon.

"How do you know so much?" I exclaimed, no longer feigning astonishment.

"I saw it on the Discovery Channel," he said before finishing his last bite of cereal and bringing the bowl to his mouth to drink the rest of the milk. "Can I be excused?" he asked me, and I nodded with a reminder to brush his teeth.

"Are you out there now?" I asked Joey out loud, back to the nothing of space that held more than even I could see in my limitless existence. "Can you see me from

Heaven?" I whispered, the sound hanging in front of me without echo.

I became aware of the possibilities that lay before me as I floated free from my earthbound body. The space that Joey once described to me was out here, and I had the ability to see it all. Earth, in the far away distance, shone at me like a star in the sky. The giant orb of Jupiter moved in a slow rotation next to me, the gasses swirling in an ever-moving sphere of colors. Beyond that were much smaller planets in their own slow-moving journey around the sun, a star that looked much smaller from this far away than it did from the comfort of Earth. And all around me were particles of rock and dust floating beside me, sparkling from the faraway sun.

But what caught my eye the most was the trail of faded stars that led further than I could see, winding toward the edges of the galaxy and beyond. My curiosity was working overtime, and I turned to move toward the Milky Way. I picked up speed as I went along, traveling faster and faster until I was plummeting through space at full throttle. If I were more than just a spirit, I was sure I'd have a tail of fire as I moved forward with increasing velocity.

I came close enough to view the stars that made up the Milky Way, still millions of miles away, and moved parallel with it. I passed planet after planet, the space around me feeling colder as I moved further away from the sun. I saw the glow ahead of me, still thousands of miles away. It was like a sheet that wrapped around space, invisible above and behind me as I traveled onward. But as I got closer, the glow got brighter. I picked up speed and flew forward with all my strength. It could only be the edge of the galaxy. Even closer, I could see space rock moving toward the glow. But with shock, I saw each rock sucked through, an invisible wind grabbing hold and propelling it into a storm that swirled around the galaxy.

I was going too fast to stop, or so I thought. Had I controlled my fears long enough to think with clarity, I would have remembered that I had no limits, that I could think myself away from this place in just a moment. But as I streamed towards the edge, all I could think of was being swept into a vortex I wouldn't be able to get out of. *This is my hell,* I thought. *I'm going to be stuck here forever in a blender because I chose to leave Earth behind.*

It was no use. I closed my eyes and waited for the end. And then I hit it. Literally. I bounced off the glowing edge of the galaxy as if it were a solid wall, propelled backward through the weightlessness of space with as much force as when I was moving forward. As I flew back, I remembered the power I had. Within a thought, I was back at the edge, examining the glowing wall without touching it. I could see the velocity of movement that existed just beyond it, pulling at anything that managed to pass through the wall I had hit with great force. Trembling, I brought my hand up towards the glow, reaching forward with some hesitation. Even as space particles passed through the barrier without effort, my hand pressed firm against it. There was no give, regardless of the amount of force I used against it.

That's as far as you go.

I turned my head around, startled at the voice that spoke when I had been alone for so long. No one was there. Once again I raised my hand towards the glow.

Rachel, you will go no further.

This time it was unmistakable. And rather than being a voice near me, it was inside my head.

"Who are you?" I yelled out. Even as I listened for an answer, I admired how the glowing barrier in front of me vibrated with my voice, carrying my sound over it with a ripple of light. I waited for a reply, but received none. What I did hear was the sounds of the Heavens, or what I perceived to be the Heavens. They were closer this time, but muffled. It sounded like they were just on the other side of the barrier, but I couldn't be sure. I wondered how long I'd been tuning them out that I was only aware of them now. I strained my ears, trying to make out the words. But it was like listening to sound above water while holding your breath below.

The barrier began to glow brighter, the wind on the other side forming a churning tornado as I both heard its thundering roar and saw all that it carried moving faster against the invisible wall. It started to pulse, and I backed up in fear of what was about to occur. Just as I was thinking of turning around and heading back to where I came from, I was engulfed in a flash of light, shocked by an explosion that went straight through me like a bolt of electricity.

And then I started to fall.

Thirteen

In one instant I was hurtling through space with nothing to grab onto. In the next, I was back in the forest I found myself in when I first came to this new reality. I wasn't sure how I got there - if I had flown or just imagined myself here. But I was glad to be back, safe in my dark and moist forest instead of being engulfed by an explosion at the outer edges of the galaxy. I tasted the air around me, breathing in the mossy textures that comforted my nose. It was a far cry from the metallic cosmos that smelled like rust and tasted like biting on a penny.

I had landed in the same spot I was in when Aunt Rose found me, where the lightening had come down, catching the woods on fire. The proof of that fire was long covered over, both by Aunt Rose and by time. But from where I sat, I could still see the exact spot where the lightening had hit, the scars of the broken tree just visible under a blanket of green.

The scars continue to be there, even after death.

Here I was, months, maybe years, after I had crossed over, and I still held onto a life I couldn't get back to. But the love remained, on my side and on John's. It was what kept us connected, what linked us despite existing in two different dimensions and separated by an invisible barrier.

And I was tired of the barrier being there. Never had I felt more alone than I had in the days, weeks, months since my death. The existence of that barrier tore at me, made me feel like nothing was ever enough. I couldn't go on just seeing a glimpse of a smile, or knowing that John was thinking of me. How could I be satisfied when he didn't even know I was there? How would it ever be enough when I'd never see my reflection in his eyes, or the way he smiled when he looked down on my face?

This time when the cicadas began buzzing, I relaxed into the song and was carried into it as if I were one of the notes echoing through the trees. I thought of John, envisioning myself wrapped up in his arms again, feeling the sandy texture of his cheek against mine and the warmth of his body wrapped around me. I nestled against him, falling deeper into his embrace so that it no longer felt like an imagined scene. Everything else felt like a dream as I submitted to the feeling of being held so close. And in the moment, I no longer felt the weightlessness of being dead, feeling instead the sweet tether of living within a human body with skin and sweat and heat and life.

But the sound of the cicadas that surrounded me kept me grounded, letting me know that they were the reality, not John. And I managed to tear myself from John's arms and set myself back on the forest floor, sinking in tears as I cried for all I had left behind.

"Oh Rachel, what have you done?" a voice asked next to me. I looked up to see Aunt Rose looking down upon me with compassion, mixed with a slight shiver of fear.

"What do you mean?" I asked, forgetting my anger in my confusion. I wasn't sure if she was referring to the voyage through space, my resolve to stay near John, or just plain failing at this existence in death. But then I remembered that she was the cause of all of this, and I set my jaw in stubborn defiance. "I'm not speaking to you," I told her, turning back to the ground and willing her to go away.

"Take my hand, darling," she said, forgetting that I had forbidden her from using the endearment. I wanted to lash out at her for even daring to come near me again after all the trouble she had caused. But something inside me urged me to trust her. And so I did. I reached up and took her hand, pulling myself to my feet. And with a tug, we were both transported from the forest to the inside of a building. It felt familiar. I took in the hardwood floors and the painted walls, the photos that hung from the walls and the light fixtures that glowed above our heads. I realized with a lurch that this was the house in San Anselmo. How much time had passed since that day?

Aunt Rose urged me forward. I walked through the house, sighing with admiration over everything John had been working on in his spare time. The kitchen was just as I had hoped, the checkered floors greeting me like they were part of a diner out of the 1950s, the red from the towels and kitchen gadgets on the sink smiling at me and beckoning me forward. Sunlight streamed through the window where I would have been washing our dishes, and I ran my hand over the smooth marble that encased a large sink below the curve of a sturdy faucet.

I moved to the next room, and exclaimed over each detail that John had placed into it with care. The brilliant white wainscoting in the bedroom complemented a light shade of blue on the walls. Large wooden blinds sat within the windows, opened to reveal the garden outside that was blooming with life. Separating this particular bedroom from the master bedroom was a tiled bathroom, the same black and white pattern on the floor below a wide claw footed tub. I climbed into the tub and lay down, the size of it large enough to allow me to stretch out my legs and soak in the imaginary bubbles. In the corner was a large glass shower encased in blonde stone with a large rainfall shower head above. A pedestal sink was in the other corner, and a large vanity lay between the sink and shower where I would have been able to do my makeup and hair.

"Darling, I need you to keep going," Aunt Rose said, interrupting my mental escape inside the home I was supposed to be living in. She took my hand once again, but this time did not lurch me away. Instead, she led me to the master bedroom. I gasped when I saw what she had been trying to show me all along, feeling stupid for being distracted by a building. There on the floor was John, crumpled in a fetal position beside the makings of a bed frame. The screwdriver had fallen from his hand and rested a few inches away. As I rushed to his side, I was afraid he was dead. Rather, I was half afraid. Part of me, the part that I hid from my watchful Aunt Rose in the corner, hoped that this meant he would be joining me soon, that I would be able to hold onto him once again and feel his breath on my face. But I also wanted him to live, knowing how he needed to be there for his son, knowing that it wasn't his time to leave earth.

I reached out and touched his face, or at least moved my hand against the barrier that separated us so that my hand hovered just above his ashen skin. In an instant, I was flooded with images of the two of us together, his mind working overtime as he flitted from consciousness and a dreamlike state, fighting to stay on his side of life.

"Rachel," he whispered, and I realized he was aware of me in this half-conscious state.

"I'm here, sweetheart. I've always been here," I whispered. I could tell he couldn't hear me, that he was just aware of my presence even if I felt only like a dream. But I lay down next to him, my back against his chest as I curled up into his body, the invisible barrier the only thing between us. And I stayed like that with him for a few moments, holding the same position I had imagined just moments earlier in a forested symphony of cicadas. The song of the winged insects was replaced this time by the sound of John's heart against my back, my ears filled with its irregular beat, the sound so engulfing I was afraid it would beat right out of his chest.

"Now do you understand?" Aunt Rose murmured from where she stood on the other side of the room.

"Understand what?" I asked her, keeping my eyes closed and wishing she'd just go away.

"How fragile life is, and how it can be broken by just one of our mere whims," she told me with quiet seriousness. I opened my eyes from the protective shell of John's body and looked at her.

"What do you mean?" I scrutinized her, a ball of fear manifesting inside me.

"If you don't stop wishing him with you, he's going to die, Rachel." Her eyes flashed with determination as she tried to get me to see what I was refusing to see.

I had caused this.

I jumped from where I was and stood over John. His breath was slow and he winced in pain. When he could speak, he said my name with each breath. I longed to stop his pain, to bring him away from all that hurt him and comfort him in his fear. I remembered what it was like to die alone, to be cast into a confusing world where nothing made sense and no one was there to show me the way. With silent vows, I promised him I wouldn't let that happen to him, that I would be there when he reached the other side, and together we could figure out what happened next.

"Do you really want to be the cause of this?" Aunt Rose asked me, beside me with her hand on my shoulder. I was reminded of the moment I realized that her wishes had ended the lives of me and Joey, and how angry I had been with this woman I had once loved like a second mother. I looked with alarm at John, realizing that I was in danger of killing him, and that he might hate me for it. I tried to reason within myself that he would have wanted this. But I knew that by bringing him to me, I was also tearing him away from everyone he loved in life, including his son.

"Is it too late?" I asked Aunt Rose with a sudden fear. I remembered the momentum that had continued even after she had changed the course of her thinking, how we had careened off the cliff even as she willed us to continue on in the land of the living.

"I don't think so. But you need to change your thoughts from wishing he were with you to wishing with all your heart that his life will continue," she told me. She moved her hand from my shoulder and took my hand in hers. I squeezed it with determination, glad she was here to guide me in something I still didn't quite understand. How would I have known what to do, or even what was happening, if she hadn't found me and led me here? I closed my eyes and thought about John, this time in a reality that didn't include me. I thought about him with his son, imagining the two of them together in this house, sharing a life of happiness that was filled with the living instead of being haunted by the dead. I created in my mind scenarios that involved him working at his job, taking Sam to baseball games, and even, with hesitation, thoughts of him falling in love again and discovering life beyond me. But as hard as I tried, I couldn't bring myself to see a face upon the girl he looked at with such care in the confines of my imagination. Instead, I saw the back of her head and his face looking down on hers. And I pushed against the feelings of jealousy that threatened to overwhelm, discovering the sweet sensation of comfort that rose up under the thoughts of him happy once again.

From the ground, I could feel him stir. He grimaced in pain as he tried to sit up, the pain forcing him to remain on the ground. My image was gone from his head, filled instead with thoughts of his son and a feeling of hope he hadn't experienced since I had been ripped from his life.

160

Without warning, a yellow lab trotted into the bedroom and went straight to John. The dog licked at his face and then looked right at me. He saw me, even if it was only as a glowing light. It was strange that he was here, though I decided to thank him in silence rather than question his presence in our home, John's home.

"Is anyone there?" a voice called from the front of the house. I was transported to the entryway where a couple stood at the open door with an empty leash in their hands.

"Hello? I think our dog is in your house!" the man called, hesitating for just a moment before stepping into the hallway. The dog barked next to John, and both of them moved forward with less hesitation. "Sandy!" the man called out as he ventured through the house. He turned the corner and saw his dog next to John. Rushing forward, he said, "Call 9-1-1!" to his wife who was already pulling out her cell phone.

I moved back into the corner, melting into the shadows, my shame making me want to be even more invisible than I was. I had caused this. It was my fault. In front of me, the man knelt next to John and checked his heart rate, his breathing, asked him a few questions that John stumbled over in his answers. The time bubble burst as I watched everything happen in both slow motion and in an eerie fast forward, all of it unfolding at the same time. The paramedics came and checked his pulse again, swarming around him like seagulls fighting over an open bag of chips as they poked and prodded him before lifting him on a gurney. The couple with the dog spoke with one of the paramedics, telling them everything they knew about what had happened. They were the last to leave, taking the keys that hung on the hook inside the kitchen and tucking a note with their phone number in John's shirt pocket as he was wheeled away, then shutting the door behind them and locking it behind them.

"Did you want to go with them? Maybe ride in the ambulance?" Aunt Rose asked me. I shook my head, too fearful to speak. "Maybe you'd like to meet them at the hospital then," she said. Again, I shook my head. I was afraid to be near him, afraid I'd wish he would just succumb to whatever was ailing him and cause him to pass over to the other side. Aunt Rose patted my cheek, and in the sympathy that shone from her sad smile, I knew I didn't need to explain anything. "Come on darling, let's get out of here." She took my hand and we were whisked away from the sunlit house that should have held so much happiness, but only carried the same ghosts that all of us – John, Sam, me, and even Aunt Rose – were trying to escape.

Fourteen

Next I knew, we stood inside a hospital, despite my insistence I didn't want to be here. I glared at Aunt Rose, who only shook her head with a smile.

"We're not visiting John. I have other plans for us," she said. She turned and walked down the hallway, and I followed despite the air of suspicion with which I regarded her. Even though I was almost as guilty as she was of ending the life of another, I still held on to a bucket of resentments, faulting Aunt Rose for the pain of all I had lost. I also knew that she could sense this, and accepted it for what it was. Knowing Aunt Rose in life, and now in death, I imagined she didn't mind the blame I placed on her head. I was talking with her again. That small concession was enough for now.

Aunt Rose turned the corner, and smiled back at me. I could hear the strumming of a guitar echoing down the corridor, young voices chiming in with the stringed notes. We followed the sound to a set of double doors that were flung open wide to allow the music from the inside to fill the hospital wing with song.

On the other side of the doors was a large room with linoleum floors and streamers hanging from the ceiling, uneven as if they had been there for ages. Every inch of the walls was peppered with colorful children's paintings. Bookshelves with books of every size and shape stood in a corner next to several bean bags, and a few forgotten books lay on the floor nearby. Beside that was a bin of toys and a miniature kitchen, a tiny frying pan on the stove holding a replica of a fried egg.

The back of the room was dark, unused at the moment, making the room appear even larger with so much vacant space. And in the very center under a large light that hung from the ceiling was a man in a white coat, who I assumed to be a doctor, playing his guitar while surrounded by over a dozen children who sang along with him.

I surveyed each child, seeing the various ways they were broken. One child sat on the floor with a blanket wrapped around him, his pale leg peeking out from under the material to reveal how skeletal he was. His face was gaunt and took on a yellowish hue under the fluorescent lights, though his smile made his face shine with joy as he laughed and sang with those around him. A girl sat next to him, her head void of any hair. She wore a nightgown that buttoned at her neck and sleeves down to her wrists. Her feet were bare, and I could see bruises in various shades of purple, green, and yellow against the fair skin of her legs. A boy lay in a wheelchair that reclined enough so that he could remain lying down while still able to view the rest of the kids and the doctor playing the guitar. He didn't sing, but every now and again his face would break out into a silent laugh. His eyes darted around the room as he took in all the sights and sounds that surrounded him.

I took particular interest in this one child, how he was trapped in a mind and body he had little ability to control, and yet was so happy among the other children. I noticed how he was set apart from the others, the children around him paying him no attention as they paired up with each other and left him out of their circle. Segregation exists even in the grimmest of places, I noted.

Every one of the kids kept a safe distance from the boy, as if his paralyzed body and mind of marbles were catching; only glancing over their shoulders when a baritone laugh would escape from his lungs. All of them did their best to ignore him as their innocent voices rose and fell in the echoing room, all except one young girl who couldn't take her eyes off of him. I watched from our corner of the room as she got up, her eyes trained on him as she began to tiptoe in his direction. The boy who sat next to her grabbed her hand, shaking his head at her while motioning for her to sit back down next to him. I realized they were paired up in buddies, as younger kids sat next to older kids in a semi-circle around the strumming doctor. This was what must have ensured a sense of order in the room. But the paralyzed boy had no buddy at all, my only explanation being he was neither able to wander off, nor prevent a younger patient from doing so.

The young girl yanked her hand away from her buddy and crept the rest of the way over to the boy on the reclined wheelchair, staring into his face.

"Abby, get back here," her buddy hissed at her, trying not to disturb the song going on while making himself audible enough for her to hear him and come back. A nurse stepped forward from the back of the room and smiled at Abby's buddy in the circle, motioning that it was okay and she'd keep an eye on them. Abby's buddy turned back around in defeat, focusing once again on singing with the other kids and forgetting Abby and the boy reclined in the back of the room.

The paralyzed boy took his gaze from the kids that sang in the room and looked at the girl in front of him. His mouth hung open in a permanent grin, the drool dripping from his lower lip onto a bib that was fastened under his chin. He grunted at her in an awkward laugh, his head flopping around without any form of control while his body lay limp underneath him. Abby reached forward and touched his cheek, causing the boy to grin wider. She laughed at his reaction and he laughed with her.

"I think Jacob likes you, Abby," the nurse whispered. Abby gave the nurse a shy smile, shrinking away against the wheelchair with her fingers in her mouth. She couldn't have been more than five years old. She wore a nightgown like many of the other little girls in the room, a much happier thing to wear than the standard hospital gowns the rest of the patients wore in the hospital. Her long blond hair hung against her back, still a bit tangled and messy as if she had just woken up. Part of it was shaved away, and a bright red surgical wound shone out from behind one ear, fastened together with black staples.

"Brain cancer," Aunt Rose whispered to me when she saw my gaze fall upon Abby's injured head. I sucked in a sharp breath, cursing a world where young children have to endure diseases that are far too ugly for a life so innocent. "Don't worry, she'll make it out okay," Aunt

Rose reassured me. "They managed to cut all of the cancer out of her brain, and her body has responded to the radiation beautifully." She shook her head with a smile. "The things these humans are capable of, you'd think they were demigods with their abilities in science and healing. Truly miraculous, the things they can do." She nodded her head towards Jacob. "Now him, that's a whole other case. There's nothing left for the doctors to do but wait for him to succumb," she said, clicking her tongue. "It won't be long, either," she added, nodding toward a figure in the back of the room.

A woman stood in the corner, separate from all of us and intent in her observation of Jacob. She glanced over at us and nodded in acknowledgement before focusing her attention back on him. I hadn't even noticed her before, and now her presence was hard to ignore.

"Who is she?" I asked.

"She's a family guide, probably an aunt or distant relative. We all have them, a familiar face that greets us in the first moments of the afterlife. Generally we give those who have passed a little solitude before suddenly appearing, allowing you to plot your own course before we come to guide you through the hows and whys of life after living. But with children, we try to be there immediately when they cross over. When that happens depends on the will of the child. For some it's immediate, as they hold little knowledge on how to hang on to life when their spirit begins to move on. But for others, they fight to cling to life, trying to remain in a world with people they love in hopes they can overcome the inevitable. So those of us called to guide them in this existence just hang around until they pass over. Sometimes the spirit of the living can even see us, like Jacob there," she said.

Sure enough, I could see Jacob's head roll every now and then toward the back of the room, his eyes straining as he tried to see the woman who stood in the back. She smiled back at him, but made no other movement at all. I could sense that he recognized her, but he was unable to voice his recognition. Instead he focused the rest of his attention on Abby, who had now mustered up enough courage to hold onto his exposed hand, curling her tiny fingers around his to make up for his inability to return the motion. And her soft, angelic voice seemed to rise above the other voices in the room as she shared a piece of the celebration with the boy who was ignored by everyone else.

When the designated music time ended, all of the children left for their hospital rooms. Many of them shared rooms with other kids, but Jacob's room only held one bed and a couch in the corner of the room that was made up with a pillow and blanket. Aunt Rose and I melted into the shadows of the room as the nurses worked together to place Jacob in a hospital lift that helped to transfer him from the mobile reclining chair he was in to the hospital bed. A woman, whom I perceived to be his mother, stood next to Jacob's bed, taking his hand once he was positioned in bed and listened close while a doctor shared a quiet conversation with her. The spirit woman from the music room stood silent in the opposite corner of the room, all of her attention focused on Jacob as he drifted off to sleep despite the commotion of the hospital.

"His condition appears to have improved," the doctor told the mother while jotting down a few notes on his clipboard. "He was well enough tonight to join the other kids during music hour, and he responded to the sounds."

"Do you think that means he might be able to come home again?" Jacob's mother asked, hope radiating from her eyes as she squeezed Jacob's hand.

"It's too soon to tell," he apologized. "We'll run a few more tests and keep a watchful eye on him for the next several days. But I wouldn't cancel Hospice just yet. We won't be out of the woods for a little while. I don't want to get your hopes up, though it doesn't hurt to hold on to hope for his sake. However, sometimes I've seen patients make miraculous recoveries only to pass away the very next day." Jacob's mother winced, and I could see the doctor regretting his words. He started to say something else, and I could hear his brain searching for just the right words. But in the end he just smiled and squeezed her shoulder and then walked away to leave all of us alone.

Underneath the beeping from the monitor next to the bed and the noisy labored air that escaped from Jacob's mouth as he slept, was the sound of his mother's gentle weeping as she continued to hold his motionless hand. She was exhausted. I could sense it when I tuned into her, feeling the weight of stress hanging on her chest like a hundred bricks. Her emotions were a mixture of grief, sadness, anger, and a tinge of relief at the notion that everything might be over soon, followed by immense guilt for even thinking that way. And drowning it all was a feeling of fear, afraid for her little boy who might cross over to a place she couldn't follow, and afraid for herself when her life was void of his presence.

She stayed that way for some time, praying next to him into the early hours of the morning, *Please God* being her most fervent request to an almighty spirit that felt light years away. It was reminiscent of the prayer breathed from John's lips a million breaths before in the church where we were to have been married.

Jacob's mother took a deep breath in an attempt to compose herself. She wiped her eyes and searched her son's face for any sign of movement that showed he might pull through this. I could see visions of Jacob in her mind, images that appeared to be from a few months earlier when he was full of life and running on his own two feet. I could see the sparks within Jacob's head, currents of electricity that didn't quite meet up, making it impossible for him to move on his own accord. The notes on the chart flung out at me as if under a microscope. *Pediatric stroke* and *blood clot* were written in dark black ink, followed by scribbles of diagnosis and instructions of care for the nurses.

Jacob remained motionless in sleep, and his mother submitted to the heaviness of her eyes as she curled up on the couch to sleep for a few hours. As she drifted off, the spirit woman in the corner moved forward and stood by Jacob's bed. She didn't touch him, but just stood there watching him. Out of the shadows, I could see the striking resemblance she held to both Jacob and his mother. I wanted to ask her how she was related to them, but was aware of how private this moment was. I looked over at Aunt Rose with a look of helplessness, asking her with my eyes if we should leave, if it was okay if we were here. She gave a small nod of affirmation, then turned back to Jacob and the spirit. I did the same.

It wasn't long before I saw his body glow, the outline of his shape appearing to expand as his spirit grew just bigger than his body. The steady sound of the heart monitor next to him started to beep fast, waking Jacob's mother with a start. She ran to his side and grabbed his arm. Jacob's face remained motionless.

"Nurse!" she shouted, grabbing the call button from the side of the bed and punching it with her thumb over and over. "Hang on Jacob, just hang on," she pleaded with him. "Nurse!"

Two nurses rushed in, moving his mother to the side as they checked his pulse. Jacob's body began to shake with violent movements. The machine went crazy as his body convulsed, forgetting the paralysis that had left him immobile for the past few months. I could hear the crackling in his brain as he underwent another stroke, his inner voice screaming in agony, images flashing through his mind of things he had seen in his life and the face of the calm spirit woman who stayed next to the bed.

"Code blue," was heard over the intercom. A crash cart was wheeled in, and they fired it up as a nurse held the paddles. The doctor rushed into the room and barked orders at the nurses who surrounded Jacob's body. One of the nurses placed a breathing mask over his mouth while another injected a clear substance into a bag of liquid connected by an IV to his arm. Jacob's body ceased moving and he lay as if sleeping. The heartbeat on the monitor slowed from its rapid rate, moving to a regular beat before slowing even more until it became one thin line with a long beep to match.

"Clear!" the doctor called, and Jacob's body jumped with the shock of electricity, the thin line jumping with it before settling back into an unresponsive scream. They tried it over and over, Jacob's mother crying in the corner as she watched in helplessness, the spirit woman waiting near Jacob's head, and Aunt Rose and me intruding on a moment that didn't belong to us.

As the chaos swirled around Jacob's body, I saw his spirit sit up and look around him. Fear was written all over his face as he looked at what was going on to his body and with all the people that rushed around him. But when his gaze settled on the spirit woman, he relaxed into an easy grin. She returned his smile with sheer happiness, the first strong emotion I had seen her express since first noticing her. Taking Jacob's hand, she helped him to hop down from the bed. He looked down at his legs, held his arms in front of him, and stretched every part of himself now that he was free from his frozen body.

"Welcome home, Jacob," the spirit woman said as they walked towards us.

Jacob didn't even notice us as he moved towards us, but he did give one last look over his shoulder as his mother sat crying on the couch, the nurses putting the paddles away while the doctor told her they did everything they could. We all watched as the doctors and nurses left the room to give her a few moments with her son's body. She stood up, hesitating with her hand over her mouth. She walked forward as if weights were strapped to her feet. She reached Jacob's body, which seemed very small amid the mess of wires and machines. One by one, she unhooked them all, removing the breathing machine last from his pale face, and holding her hand against his cheek with the gentlest of touches. Jacob's spirit broke free from the spirit woman's hand, rushing to be near his mother. He touched her face in the same way she was touching the cheek of his body, and his mother shuddered into tears from a feeling she couldn't quite place.

"Take care of him, sis," she whispered, certain she was heard as she relinquished her boy to the sister who had already passed on. Jacob kissed her on the cheek, smiling at his mother with love, and then ran back to his aunt. Together they evaporated from the room as his mother collapsed in a shaking and silent cry with her head on his lifeless chest.

"Where did they go?" I asked Aunt Rose.

"She's leading him towards Heaven," she said. I sighed and shook my head at the great irony that we have so many answers about Heaven in life, but knew nothing about it in death.

Fifteen

"I don't understand," I said to Aunt Rose. "All this time I've been asking questions about Heaven, and no one seems to know anything at all. And then this kid gets to go to Heaven just like that, and you know exactly what is going on? What about Joey? You didn't seem to have any answers for me then!" My mind was racing overtime, the world opening up in a whole new light and presenting me with so many questions I didn't know which to ask first.

We stood in an empty room now, the hospital long faded away. I didn't know where we were, but it was clear we were in utter solitude. Aunt Rose smiled at me, waving her hand next to her to reveal a plush couch. She sat down and patted the seat next to her. I joined her with caution, still having a hard time trusting this woman who both made everything feel more difficult and was the only one who could guide me to real answers.

I started. "Where is Joey?"

"I don't know."

My frustration, never far below the surface, exploded. "What do you mean you don't know?" I demanded. "You knew where Jacob was headed, didn't you? So why don't you know where my son is?" Aunt Rose sighed, giving me another one of her patronizing smiles as if I were but a child and she were about to teach me the ins and outs of the universe. The worst of it was that I felt like a child.

"Rachel, you want me just to say he's in Heaven, right? Well I can't be certain he's there," she maintained. "I can assume, as can you. It's likely that's where he is, being that he's a child and leaving the world behind just seems to come easier for them. But can I guarantee it? No. Just because we can't find him doesn't mean that he's moved beyond this divide to get to Heaven. He may be doing some exploring of his own or he may be stuck in his own attachments. He could be anywhere."

"Why doesn't anyone know anything concrete about Heaven?" I asked Aunt Rose. I was thinking back to conversations with Jane, when she told me she felt like there was a Heaven but couldn't be sure.

"Because none of us have been there," Aunt Rose said. "If we had, we wouldn't be back to this divide. We'd be there to stay for good."

"Okay, look. My friend Jane, who also exists in this divide, didn't seem to know much of anything about Heaven. In fact, she seemed to believe in it through faith alone. But when pressed for facts, she couldn't be sure there was a Heaven, a God, or anything beyond this place we exist now. She just felt it was true. But here you are, speaking with certainty that there is a Heaven, that this is only the resting place before we move on, that Jacob was being led by that spirit to this Heaven, and that Joey may or may not be there. How can you be so sure of these things, and yet you're here in this world and not there?"

"Now you're getting to the real questions," Aunt Rose said, her eyes twinkling at my confusion. "Do you know who that spirit woman was that led Jacob from the room?" she asked me.

"She was his aunt, I think," I said. "It seemed like he knew her, she looked a lot like him and his mother, and his mom referred to her sister, so I can only assume she passed away and was now there in the room when he passed."

"Yes, she was probably his aunt. But do you know her purpose there?" Aunt Rose pressed on.

"You said she was a 'family guide', someone who guides a loved one through the afterlife," I said.

"Yes. But with children, their time in this divide is very brief, sometimes serving as just a pathway to Heaven. You saw how Jacob kissed his mother and then left with the guide. He was leaving her for the last time, and he was okay with it. His guide's responsibility is to help him through the transition of life to death. And when he's ready, she leads him to the entrance of Heaven where he will stay forever."

"So he's trapped there? What kind of Heaven is that?" I asked Aunt Rose, and she laughed at my naivety.

"No, he'll choose to stay there. Once you enter Heaven, it's so magnificent you won't want to leave at all. But the only way to be able to pass through those gates in the first place is to let go of everything that exists on this side of Heaven. That includes the people you once loved and the life you once led. So you have the ability to come and go, but no one wants to come back to the darkness of this world once they've let it go and moved to the next."

"How do you know so much when you haven't been there?" I asked her.

"I told you before, I'm a guide," she told me. "I'm your guide, and I've been the guide of several before you." She paused and counted off on her fingers. "Let's see, there have been four I think. It's been so long I can hardly remember. I led one of my good friends when she passed on. She didn't linger much at all, being ready to die in her later years of life. One of my neighbors passed away some time ago and that bitter man had no family or friends at all who he'd be comforted by. So I helped him to get to the peaceful side of death and transition to Heaven. And there were a couple more. All of them, once they were done peering into the window of the living, were led by me to Heaven where we both got a glimpse of what's to come before they left me and moved on. Let me tell you, darling, what waits for us on that other side is better than anything you've ever imagined."

"But if it's so great, why are you here and not there?" I asked her.

"Because you have to be able to let go of the living and the world they live in before you can move on to Heaven," she affirmed. "And, well, you know how that goes."

"That's why I'm here, too," I mused.

"That's correct," she nodded, free of judgment.

I was beginning to understand. Her obsession with my sister and me, her inability to detach was being mirrored in my feelings for John. I thought about how I couldn't tear myself away from being near him and Sam, and how involved I got in the living world even though I was no longer a part of it. All of a sudden, I was having a hard time holding my death against her, having just risked John's life through my own attachment. I was even having a hard time staying angry over the death of my son. Remembering the intense pull to bring John over, the way I had to struggle to stop killing him, I could get a sense of what Aunt Rose had experienced in my final moments of life. I realized she couldn't overcome the intense emotions that existed in this world, the feelings we clung to when we were able to grasp onto little else.

Even now I was being tortured by my own longing. More than anything, I longed to see John, to be by his side as he recovered in the hospital. But just as strong was the fear that my presence would put his life in peril. It had taken so much for me to be able to pull away from dragging him down. What if I found myself in the same position I was in before, leading him down a road he could never return from, leaving behind Sam and everything else he held dear in this life? I couldn't do that to him. And yet, I needed to be next to him again.

"Come with me?" I begged Aunt Rose. "Stay near me while I visit John? I don't think I can do this alone." I could tell in her eyes that she wanted to protest this, to persuade me to leave him behind and focus on moving on. I could also tell she wasn't going to say any of this out loud. Instead, she nodded.

"But darling," she cautioned, "if you start pulling him back down, I can't stop you. Only you have the power to refrain from that. And he's in such a weakened state, any thoughts you may have of him being with you in this existence will surely kill him. So go ahead and visit him, but practice restraint. Keep your mind clear and your intentions pure. And think of his needs before your own."

I nodded and grasped her hand, squeezing it tight and drawing comfort from the safety net I gathered from her presence. Together we left the empty room and went back to the hospital where Jacob had just passed only moments before. But this wing was different. There were no guitars playing or children singing. No streamers hung from the ceiling, no drawings were taped to the wall. This wing of the hospital had a far more serious air, where doctors and nurses rushed from room to room, family members shuffled in and out with somber faces, and the most prominent sounds were the voices over the intercom and a steady stream of beeps from the nurses' station and each room we passed by.

J. Hanlon was on the wall outside his room, and I peered in as if I were visible and afraid to wake him. I jumped with a start when I realized someone else was in there with him, a woman holding his hand. A dangerous feeling of jealousy began to bubble up before I realized it was only my sister. I let out a long breath, realizing just how hard this was going to be.

John was sleeping, his appearance fragile in his hospital gown. He was hooked up to an IV at his arm and wires attached to his chest to monitor his heart rate. The machine beeped beside him at a steady pace, almost as if nothing had happened. Sara sat next to him, rubbing the top of his hand with her thumb as he slept. She stared off at a wall, her mind traveling a million miles a minute. I did my best to tune out her thoughts, but captured a few fragments of the troubles she'd been having with Kevin, fears about joint custody, and the terrifying thought of supporting herself on one income instead of two.

John stirred, shifting under the thin blanket before opening his eyes and blinking with heavy lids. He saw Sara and smiled, his murmur so soft she couldn't hear what he had said. But I heard it glisten through the air to my ears.

"Rachel."

He opened his eyes a little wider as he woke, and realized with a start where he was and who was holding his hand. "Sara," he said, praying she didn't hear him call her by her sister's name. She smiled and squeezed his hand. "How long was I out?" he asked her.

"Half of yesterday and pretty much all of today," she said. "But that's mainly because they've been keeping you sedated. I'm supposed to let them know when you come out of sleep."

"Not yet," he said. "What time is it?"

"It's late, about eleven o'clock at night. They allowed me to stay when I said I was your sister." Her smile held notes of guilt. He chuckled.

"You're a bit fair to be my sister, but whatever works. I'm glad you're here. Does Sam know?"

"Yeah, they called your ex-wife first and she told him. He's the one who called to let me know," she informed him. John was startled by this, so was I. It seemed so out of character, strange even, that Sam would even think to call Sara. "I assume it's because he needed someone who wasn't his mom to be here," Sara explained, making sense of the confusion. "I think..." she began, hesitating before she continued, "I think, that I just happened to be the closest person to Rachel he could think of to be here with you and with him." She said it in one breath, hoping that by doing so, John would be unscathed by the reminder that she was just my stand-in. It didn't stop John from wincing, hiding it under an exaggerated yawn. "He was here earlier today, but needed to get home since he has school tomorrow."

"It's nice to know he cares," John said, and grimaced, regretting the words as soon as they left his mouth. "I mean...I didn't mean that. I guess I just meant that with him being a teenager and all, and especially now that he lives with his mom, it's hard to know exactly what he's thinking. It's just nice to know...that he cares," John said, followed by an awkward chuckle.

"He cares," Sara told him. "He was worried about you. He stayed here for a few hours while you slept, and we chatted about how things are going at his mom's house."

"He talked with you?" John asked. As he said it, he tried to sit up with his elbows, only to have his face twist with pain as he collapsed on the bed.

"Don't overstrain yourself; here, let me help you with the bed." Sara reached over him and pushed a button on the railing of the bed, and the back of it raised so he could sit in an elevated position with no effort. "You had a heart attack, John, which is not normal for a forty-year-old man. It was likely caused by stress, but the doctors still need to run a few more tests." She paused, looking uncomfortable. The shift in her demeanor wasn't lost on John, even as he fought to stay awake under the lingering effects of the sedatives.

"What's wrong?" he asked her.

Sara gave him an embarrassed smile, and I could hear her thoughts mulling over how to ask the question. She took a deep breath and let it out before speaking.

"I don't know how to ask this, and hate to even bring it up while you're just waking up. But your ex-wife was the first person they called. Apparently she's still listed as your next of kin. You didn't have Rachel on there?"

It was John's turn to be uncomfortable. I waited for his answer, though I could hear his mind tumbling over excuses loud and clear. He had Wendy on there instead of me? Aunt Rose touched my arm, and I was reminded to still my thoughts and just be an uninvolved observer.

"I know," he admitted. "It's not that I didn't want Rachel on there. I blame it on laziness more than anything. It's my downfall, putting everything off until last minute. In the weeks before her death, I had planned on adding her to all that I owned, including power of attorney and next of kin. I just hadn't gotten around to it."

"Well, I guess it's a moot point now. Besides, it was probably a good thing Wendy was still on there since they may not have known who to call otherwise," Sara said, smiling. He squeezed her hand with a returned smile, and she was reminded that her hand still grasped his. Embarrassed, she pulled it back in her lap.

"So, Sam talked with you about life in Sebastopol," John said, changing the subject. "What did he say? Does he like it? Is he miserable? Is his mom a tyrant and he realized he made a huge mistake?" Sara laughed at this.

"Well, he seems to enjoy his new school," she told him. "He's made a few friends that he already sort of knew from his mom's neighborhood. And he says there are a few cute girls there, even though he misses one girl in particular from his old school. His mom is okay, not bad but just different. And even though he'd never admit it to you, he told me that he misses living with you. He says you don't visit him that much, blaming it on you being busy with work and the house in San Anselmo. But I think he'd like the two of you to hang out more."

"I guess I didn't...I mean, I didn't realize... I didn't think he wanted to hang out. I don't know. I mean, I feel like a total idiot now. I thought that since he didn't hang out with me much before he moved out, he wasn't going to want to see me much after. And...I guess I just didn't know how to call him up and ask him to go do something." John moved his arm to run his hand through his hair, wincing at the pain of the simple motion. The wires attached to his arm brushed against his face and rattled the IV bag. Sara reached over and helped him to untangle from the awkward wires.

"I think because he doesn't live with you, he especially wants you to call him up and ask to hang out. He's testing you, trying to see how much you care."

"I know," John admitted. He made an inner resolution to try harder with Sam. He wasn't sure how - maybe a phone call or a lunch out, perhaps an afternoon to work on his throw even though Sam's interest in baseball was starting to wane. But once he got out of this hospital he swore to himself he'd be a better dad. It seemed like he was always making promises like that, something he realized even as he did it again. This time, he swore, he would follow through.

"I should really let the nurses know you're awake," Sara said. "They're going to want to poke you in all sorts of fun places to see how you're doing."

"Sounds kinky. Any of them cute?" John asked. Sara grinned.

"You're such a pervert. I'm going to take off now, but I'll be back tomorrow to check in on you. Don't go anywhere, okay?"

"Heck, no. I got ladies waiting to fulfill my every whim. I'd be a dummy to take off now." Sara grinned, leaning over to kiss him on the cheek. Without thinking, John inhaled, catching once again the familiar scent of my hair in my sister's blonde locks. It stirred something inside him, just as it had before. Except this time, instead of seeing my face in front of him, he saw Sara's. The feeling caught him off guard, but he managed to tuck it away. Sara didn't see it, but the newness of this emotion inside him felt like a slap in my face.

The struggle to keep my emotions at bay became too heavy a burden to control. I felt the bitter acid of jealousy brewing inside of me, the taste of it sparking on my tongue at the reality that John *could* move on, and my sister could be the one to help him do that.

Before I could jeopardize him any further through emotions beyond my control, I knew I needed to escape. And I needed to go alone. I moved out of Aunt Rose's reach and focused on a place as far away as I could manage. Only when the room began to evaporate around me did Aunt Rose turn toward me. Her saddened eyes were the last thing I saw before I was cast into darkness.

Sixteen

"What do you want from me?!" I screamed to an invisible God from where I stood. "You've taken everything else from me. Why this? Why now? Why her?"

So that I would not affect John with the ridiculous feelings that threatened to devour me, and ultimately him, I had to get far away from the hospital. I knew I could have gone farther, that I could have traveled to the farthest corner of space where I'd gone before, but I was afraid of the voice that spoke to me within that emptiness, and of the churning tornado on the other side of the barrier. So I envisioned a different point that was still safe on earth, choosing to keep my feet grounded in the familiar rather than exploring the unknown.

Well, sort of.

I'd seen pictures of Mauna Kea, the tallest mountain in Hawaii, in a National Geographic when I was young. The article read of tours to the domed observatories at the top of the mountain with a view of the surrounding islands and an uninterrupted night sky that boasted millions of stars. In the colder seasons, the bald peak of the mountain was covered in snow.

The fact that there was a mountain in Hawaii that had snow fascinated me. Though I had never been there in life, it seemed like the perfect escape for me. I needed to be able to process my thoughts without killing anyone, and to remain hidden for at least a little while. So this was where I now found myself – on the top of Mauna Kea in my escape from whatever was manifesting itself between my sister and John in a hospital in San Francisco.

It must have been autumn on top of the Hawaiian mountain, because, much to my dismay, no snow could be found. The air was cold, with a slight drizzle wetting the ground. But the whole top of the mountain remained bare. I clenched my hands in anger and willed time forward. In my determination, the motion was effortless. Day became night, night became day, and the stars moved across the sky in mere minutes. The air around me changed from cool to colder. The light rain changed into snow flurries. Soon, the ground was covered in white, the season having changed from autumn to winter on the Hawaiian peak of Mauna Kea.

My feet left no footprint in the frozen slush, but I still slipped through the ice, kicking at it with anger. I yelled out at the ocean far below, screaming with everything I had. A few explorers wandered around the observatory, passing right by me as I shrieked into their ears. But they heard nothing as I bellowed against a life I didn't ask for and circumstances that were beyond my control.

"God damn it all to hell!" I blasted into the air. "Why? What the hell is the reason for all of this? As if being dead wasn't enough? You give me all this power in exchange for life, but you've placed too many limitations on me! I can't touch John. I can't even get him to hear me. And I definitely can't feel too strongly about anything around him or else I'll kill him. What kind of joke is this? It's not fair! I have shackles on me when I'm supposed to be free!" I cried out. I breathed hard against my anger, feeling the fury racing through me. Here I was, unbound from the laws of gravity without an earthly body, and the ability to travel anywhere and be anything. And yet, the rules of this world kept me in an inescapable prison. I was trapped, unable to just dive deep into my yearning so I could mourn all I had lost.

"And then Sara? Why Sara? Why her? Please God, anyone but her!" I pleaded. I couldn't bear the thought of my sister wrapped in John's arms, even though I knew that any girl who replaced me in John's heart wouldn't be worthy in my eyes. But Sara? This truth stung. Why did she have to visit him so much, attaching my memory to her presence to make him fall for her? Why did so much about her have to be so similar to me, and so familiar to John?

I screamed into the wind, haunted by the inequities of the situation, and the atmosphere shook around me as sound waves rippled through the air. A few adventurous birds that had traveled to the top of the mountain looked in my direction. But even they steered clear of me, afraid to come close to the crazy ghost causing such a racket. Storm clouds brewed in the sky, threatening to break open and envelop the earth and all the injustice it held. But they just churned as a covering to the heavens, becoming a fogged-up mirror to the storm within me. The torrential rains were restrained from spilling over, just as I was forced to bottle up the pain from my sorrow and devastation.

When I had no more words left, my emotions having drained me of anything else I could scream to an uncompassionate God, I sat on the icy ground and stared out at the horizon. The fog was just starting to creep in, covering the ocean and lopping off the bottom of the mountain so that I appeared to be standing on just a mere hill. The carpet of white went as far as I could see, and I had the sudden urge to just jump out at it and land upon the fluffy covering, curling up inside until I could sleep away the injustices of this in-between world. Only one thing stopped me as I stared out at the inviting cloud of white, and that was a memory of my father.

As a child, I once asked my father why we couldn't just drive across the foggy covering of the valley that led to our home. I was around five years old, peering out from my passenger side window of our family's car, trying to catch a glimpse of the vineyards that were concealed under the thick white cloud. We had just rounded the bend towards our home in Sonoma, and the fog looked more like a solid blanket than a fluffy cloud. He chuckled, a deep baritone sound that filled my soul with gingerbread and hot cocoa, a laugh I hadn't heard in so long that just the memory of it warmed me on this morning atop a snowy mountain in Hawaii.

Back then, he'd taken the time to describe the way moisture and the different temperatures of the air created the fog, and how we were able to pass right through it. He explained that it wasn't a blanket at all, though it did help to keep the ground warmer than it'd be without it. He always was one who believed the truth in science was more important than the magic of the imagination, even when explaining things to a five year old child. He figured that bypassing childhood "lies" would ensure my education wasn't tampered with, giving me an edge compared to my classmates. To him, magical things were a waste of time.

As I sat looking out at the Hawaiian fog, I knew that I could curl up within it and sleep hidden within the confines of the misty padding. Escaping within the magic of the impossible seemed like the perfect game of pretend. But just as important, I needed my dad to be right - even in my death where the impossible was possible. And right now, I wished more than anything that he could be here next to me, telling me the science of air and temperature, and a better truth - that everything was going to be all right.

I hated that I was having such a strong reaction to the mere passing thought that was shared between John and Sara. It didn't mean anything. So what if John smelled me in Sara's hair? It wasn't as if they were having an affair, or even entertaining the idea of one. At least, I didn't think so.

But what if they were?

I shuddered at the thought, trying to pinpoint what it was that was bothering me so much. He was going to move on at some point or another. I knew this to be true. And if I claimed to care about him, I would want him to find someone else and not be alone for the rest of his life. Of course, the selfish part of me still had to get on board with that notion, because all I wanted him to do was dress in black and wait until he could be by my side once again. In my imaginary reality, it was all very dramatic and full of angst.

But the twinge of jealousy I was feeling was more than just the thought of him finding someone else. It pained me to think of John moving on. But it killed me all over again to think of him with my sister.

Sara had always been the beauty queen, the one who had all the friends and was the center of everyone's attention. Being only a year apart, we'd been raised almost like twins. She was the older of us, claiming the spotlight right from the beginning as the oldest, and holding that spotlight tight when I was born. My mother used to boast that I was such a great baby right from the beginning, how she would prop me up in a chair with a bottle to entertain myself while she tended to my sister's many needs. She bragged about how easy I was compared to my temperamental sister.

All I heard was how easy I was to forget.

We shared a room growing up, from our early years all the way through high school. My side of the room was always a pile of clothes I had worn throughout the week, some more than once, even in their wrinkled state. Sara's side was clean to a fault, from the hospital corners on her tidy bed to the clothes that were color-coordinated in her closet. She saved her money to spend on the latest fashions, wearing the latest trends with the rest of the school while I opted for more of a t-shirt and jeans motif. I found that books and junk food were a much better investment, even if they were also the reason behind my pudgy appearance.

It wasn't until my freshman year of high school when I began to feel the pains of Sara's beauty and popularity. I'd already experienced what it felt like to stay home while she attended party after party. But I was glad to stay home. Parties full of people drinking, making out, or whatever else they were doing behind their parents' backs freaked the hell out of me. The one time Sara had asked me to come with her, I was ready to leave within the first five minutes. I ended up sitting on a couch and pulling out one of my books I carried around, sandwiched between a guy who kept offering me a doobie despite my insistence that I didn't smoke weed, and a couple who appeared to be trying to find something down each other's throats with their tongues. On the way home, Sara lambasted me for embarrassing her in such a heinous manner, for having the audacity to nerd out at one of the coolest parties of the century. From then on, I was excused from any other social obligation with Sara, as far as she was concerned. And I couldn't have been happier.

But in that same year of high school, I met *him*. And everything changed.

****

His name was Eric. He had the dreamiest blue eyes I had ever seen and was one of the few sophomores in our advanced English class reserved for freshmen. But he read from Ernest Hemingway as if he were right there in the twenties, attending a bash with Daisy on his arm. Once he even caught me staring at him as he stood in front of the class, taking his turn to read from the chapter of *The Great Gatsby*, and he caught me smiling like a dope from my seat in the third row. I had blushed something fierce when his eyes met mine, and smoldered in my seat when he didn't look away. I almost died on the spot when, instead of glaring at me or calling me out in front of the class, he just gave me a private wink, smiling at me from the corner of his dimpled mouth before diving back into the messy triangle of romance that existed in a book I'd already read three times through.

"What are you doing this weekend?" he asked me after class, and it took everything I had not to run to the bathroom and vomit from the caffeinated butterflies that attacked my insides.

"Nothing really," I managed to squeak out, and he got my address so we could hang out.

The weekend came, and for the first time I had nothing to wear. All of a sudden, my crumpled t-shirts were too tomboyish for such an occasion, my jeans cut way too high unlike the low-waisted fashions my sister and all her friends wore.

"Let me borrow something!" I pleaded with my sister, who held her ground as she lay on her bed with a magazine.

"You'll stretch out all my clothes," she told me, snapping her gum with impatience. "Besides, what do you want to borrow them for? You're just going to get them all dirty outside."

"Eric is coming over and none of my clothes look good enough," I said, praying that the mention of a boy would jump her into high gear. It worked. She leapt off her bed and started rummaging through her closet.

"Why didn't you say so, Rachel? How exciting! Tell me everything about him!" As she searched her closet for the perfect outfit, I described how his eyes were the perfect shade of blue forget-me-nots, how he loved to read in his spare time, and that his hero was Ernest Hemingway. I made up most of this, of course, since I still knew nothing about him. But because that description illustrated the perfect guy for me, it only made sense that it defined him to a T.

"Sounds boring," Sara said, wrinkling her nose. "How's this?" She pulled out a light colored dress with pink flowers and an empire waist. I grimaced at the prettiness of it, the exact opposite of everything I ever wore. She caught my look and explained. "It will fit you up top and hide your belly, and you can wear jeans underneath to jazz it up and make it less girly." I took it from her with caution and slipped it over my head. I pulled on a pair of jeans, and she bent down to cuff them so they landed between my ankles and knees. Afterwards, she showed me how to apply a little mascara and lip gloss, offering a natural look under a hint of femininity. Then she pulled my long auburn hair into a loose bun at the base of my neck. "If it looks like he's getting bored, take your hair out of the bun and shake it out. He won't be able to look anywhere else." I blushed with embarrassment, though I was memorizing every single thing she told me.

The doorbell rang, and we both squealed with excitement.

"Oh my god! How do I look?" I asked her. I hated the way it sounded, like the dress had turned me into one of her ditsy friends. But in the moment, it mattered more than ever.

"You look great," she told me. "Now don't keep him waiting too long."

I bounced down the stairs, shooting like a cannon towards the door once I reached the bottom step. But just before I got there, I stopped to catch my breath. After a few seconds, I opened it. There he was. He was looking over his shoulder when I opened the door, and then turned back towards me at the sound. The sight of his grin made me breathless all over again, and I couldn't help but let a goofy smile fall from my lips and drown out any coolness I might have possessed. I was grateful when he didn't notice.

"So what do you want to do?" he asked me, and I started to shrug. "Now come on," he laughed. "I made the move to ask you out. Now it's your turn. Plus, this is your turf. Next time we'll hang at my place and I'll decide what to do, I promise." Just the mere mention that there would be a next time when the first time hadn't yet happened made my heart soar into my throat.

"Well, we could look through my library for a book to read," I said, forcing a laugh when I saw the awkward look on his face. "I'm totally kidding, of course," I said quick, covering my tracks. He laughed with me.

"Funny," he said. "What else you got?"

"Well... I know. We could take a hike up into the hills and then come back and watch a movie," I said. His eyes lit up at the suggestion, and I grinned. "I just need to let my mom know I'm going." I called into the house to my mom, who insisted on coming out to meet Eric right away.

"So you're from Rachel's class!" she exclaimed, as if she had thought I was the only one who even took English in high school. "That's great! Have you lived in Sonoma long?"

"All my life, ma'am. I just went to a different school until this year," he said.

"Oh? Did you all move or something?" she asked.

"Mom!" I exclaimed. "You don't need to ask him his life story!"

"It's all right," Eric offered. "No, we didn't move. There were just some mean kids there and it was getting too hard to stay. My parents finally caved and let me come to this school."

"Ugh, kids can be so cruel," my mom scoffed. "Well, are you happier here? Are the kids nicer to you?"

"Much nicer," he said, looking straight at me. I blushed under his gaze, looking down at my shoes. The look wasn't lost on my mom, who hid a smile behind her hand.

"Well, it was nice to meet you, Eric," she said. "I have to get going, though. I'm baking bread, and if you know anything about the rising process you know how finicky it can be." I did know about rising bread, and I knew that it wasn't that finicky, and in fact needed no attention at all. I gave her a grateful smile before she turned to leave.

"Nice to meet you, ma'am," he called after her.

"Please, call me Maureen," she shouted back through the screen door, disappearing inside and leaving us alone.

"Your mom's nice," Eric said.

"Seems that you've charmed her," I teased. He laughed.

"Well, I guess that's a good thing if your mom likes me."

We took off for the hills, climbing through the barbed-wire fence that did little to keep anything out. His stride was long, and I had to jog to keep up with him. I was glad that I had worn jeans under the dress, and tennis shoes instead of the sandals Sara had suggested. I raced alongside him and we made a game to get to the top first. I beat him by only an arm's length, of which he grabbed me and pulled me back towards him. My mouth was open in laughter when he placed his lips against mine, resulting in an awkward first kiss. I almost bit him when I pulled back in surprise. He laughed.

"Should we try that again?" he asked. I was too embarrassed to speak, so I just nodded in wide-eyed silence, closing my eyes as he put his lips against mine once more. I could hear the echoes of the cars racing on the country road at the bottom of the hill, the call of the birds as they soared overhead, and the song of the cicadas within the gold of the weeds. I could feel every single wisp of my hair dancing against my cheeks, the wind moving them from the safety of the bun at the base of my neck. I could feel his hands on my hips, my arms around his neck, his tongue pushing though my lips, the strange softness that entered my mouth. Everything was happening all at once in this amazing first kiss with a boy I liked who also liked me back. He pulled away to smile down at me. I looked up at him and saw a glimpse of something sad and distant, the moment lasting for just a second before he relaxed back into his smile.

"Want to hang here for a while?" I asked him.

"Absolutely," he said. We both sat down at the same time, and he offered me his chest to lean against as we both stared out at the same horizon. As we sat, we shared our hopes and likes. I was pleased to know that, in truth, reading was one of his passions, though he admitted to finding Hemingway a little too simple. I forgave him in an instant, apologizing in my mind to my literary hero. He told me about being an only child, how his dad had high hopes of him joining the military like he did, but how Eric's hopes were to become an architect and live in New York. I told him about my dreams of one day writing the great American novel, skipped the parts about my beautiful sister, and admitted that this was the first time I had ever been willing to wear a dress in my teen years.

"It's really pretty," he said.

We walked back hand in hand, sometimes talking and sometimes just taking in the nature that surrounded us. When we reached the house, I prayed that my sister had already left for one of her many friends' houses. But there she was, swaying back and forth on the swing that hung from the tree outside our house. I groaned and held Eric's hand tighter.

"Who's that?" he asked.

"That's Sara," I said. "She's my older sister." I tried to ignore the way he looked at her, seeing something in her that I thought he had seen in me. I told myself it was just because she was pretty, another version of me, and it didn't mean anything.

Sara waved from the swing. "Hey guys!" she called out. She hopped off and then ran towards us. "I was just getting ready to go downtown with a few friends and wondered if you wanted to come along." I fumed inside as she tried to sway Eric's attention from me to her through her bubbly demeanor. She never asked me to go anywhere with her anymore, and I narrowed my eyes in suspicion at this uncharacteristic invitation.

"Sorry, Sara," I smiled, glaring at her in a way only she could see. "We were just about to watch a movie. Maybe next time." She smiled at me, and I couldn't tell if she knew I was angry with her, or if, in her mind, she thought she was being charitable by asking us to join her.

"But wait, Rachel, it could be fun," Eric said. I tried not to appear annoyed when he jumped into the conversation, and I felt his hand loosening a little in mine. "I mean, I don't know a lot of people from our school, and this might be a good way for me to make some friends."

"Oh, you don't want to meet Sara's friends," I told him, keeping a sweet tone to my voice. I could feel Sara's eyes drilling holes in the side of my head. "They're all into superficial stuff, like celebrity gossip and fashion. Totally lame. You'll be bored out of your mind."

"At least my friends can drive," Sara shot back. "Unlike yours, who depend on their mommies to drive them where they need to go."

I held my ground, giving her a look that said *'leave us alone, he's my boyfriend.'* She sighed, reading it loud and clear, and then smiled at me. *'Sorry,'* she mouthed to me when he looked away. "Whatever, never mind. I don't think there's enough room in the car anyways. Forget I asked." A black Mustang barreled down the road, and Sara jumped up to greet the driver. "It was nice meeting you, Eric!" she called over her shoulder. I felt Eric stiffen next to me, sizing up the driver of the car as they started to pull away. I realized that watching a movie with him wouldn't be any fun under the circumstances, and that I'd had enough for one afternoon.

"Wait!" I called out. I saw Sara motion to the driver to stop before poking her head out the window.

"What's up?" she yelled back over the sound of the roaring exhaust. I turned to Eric and smiled.

"Do you want to go?" I asked him, and he didn't even try to hide his enthusiasm at this suggestion.

"Sure," he said. "Do you?"

"Not really. But you go ahead. I'm actually getting kind of tired, you know, from all that hiking. But that doesn't mean you shouldn't go and have fun," I said. I blinked a few times to ensure I didn't start crying, and I knew my smile must have looked funny, as wide as I was grinning. He didn't even notice. He hugged me hard, pulling me in so that my face was mashed up against the zipper of his sweatshirt.

"Thank you, Rachel! I promise, we'll watch that movie together next time," he swore, and then jogged off to the waiting car. Sara gave me a helpless look, but I just looked away from her. "Bye!" Eric called out, and they all waved as they sped away. I waved back until they couldn't see me anymore, the tears already rolling down my cheeks before they were even out of view. Then I ran in the house, past my bewildered mother, and into my room where I flung myself on my bed.

He never did call me back, and at school, his blue eyes looked everywhere but in my direction – much to my relief. It made it easier for me to avoid him and never talk to him again.

However, Sara was a different story. I spent weeks treating her with icy contempt despite her best attempts to sweeten me up and get me to like her again. She didn't even protest when she found the dress I had borrowed at the edge of my side of the room, a huge tear in the side as if it had been shredded at the seam on purpose. She just placed it in the garbage on her side of the room as if it were nothing.

"He's gay," Sara told me later when I broke the silence and confronted her.

"That's not funny," I told her.

"No, it's true!" She described how they had gone to the party and he had met up with someone from his old school. They had disappeared, but her friend, Tyler, caught a glimpse of them kissing in a bathroom. "That's why his dad made him switch schools, because Eric had come out among the kids and even had a boyfriend. His dad was trying to get him to leave all that behind, hoping he would straighten out at a new school, if you know what I mean."

"How do you know all this?" I asked her.

"He told me when Tyler and I confronted him. He swore us to secrecy, and so far you're the first person I've told."

"But he kissed you, too!" I blurted out. The rumors about Eric's sexual orientation may not have spread around the school, but the story of Sara and Eric making out on a couch while his hand covered her breast had made the rounds. Sara blushed, smiling with both embarrassment and pride.

200

"I guess I was just an experiment, to see if he really was gay. Turns out even I can't get a guy to bat for our team." That meant the kiss we shared on the top of the hill behind our house, the very first kiss I had ever received, was only a lie – part of his experimentation.

"I can't believe you even let him kiss you, knowing that I had a huge crush on him," I said. It no longer mattered as much, seeing that he wasn't interested in either one of us. But it still stung that Sara had betrayed me, knowing how much Eric had meant to me.

"I know," Sara said. "That was pretty shitty. I'm really, really sorry." I was never one to hold a grudge, and her sincerity helped me to fold into forgiveness. "Tell you what, let's make a pact," she said, holding out her pinky. "I promise to never, ever go after a boy you like, are dating, or even have dated in the past. Anyone you have kissed or you claim as off limits, is off limits. Can you promise the same?" I promised her, linking my pinky in hers even though I was sure I would never be faced with a similar problem.

But the promise remained true for the rest of our lives, or rather, my life. Sara grew out of her flirtatious teen years. I grew out of my mousy, bookworm state of fourteen and began to care about my appearance and making friends. Soon I was discovering the ups and downs of dating, and Sara became my ally as we both backed each other up when, without fail, a heart would get broken.

But I was always a little cautious around her, especially when bringing a new guy into the house for the first time to meet my family – to meet Sara. The ultimate test always rested in their initial reaction upon meeting my sister. The ones who couldn't help but admire her even while standing next to me were almost always gone before the month was over. But the few that took more notice of me than my sister were the ones I allowed myself to fall for until the relationship had run its course. Just two men passed the test, resulting in the only long-term relationships I ever submitted myself to – the one with Joey's dad, Tony, and the one with John.

****

And yet, here in the present, Sara was moving in on the love of my life, causing him to fall for her through her kindness and the smell of her hair.

Seventeen

Picturing the way Sara sat at John's side in the hospital, I kicked myself for not seeing it sooner. She was falling for him. And how could he not help but fall for her?

In life I'd had golden brown hair, cut just below my shoulders, and a dozen paths of laugh lines around my eyes, enhanced by years of being in the sun. My nose and cheeks held a hint of freckles that were invisible to me as I looked past them in the mirror, but they were the first thing most people saw when they looked in my direction. Sara was my exact opposite. Her unblemished skin was kept fair by hiding away from the sun starting when she was still young, and she kept her blonde hair cut short, framing her face with just a hint of curl. While I took the darker features of my father, right down to my amber eyes, she had the same blue eyes as our mother's side of the family, a hint of aquamarine in the cerulean of her irises. She was always the fairer of the two of us, the one who was noticed first.

But while most were drawn to Sara's beauty, she had never even fazed John. From the first day, John seemed only to see me. His devoted attention took some getting used to at first, but that only deepened my love for him as time went on. He never even flinched when he first met Sara, unaffected by her beauty as he stood next to me holding my hand.

Just that glimpse of stirring within him at the hospital felt like a betrayal. He knew the years of torment I'd faced being Sara's younger, unnoticed sister. He knew that even in my adult years, I struggled against the jealousy of not being Sara. While I hid from him just how much I was haunted by our childhood, the few times I had revealed my insecurity he was right there to assure me that I was beautiful and deserving of love.

But now with me out of the way, Sara was able to move in and make a kill. She could claim for her own the man who was supposed to be my husband, even when the body of her own marriage wasn't yet cold.

"You're going to kill yourself if you think this hard," a man said next to me, startling me out of my head with his sudden presence, and bringing me back to Mauna Kea. His eyes twinkled at his joke, and I chuckled politely, finally getting it.

"It sure feels like I could die all over again," I told him in all seriousness. "I'm Rachel," I added.

"The name's Frank," he said. He wasn't a very tall man, and lacked any hints of youth. His skin was the color of coffee, weathered by the sun with a few age spots that existed on his bald head. Despite our wintery surroundings, he wore a button-up shirt over a pair of khaki shorts, with sandals on his feet.

"Did you once live here?" I asked him. "I mean, not here. But on the island?"

"A long time ago," he said. "Around twenty years ago. My wife and I lived in a town about thirty minutes from here. We used to visit this spot often when we were younger, bringing the kids with us to see the whole entire island so they knew how lucky we were to live here." He smiled at the memory, pausing for a moment as he lived in it. His focus returned to me. "Mona still comes here sometimes, and in fact, she's coming here today. I'm just waiting for her."

"That's nice," I said, still wallowing too much in my own misery to be able to engage in the life of someone else.

"So what is it that's killing you?" he asked, and I sighed.

"Love," I told him. He nodded with appreciation.

"Ah, the greatest weapon of all time, the one power that can leave you feeling so good and so bad, just depending on which way the wind leans you that day," he mused. "I've been killed many times over with love. What a sweet death it was, too."

He leaned back and looked out at the horizon, the sky turning a delicious shade of pink as nightfall passed us by and the sun glimmered just below the morning fog. He looked to his right, and I heard his breath catch.

"There she is, my Mona."

I turned in the direction he was facing to see a caravan of cars parking in the lot near the observatory. An elderly woman was helped out of the car by the guide, followed by an older man. The man accompanying Mona linked his arm over hers once they were both safe on the ground. I could tell how much he cared for her in the way he held onto her, ensuring she had no way to slip on the icy ground. With careful steps, they made their way to a place where they could see out over the entire island once the fog burned off.

"Who is that?" I asked Frank.

"That's her second husband, Oscar," he told me, smiling with kindness in the direction of the man who now held fast to his wife.

"You're not jealous," I stated with surprise. "Doesn't it hurt to see someone else looking at your wife that way?"

"It used to," he admitted. "When they were first getting to know each other, I thought I would die a new death every time I saw them together. But I've learned to be okay with it over time. I mean, look how happy she is."

He nodded in her direction, and I watched the couple. Sure enough, Mona smiled when Oscar whispered something in her ear, moving closer to him so that they were supporting each other's weight in the brisk cold of the morning. Their breath came out in puffs of white, but they didn't seem cold as they stayed near each other. "He loves her so much. It makes me happy to see her taken care of by a good man, since I no longer can," Frank said with a smile. I expected his face to hold a note of sadness, for his smile to harbor secrets of regret that he wasn't the one holding on to her and whispering in her ear. But he wasn't sad. I was amazed at his happiness as he watched his wife in the arms of another man, finding joy in her joy and laughing when she laughed.

"I don't know if I could ever be happy if John moves on," I said, looking away from Mona and Oscar and down at my snow-covered shoes.

"Is John your husband?" Frank asked.

"Almost-husband. We were to be married in just a few weeks when I died."

"Oh, that's unfortunate," he said. "So you didn't get that much time with him, did you?" I shook my head no, feeling even sorrier for myself in the moment. "But you do know he'll move on," Frank said with certainty. I nodded. I knew it to be true. I just didn't want it to be true.

We sat there without speaking for quite some time. The sun rose above the fog, burning it off until we could see the beautiful island lying below us, surrounded by the green and blue water that appeared still as glass from this high up. The air was now warm and clean, and more people came by car to see the view and take a few pictures. I could see Mona and Oscar beginning to make their descent back to the car they came from, a guide staying near them to ensure they didn't lose their footing. Frank got up, too, preparing to leave as well, since his reason for being here was about to be driven away. But he turned to me before disappearing.

"When you love someone, what you love most about them is how they make you feel," he told me. "You're not only in love with them, but you're in love with the person you are when you are around them. This is a one-sided existence we live in, where we don't receive the kind of love we used to get when we were in the world of the living. You would do best to adapt the way you love John to fit in with your afterlife, because you're confining yourself to a world of hurt and disappointment if you keep going on expecting him to give you what you need. He can't do it. But you can love him selflessly. If you can find happiness in his happiness, even if it's from someone else's love, you'll find peace with him moving on. After all, a selfless love only wants the best for the object of adoration. And in our state, the best just isn't us." With these words, he gave me a solemn bow in a ceremonial gesture, and I nodded my head from my seated position. He took my hand in his and kissed it, his kind and smiling eyes the last thing I saw of him before he disappeared altogether.

I knew he was right. If I loved John like I thought I did, I needed to start thinking about his happiness and leave my own happiness to the side. Well, no, that's not what Frank was saying. I needed to find my happiness in John's happiness, receiving love and joy back with each blessing that came John's way. If this joy happened to come from Sara, so be it. I needed to let go of the childish jealousy I felt towards her, letting go of the past because that's all it was – the past.

I didn't realize I was crying until the tears from my cheeks dropped down and splattered on my bare knee below the hem of my dress. My heart was breaking all over again, but this time it was cleansing. I let go and immersed myself in my sorrow, grieving for the romance John and I shared. I knew the next step was to let it go and make room for a different kind of love. *Such a human emotion, this crying is*, I thought to myself, even as the tears and sobs continued at a steady pace. I wondered why, when we had to give up all other attributes of human life, we were allowed to keep our emotions – and even stronger emotions than we had in life. It seemed both a blessing and a curse, allowing human life to be held onto by a thread while keeping the fullness of it just out of arm's reach. I wanted the freedom to feel nothing for my human life. But in a contradicting desire, I wanted to seize life so it would stop slipping from my grasp.

The sun rose and set, at times in a rapid spiral of motion as an immeasurable length of time passed me by. I wasn't sure how long I'd been there when the tears ceased their steady stream down my cheeks. But when the last tear dropped, I felt a sense of relief as I realized I was ready to begin a new chapter.

I took a deep breath, blew it out, and stood up and brushed the snow off my dress, taking one last look out at the ocean that surrounded the big island of Hawaii and my perch atop Mauna Kea. The fog had just begun to form at the base of the mountain, and I watched as it grew, gathering strength in its manifestation. Soon, the whole expanse in front of me was covered in the white blanket of clouds.

"What would happen if I walked out upon the fog, Daddy?" I had asked my father that day driving above the covered valley.

"You'd pass right through and fall to the ground," my father had told me, stripping away all the magic my five year old self still held when it came to science and life.

The fog touched the edge of Mauna Kea, inviting me to test my father's theory and prove him wrong. I placed a cautious step forward onto the filmy cloud, touching the solidity within the mist that existed only for me. I moved forward so that both my feet were firm on the fog. A gap in the cloudy substance showed I was standing thousands of feet above the shadowed island below, with nothing to break my fall should I plummet from my space in the sky. I found pleasure in this dangerous thought, smiling in the freedom that existed in this one simple realization. And then I ran across the fog at full speed, skipping over the covering of the earth until I reached the end and jumped off into the ocean below.

Eighteen

John came home after a grueling day of work in the summer heat. He kicked off his shoes at the door to keep from tracking dirt any farther than the entry way of the apartment, shedding clothes piece by piece as he walked up the stairs to his room. At the top of the stairs, he tried to ignore the view of Sam's room from the corner of his eye, though it was getting harder and harder to do in the emptiness of the house. His son's room was added to his list of ghosts that haunted him, sitting as it did beside the ghosts that lay within the door of Joey's room.

It had been just over a year and a half since my death, and a year since Sam had moved out. At times, John felt like time was passing at a rapid pace. Other times it stood too still. He was glad he would soon be free from the clutches of the apartment, fleeing the memories and starting fresh when he moved to the finished house in San Anselmo. The whole apartment was packed up, save for the few belongings he still needed in his day-to-day life – as well as the contents behind the door of Joey's room.

This forbidden area of the apartment had become something like a shrine since my departure, unseen by human eyes since Sam had moved out. While John refused to view the contents of the room, Sam had often gone in there when he lived in the room next door, rifling through Joey's video games and belongings in secret, just in case there was anything of interest to him.

I also visited the room. Often I would find a hollow sense of solace among the clothes on the floor, the unmade bed, Joey's things strewn below boxes of my things. His smell still existed in the walls and the bedding, and I would sit for hours, days, weeks, just pretending I still held a connection with my son. I had given up on finding him in this divide, knowing that when it was time, if it would ever be time, he would find me instead.

As John showered, his mind drifted to Joey's room. He knew he needed to do something with the room, but wasn't sure if he could bring himself to open the door and face all the things he'd packed in there to keep my memory at bay. While it hadn't worked – I haunted him even when I stopped trying to do so – he found comfort in knowing the solid proof of my existence was hidden behind a closed door.

But he couldn't move from the house until he had packed up everything. And that included Joey's room. He needed to decide what to give up forever, and if anything within that room would make it to the new house. He knew this was a task he couldn't do on his own.

John finished his shower and dried off with hurried movements. I knew who he was going to call before he even picked his cell phone up off his bed.

"Can you come over? I need your help with her things," he said without even saying hello.

"Of course," Sara replied.

He'd only seen Sara a handful of times since he came home from the hospital eight months earlier. She had helped him to settle in to the apartment, but he made it clear that he was okay to take care of himself. Sam had stayed with him for a while back then to help monitor him until he could get back on his feet. And because of Sam's involvement, his ex-wife, Wendy, had lost the iciness she'd developed in the beginning stages of their divorce, and made herself available to him should he need any help.

Still, Sara called every now and then just to check in on him. He had let her calls go straight to voicemail each time. Then he listened to them as soon as his phone signaled a message, hearing my voice within hers as she let him know she was thinking of him and hoped everything was going okay.

The intent wasn't lost on Sara, either. She knew he was avoiding her. She tried to respect the distance he was keeping, but she couldn't help but feel disappointed in the wall between them. Kevin had since moved out, and she was forced to be away from her girls every weekend as a result of the custody arrangement. She tried to immerse herself in work to keep from going crazy in the empty house on the days they were gone. But the evenings felt unbearable as she ran out of things to pick up, dirty dishes to clean, unmade beds to make, and a bathtub void of bubbles and giggling girls.

It was on those nights she called John, even just to hear his voice in his message on the phone, giving her a sense that she wasn't alone.

The doorbell rang thirty minutes later, and John let Sara in. He gave her a quick hug, turning his face far away from hers in their embrace.

"Thank you for coming over," he said.

"Anytime!" she exclaimed. Both of them moved around each other with caution, acting as if this were more of a first date instead of a friend helping a friend. "So what's going on?" she asked.

"Well, you know how I'm moving?" he asked, and she nodded

"You want me to lift heavy furniture, don't you?" she joked. "I knew these muscles would curse me one day." He chuckled with her, grateful for the break in the tension.

"Not exactly. But I do need you to move some things with me, specifically Rachel and Joey's things," he said in an apologetic tone. Sara smiled in reassurance and nodded. He led her up to Joey's room and took a deep breath at the closed door. With great force, he turned the knob and pushed the door open, the boxes behind it shifting so that a few things fell over in the process. "Oops," he said, wincing.

Sara moved past him and looked around. Step by step she maneuvered through the crowded room, taking in every single thing that had ever been mine. John, on the other hand, kept a safe distance on the outside of the door.

"Wow," she said after she drank it all in. "This is everything, isn't it?" John nodded, running his hands through his hair in embarrassment. "Have you even been in here since Rachel died?" she asked.

214

"Just to put stuff in here as I found it. Other than that, no. I couldn't bring myself to give anything of hers away. But I couldn't look at it anymore, either," he admitted.

Sara moved a few of my belongings around in a box, seeing glimpses of me in things she recognized, running her curious hands over the things she didn't, and feeling overwhelmed by the task as a whole. She was beginning to regret even answering her phone when John called. But she could also tell that if the physical task of this job seemed daunting to her, the mental portion of it might be impossible for John.

"Did you want to do this together? Do you think you can handle deciding what goes and what stays?" she asked him. He nodded, though the look in his eyes lacked conviction.

"I, uh… I was thinking we should just get rid of it all. I can't keep any of it. It's too painful. But I figured that if there was anything in here that you wanted… You know, since they were your family and all."

Sara started to protest at this, sure that there was something in here that he wanted to hold on to. But when she looked at John's face she could tell he'd been haunted enough. Keeping anything around would only serve as an anchor for that ghost that wouldn't allow him to move on.

It would keep *me* from allowing him to move on.

I watched as they rifled through my belongings. At first they moved in silence, going from one box to the next as they divided things to give away and things that Sara would take home. Sara made faster work of the task than John, many of the possessions I'd once owned holding no meaning for her as she held them for the first time. Others brought back a flash from a past event, and she'd stop to remember what we had been doing, how I had smiled that day, the sound of my laugh. Many of those things found their way into her pile.

John was cautious in the task, afraid to touch anything should it tear at him with another memory. But as he watched Sara move through the boxes, he realized he needed to pick up the pace. He tried to ward off the thoughts that came with each piece, knowing that I had touched each one of these things he now held in his hand. He stopped looking at my things, seeing through them as he grabbed and dropped items into a box close to him. Sara retrieved a few of the items, explaining to John the memories they brought back to her. And John was happy for the distraction from his own thoughts of me. But as his memories became less painful in the act of going through my things, he began to understand the therapy in this simple process. Soon he was allowing visions of me to come at him unharnessed, laughing as he held the sweater I had ripped when we thought sliding down the banister might be a good idea, and shedding a tear over the blanket I wrapped myself up in every night on the couch. He tucked the blanket away in his own "keep" pile, one that held only a few items.

"I think Sam might want all of Joey's games and gaming equipment," John said. "And I suppose if there's anything else in here that a teenage boy might want, we should save it for him." Sara nodded, pulling out another box and placing a few of Joey's things inside.

"What about the dress?" Sara asked. It still hung from the frame of the closet, the ivory material glowing in bright contrast against the darkness of the room. Sara got up from the boxes that surrounded her, running her hand over the fabric. She paused at the part that was cut away, glancing over at John to give him a curious look. She looked away when she saw the pained look on his face. "I suppose we can decide later…" she mumbled, but John shook his head with determination.

"No, it all needs to be done now. I can't let this go any longer," he insisted.

"Did you want to keep the dress," Sara asked. "You don't need to keep it out, but maybe store it until you are able to part with it?" She had already figured out that the missing square was his doing.

"I can't keep it," John winced. "Do you want it? Can you take it?" Sara didn't want it either. She had no idea where she might put it, or what she could do with it. Her natural impulse was to donate it. Even with the missing material, someone would be able to use it as a discounted gown for their own wedding should they be lucky enough to find it in a thrift store. But she could tell that even the suggestion of giving it to someone who didn't know Rachel would tear John apart. So she just nodded, bringing the dress down from where it hung and laying it with care over the top of one of her boxes.

Hours later they were done. It was almost midnight when John glanced at his watch, and he sucked in a quick breath.

"Shit, Sara. I'm sorry. It's really late. Are the girls with a sitter right now?"

"No, they're with Kevin tonight. And it's okay. I think we both needed this for closure. But I guess I should get going." She didn't want to go, dreading the emptiness of the dark house across town. So when John offered to make up the couch for her, she didn't argue.

"I can let you use one of my t-shirts," he suggested. "Or... I guess Rachel's stuff would probably be better." She nodded. There had been a few items of mine that she'd tucked into her box, including a couple of her own clothes that had somehow made their way into my closet. She pulled one of my night shirts out of a box.

"This should be fine," she told him. He gave her an extra toothbrush and then made her bed up while she got dressed in the bathroom.

"Goodnight," he said to her when she emerged, giving her a hug. He caught a whiff of my smell mingling in with her perfume, a new aroma that both caught him off guard, intriguing him.

"Goodnight," she murmured. She looked up at him with curiosity when he paused without letting her go. There was no mistaking the look in his eyes. It had been so long since anyone had looked at her that way, she missed the part where he saw me, and she only saw the part where he found her desirable. Without thinking, she closed her eyes and leaned in, feeling the way his hands gripped her shoulder and moved to comb through her hair before lining her cheek with his finger and tracing the outline of her lips.

John knew he was making a mistake. He knew it was Sara in front of him, trembling in a shirt I used to wear often. But he looked past her blonde hair and saw me in the similarities of her features. He hadn't been this close to a woman since the last time we'd been interrupted during our love making, a moment that felt centuries old. And beyond wishing I were the one in front of him, he felt the natural pull of needing to be near the softness of a woman. When he looked at Sara, he knew it was her. But the familiarity she presented in her appearance and fragrance overwhelmed him into losing the ability to think. He leaned forward and caught her waiting lips with his own, crushing against them in a dance of tongues and passion.

I crouched in the corner, frozen by the scene unfolding in front of me. I was afraid to stay, but more afraid to leave. I could feel everything – the way it felt to be touched after countless nights alone, the elation of being in each other's arms, the confusion that went alongside it, and the sadness that each of them stuffed down as they pretended in the moment that this was something it wasn't. I wanted to tear myself away. My biggest fear was unfolding in front of me in a way I knew would haunt me for eternity. But something new was emerging from this nightmare. I found peace in their relief and growing passion, feeling more human than ever as their emotions transferred over to me. The irony didn't escape me. All this time I had affected John through my presence. Now he was affecting me.

They made their way to the couch, their mouths and hands never leaving each other. John knew he couldn't bring her up to the bedroom, feeling it would be like stepping on holy ground. But the made-up couch served as a middle ground for the crime he was about to commit. Her hands tore at his shirt, and he slipped it over his head. She ran her hands across his chest, pulling her fingers through the hair that covered it and tugging to send a shivering shock through his body. John unbuckled his belt and stepped out of his pants, then pulled Sara's shirt over the top of her head. She stood naked in front of him, her pale skin trembling in the shadows of the room. John pulled back the covers and she laid down within them, drawing her breath in as his skin made contact with hers within the warmth of the blankets.

Sara's hands traveled the whole of John's body, running them along the pulsing muscles of his back down to the curve of his hip as he hovered over her, afraid to let his whole weight press against her. Sensing this, she pulled him closer, feeling the release of tension as his body crushed down on hers. She could feel his heart pounding against her own, beating faster as she sent a flurry of kisses across his cheek, his neck, his chest. Unable to get close enough, she arched into him as his hands smoothed over her body, exploring every inch of her skin.

He couldn't find the raised scar that blemished my back. It was what kept him grounded, knowing that, enveloped by my scent, it was nonetheless Sara he lay against in the darkness of the room, and not me. When he found himself immersed in thoughts of me, he searched for the scar again on Sara's back, both relieved and disappointed when he couldn't find it. But Sara felt good to him, the softness of her body differing from the tightness my muscles had possessed in the weeks before my wedding, a result of a quick series of workouts rather than a lifetime of exercise. Sara's body, while slender, remained soft from afternoons chasing children rather than working out at the gym. It matched the downy texture of her skin, and John ran his hands over every inch of it, pausing when his fingers found the hardness of her nipples. She gasped at his touch, arching her back even more in the process. Leaning down, John took her nipple in his mouth, pressing it between his lips before letting his tongue flick against it. Sara could feel the sensation at the tip of her breasts washing over the top of her head and radiating throughout her body until she was burning with desire. She grasped at him, pleading to come closer with every kiss she peppered across his skin, unable to find her release until he entered her in an explosion of passion. The room was ablaze as they made love to each other, searching for comfort in a world that had swallowed them whole. John buried his face into her hair, breathing in as their bodies moved together in one fluid motion.

"You smell like her," he whispered, his movements slowing as he voiced his thought. She tightened her hold on him.

"Please, just go with it," she said. She didn't elaborate, afraid that too many words would take away from the moment. She knew he missed me, even as his body molded against hers. He needed this to be able to move past me, but also to feel close to me. She needed this for a different reason - just to feel wanted once again. She couldn't bear the thought of being rejected, and in her mind she begged him to forget me for just a moment and continue making love to her – or to remember me in secret as he found comfort in her body.

John lost himself in the scent of her hair, grasping her skin so tight it reddened in patches that would bruise later.

The room evaporated around them as they became one breath together. And in a final moment, they burst into flames within a frenzy of ecstasy, mounting to a final explosion that both gave them life and left them breathless.

No words were spoken as the passion subsided. John stroked Sara's hair against her back as she lay against him. Sara ran her fingers against the damp hair on his chest as her eyelids grew heavy. I remained a connecting thought between the two of them, feeling the different edges of guilt as they drifted off to sleep. But more than that, they both found comfort in being able to help each other in a pain that no one else could ever understand.

Nineteen

Johan had left sometime during the night to go to his own room. Sara had felt him get up, leaving behind not only more room for her to sleep but also a cool void, and she burrowed under the blankets to get away from it before falling back asleep. But in the early hours of the morning, she found herself awake in a house that wasn't her own, questioning the wisdom of their actions the night before. It was more than the fact that I existed in the very fiber of this house, even after John had gone to great lengths to keep me boxed up behind closed doors. It was more than the fact that she had just gone past an invisible boundary with the man her sister was supposed to have married. It was more than the fact that John was the first man she had been intimate with since her husband moved out. Of every fear that tumbled through her mind, the biggest worry she held was the realization that once the sun crested over the San Francisco hills they would be faced with the morning after – and it would likely end with a speech that sounded like "It's not you, it's me."

****

"I just can't do this anymore," Kevin had told her in the privacy of their bedroom after the girls had gone to bed. "We're just going through the motions, and it's killing me." It had been coming for a while, and on this night these words were spoken after a long and drawn out argument about Kevin's hours at the office and the distance he kept even when he was in the house. But still, when Kevin spoke the words out loud, it drove salt into the already gaping wounds of Sara's heart.

"You can't just give up, Kevin. This is a marriage, and you're not even trying," Sara shot at him, her words solid stone even if her insides were tumbling pebbles.

"This is no marriage, Sara. I feel like an outsider with you and the girls. Ever since you became a mother, you have shifted toward that role one-hundred percent, and there's nothing left for me."

"That's not fair!" Sara shouted through a whisper, afraid that her anger would wake the girls across the hall. "Because you're gone so much, being their parent has been totally left up to me. I spend most of my time here taking care of them, even with the flower shop! Even though that shop is taking up so much more of my time now that Rachel is dead and I'm left with a whole business to flounder in on my own! You don't do anything except go to work, come home, then plop your ass on the couch and expect a hot meal to be placed in front of you. You haven't looked at me the way you used to in months, maybe years. Fuck, I can probably even count on one hand how many times we've had sex in that amount of time. There's nothing left for *you*? What the fuck are you giving *me*?"

"I have nothing to give you, Sara! That's the point!" Kevin yelled. Sara raised her hand in fury, looking toward the girls' room through the closed door.

"Shhh!" Her whisper was icy. "We don't need to wake them up."

"I have nothing for you, Sara," he hissed.

"Then why are you pinning all this on me?" she asked him, her eyes flashing. He hung his head at the question, the silence hanging between them like fragile icicles ready to drop. She waited for his answer, the fury inside of her ready to pounce at any word he spoke.

"I don't know," he said in a soft voice. "I guess I thought things would be different, or that things would go back to the way they used to when the girls grew a little more."

"But things are always going to be different than they were then," Sara said. "We were young and selfish back then. We had nothing to focus on but ourselves and each other. Things changed forever when we chose to have kids. Now the focus is on Lily and Megan. That's never going to change."

"I know, Sara," he sighed.

"So what is it? You don't want to be a dad anymore?" she demanded. "It's kind of late for that, isn't it? Leaving me isn't going to take that away."

"No, that's not it," he shot back. "Of course I want to be a dad. But I can't stay in a marriage where I feel like I'm just the paycheck, coming home to your little family of three while I am merely the outsider."

"What are you talking about?" Sara demanded. "Those girls adore you! They wait for you to come home every single day and pounce on you once you walk in that door! When you come home, they don't even see me anymore. It's all about Daddy."

"I don't love you anymore!" Kevin blurted out. Sara gasped, the words slicing right through her. They both stared at each other, neither one able to believe the words had been spoken. Her hands trembled as she lifted them to her mouth, her eyes filling with tears. The regret was evident in Kevin's eyes, but it was too late. "I'm sorry, Sara. I didn't mean that. I—," but she waved him off with a flip of her hand as the tears broke over the barrier of her eyes, spilling down her cheeks.

"Don't. Don't even try to take it away. You said it. You finally said what I knew was true." She sank down on the bed, fighting with all her strength to keep from breaking down in front of him. "Is it someone else?" she asked him. "Is that why you've been spending more and more time at work?" He shook his head.

"No. There's no one else."

To Sara, that was almost worse. He wasn't leaving because his heart was being pulled in two directions. He was leaving because he couldn't stand to be with her anymore.

"I suppose we could try counseling," he offered as a weak gesture. She shook her head.

"I think it's too late for that," she told him. "I think you should just go."

"I'll go in the morning," he said. "I want to say goodbye to the girls."

"And say what?" Sara demanded. "That you're giving up on this family? That you don't love their mother anymore? No, you need to leave now, tonight. I can't have you in this house for another moment." She got on the floor and dug a bag out from under the bed, flinging it on the bed in front of him.

"And what are you going to tell them?" he asked her.

"I'll think of something. After all, I'm the one who is solely devoted to the kids, so much that my own husband doesn't want me."

"Sara, wait. This isn't fair. You can't make me leave without any kind of defense at all. They're my kids too. Please don't make them hate me," he pleaded. She looked at the ground, then up toward the ceiling to keep from losing her emotions.

"I'm not going to make them hate you," she said after some hesitation. And she made an inward promise to try her best to make this as fair for Lily and Megan as she could. "I'll tell them something, that Mommy and Daddy need some time apart, like a vacation or something," she said in a quiet voice. He nodded.

"And what if this isn't a vacation, Sara? What if this is the end?" He opened his drawer with reluctance, pulling out socks and shirts and placing them in the bag on the bed. Sara digested the reality in the words, reading the final answer that lay in the concealing folds of the question.

"One thing at a time," she told him.

True to her word, Sara had let the girls know that she and Daddy were taking a vacation from each other. She answered their frightened questions as best as she could, trying to keep the answers lighthearted and full of hope, unable and unwilling to hint that the end was inevitable.

She promised they both loved them very much, and that the girls could see their Daddy anytime they wanted.

"Now?" the girls had wondered, and Sara had to shake her head no.

"Not now, but soon," she promised.

At first, Kevin had stayed in a hotel, living out of a bag of things he refilled on occasion when he would come to pick Lily and Megan up for a weekly visit. Sara would offer to do his laundry, the offer serving as a secret effort to get him to see how much he needed her. But he always refused.

"They have a laundromat near the hotel," he said.

Soon after, Sara's heart broke all over again when he let her know he had left the hotel and was now living in an apartment several miles away.

"It's close to Megan's school," he told her, as if the convenience of his location took away from the fact that he had signed a lease promising he'd never move back home for at least a year. While neither one could utter the word "divorce", they did seek out a mediator to help them divide their time with the girls. At first it was suggested they do an every-other-week rotation. Sara had balked at this, unable to be away from Lily and Megan for seven whole days. That was how she lost her weekends with them.

"They need to be able to spend some time with their dad," the mediator had said, and Sara caved, allowing Kevin to have the girls two and a half days each week to keep them from being gone for any longer. And while it proved to be convenient on her busiest days at the shop, Sara discovered that she didn't know what to do with herself when the girls were away. She had spent their whole life being the center of their world, so that when she got a break from being a mother, she no longer knew who she was.

And this terrified her more than anything.

****

Sara lay still in the dark of John's apartment, letting her crumbling marriage unfold in front of her, evaporating like the fading shadows against the patches of light from the rising sun. It had been two months since Kevin had filled his bag with a few belongings and left between the time the girls went to sleep at night and woke up in the morning. And now here she was, lying naked on John's couch, alone in the dark, waiting with shaky breath for him to wake up and tell her it wasn't going to work out. She hadn't planned on this, for things to get this far. She'd be lying to herself if she said she hadn't felt a few murmurs in recent months when she was near John. But she was sure that was only because she'd felt so alone in the time before and after Kevin had left. And now her vulnerability lay around her in scattered clothing across the room…and in the reality that Kevin was no longer the last man who had left fingerprints all over her skin. She had to decide what she was going to do about this new path she had taken with John. Everything was different now.

A few creaks upstairs signaled that John was awake. Sara kept her eyes closed when she heard him coming downstairs, forcing her breaths to be slow and steady in feigned-slumber as he peeked his head over the couch to see if she was still asleep.

John poured out the cold coffee in the coffeepot from the day before and filled it with fresh water, setting up the pot to brew as his thoughts formed their own dark roast in his head.

Flashes of my face and Sara's mingled in the memories of last night. Being that close to her had felt good. Really good. He wanted to believe it was just because Sara was the closest person to me without actually being me. But it was more than that. She was familiar, not just because of the scent in her hair or the way her lips held the same shape as mine, but because she was someone who knew him and the pain he was going through. They both knew what it was like to lose me, the person they both claimed as their best friend. John realized that more than anything, he missed having a connection with someone. And through the past year and a half of friendship, he'd had that with Sara.

Hearing her stir on the couch, John poured them both a cup of coffee and crept into the living room. Placing her cup on the coffee table, he sat down on the couch where the curve of her belly created a small space and rubbed her shoulder. Sara smiled, but kept her eyes closed at his touch, inhaling the aroma of the coffee as she stretched.

"Mmmm…coffee…" she murmured, trying to gauge how groggy she would be if she really were just waking up. She opened her eyes half-way and smiled at John.

"Good morning," he said, leaning forward and kissing her on the forehead. She sat up, clutching the blanket to her chest. John reached over and picked up her cup of coffee and placed it in her hands, waiting for her to take her first sip before barraging her with his thoughts on the night before. He wanted to tell her how wonderful she was, how he had appreciated all her care as he grieved for me, how he loved how close they had become since my death, and how much it meant to him that they were able to become even closer last night. He wanted to admit that he had no idea what the future held for them, admit that he knew this was weird and unconventional, that, without a doubt, their family would wonder what was wrong with them. But he wanted to tell her he didn't care about all that, and he was curious where this road would lead them. Most of all, he wanted to tell her how beautiful she looked in the morning, how waking up to her unbrushed hair and flushed cheeks was a treat he wanted to experience over and over, and how he could probably live in her eyes should he be allowed to stare into them long enough.

"About last night," he began, taking in a deep breath as he worked up the courage to spill segments of his heart into the coffee she drank. But he never got the chance. Sara held up her hand, smiling as she shook her head.

"Say no more," she said, stopping him in his tracks. "It was just a one-time fluke that never should have happened."

"B-but...I don't think it was a mistake," John stammered.

"Neither do I!" Sara's enthusiasm made John's eyes widen. "We both have been through so much; I think it was great for us to let off a little steam with each other. I didn't realize I needed that as much as I did," she giggled.

John was confused by her reaction. The Sara he knew wouldn't be this casual about a night of passion. Or would she? He'd never been intimate with her before, so how would he know how she'd react? John realized he might not know her as well as he thought.

"How are we going to move forward?" he asked her, wincing at the way he said "we" with presumption. But she didn't hear his question the way he asked it, only hearing what she thought he was saying.

"Don't worry about it John," she said. "I mean, I don't want things to get weird between us, and I really enjoy our friendship. We can just pretend like it never happened. I promise I won't start acting like I'm your girlfriend or anything," she said with a light-hearted grin.

John hid his embarrassment as she spoke. He had misread the whole situation, and felt stupid as he remembered how he'd been acting like a horny teenager experiencing love for the first time. In an effort to hide the fool he had almost made of himself, he just nodded with a chuckle. He thought he saw a glimmer of sadness in Sara's eyes, but realized she was only looking down for her shirt. He retrieved it from the ground and handed it to her.

"Thanks," she said, slipping it over her head to hide her nudity despite the fact that he had kissed every inch of her body the night before.

"Did you want something to eat?" he asked her. "Some cereal, maybe some eggs? How about pancakes? I know how to flip some mean flapjacks," he said. She shook her head.

"No, I've taken up enough of your time already. I really should be getting home."

"Are you sure? I mean, it's the least I can do after all the help you gave me with that room," he said, doing his best to persuade her to stay a bit longer, hoping that a little more time might help her see things in a different light. But she wasn't having any part of it. He hid his disappointment when she shook her head again.

"I have to get into the shop today, and the girls are coming back tonight. I'd like to get home to have enough time to put stuff away and get freshened up," she got up and started to fold her blanket, but he waved her away.

"It's okay, I got it," he said. "I know you're in a hurry." She gave him a grateful smile.

Ten minutes later he was helping her carry boxes to her car parked a few blocks downhill and waving goodbye as she drove away.

Sara let out a deep breath as she watched him disappear in her rearview window. She wasn't sure how to read him, but was certain he was only being polite in what could have been a very awkward morning. At least she knew how to hide away her feelings before she made herself out to be some foolish school girl. However, her intention to protect herself from being rejected all over again had failed. As she drove further from his apartment, she couldn't help feeling like she was losing in love all over again.

And despite the fact that I had never wanted them together in the first place, I wanted to reach inside her head and shake her for being so blind.

Twenty

"There are my girls!" Sara cried when she heard the doorknob turn and footsteps pounding toward the kitchen where she sat. She had been eating a bowl of cereal at the table, reading a book and trying not to stare at the clock too much until they arrived. Before they burst through the door, she had done her best to keep the thought of John's hands on her from her head, only resulting in happy and melancholy shivers as she remembered the feel of John's lips across her mouth, her neck, down her stomach…

"Mommy! Mommy!" Megan called out, colliding into Sara with great force, Lily running at her heels and copying her sister's enthusiasm.

"Wow! I think you both got taller!" Sara exclaimed. They both grinned.

"Mom, it's only been two days," Megan pointed out in her seven-year-old wisdom. Sara laughed.

"I know. It just feels like a long time," she told her, ruffling her hair.

"Knock knock," Kevin called from the doorway. Sara shot up and smoothed out her hair, wiping at the bit of milk that had spilt on her shirt. Usually she did her best to look decent when Kevin showed up; attempting to give him a taste of what he was missing and couldn't have. Today, however, she put on her sweats as soon as she got home from work, and looked as though she had been sleeping all day long.

"Come in," she called out even as she walked toward the door. Kevin stepped over the threshold of his former home with caution, smiling an apology when Sara appeared around the corner.

"I'm sorry, I should have knocked before they bounded in. But they barreled through the door before I had a chance to stop them," he explained. Sara waved her hand in dismissal.

"Don't worry about it," she said. "It's their home too."

"I know," he said. "But one of these days you might have someone over and..." he drifted off. Sara looked up in alarm, wondering what he knew. But she realized he was only making an observation about the future. She also read into it that the same might be true of him, perhaps already. She shook away that thought, fighting off the urge to be jealous over things she held no facts about.

"How was your weekend?" Sara asked him.

"It was great," he said with a smile. "I took the girls to the zoo this weekend, and Megan decided she wants to be a large animal veterinarian when she grows up. She's so dang bright, it kills me! Lily, on the other hand, decided she wants to be a tiger when she grows up. I didn't have the heart to tell her that being a monkey was a better choice. You know, more fun."

"That's our Lily," Sara said, shaking her head in amusement. They both watched the girls playing lion-keeper in the corner of the room, Lily on all fours growling up at her older sister, Megan pretending to fling a whip at her to make her do what she needed her to do. "It sounds like you guys had a great weekend."

"How about you? I mean, unless it's personal," he said.

"I'm not seeing anyone, if that's what you're asking," she said in a tone that was a little harsher than she intended. She decided that she didn't need to even hint that she had slept with John, concluding that it didn't count if it wasn't planned and would never happen again. "And I didn't really do much this weekend, just worked and then helped John clear out the spare room at his house of all Joey's and Rachel's things."

"Oh, jeez. That must have been rough. Are you okay?" he asked with genuine concern. Sara was taken aback by his altruism. Even though they had been kind to each other in the months that followed their split, it felt foreign for him to show any kind of concern for her since they were technically in the midst of a long and drawn-out break up.

"Do you really care?" she asked him, unable to mask her skepticism over his sincerity.

"Sara, just because I left doesn't mean I don't care about you," he told her. He looked at the girls in the corner of the room, then back at Sara, and raised his eyebrows. "Can we not do this right now?" he murmured. She nodded, still scrambling to figure out Kevin's change in demeanor.

"Sorry," she murmured back.

"Look, I think you and I are due for a long talk about everything. Perhaps we can meet up for coffee this week or something?"

"I think that would be a good idea," Sara lied. What would they talk about? How their marriage had failed? Filling out divorce papers? How she was a horrible wife? She couldn't think of anything she'd rather do less than to meet with her ex-husband.

After Kevin left, Sara spent the final hour of the day hanging with the girls and listening to their stories. They all hung out in the bathroom while Lily took her bath, Megan leaning over the side of the tub and playing with the bubbles that surrounded Lily. Megan had outgrown taking baths with her sister, as they had done for years when the girls were small. Somewhere in the past few months, Megan had become hyper-modest about her body, especially around her mother. Even in the midst of her wonderment at these tiny glimpses of Megan's future self, it made Sara a little sad to see her daughter moving beyond her younger years.

They both took turns telling Sara about the different animals they saw at the zoo. And Sara listened as best as she could, fighting the urge to delve into the swirling thoughts spinning a tornado in her mind. Soon she was filled with images of giraffes and monkeys, coffee talk with Kevin, feeding pigeons with leftover popcorn, the weight of John's body hovering over her, bears sleeping in the sun...

"Mom, are you listening?" Megan asked, bringing Sara back to where she was, running the washcloth over the same spot on Lily's back as her four-year-old played in the bubbles.

"Of course, sweetie," Sara said, putting the washcloth down and unplugging the tub to let the water out.

"Then what did I say?" her older daughter asked, hands on her hips, acting very much like the parent.

"Uh…" Sara racked her brain. Bears? Giraffes? "You were telling me about the lemurs?" Sara asked with a hopeful grin. Megan pushed her lips out in disappointment. "Busted," Sara said with a chuckle. "Sorry Megan, I guess I got caught up in a daydream."

"What were you thinking about?" Megan asked.

"Nothing, really. Mostly how good it was to have you both back. The house is so empty without you!" Megan's face beamed at the answer, and Sara breathed an invisible sigh of relief that the girls couldn't read her mind. "So what were you saying?"

"I was asking you what divorce meant," Megan asked. Sara did a double-take at the question. What the heck were they talking about this weekend?

"Why do you want to know?" Sara asked after a moment's pause to control her voice.

"I heard Daddy talking about it on the phone. He said he might be getting a divorce. One of my friends said her parents got a divorce but I never asked them what it was. Do you have a divorce? Do you know what it is?" she peppered at her mother. Sara thought about how to answer her daughter, and realized that her daughter needed the full truth. But first, she couldn't help but gather a bit of information on Kevin.

"Was your daddy sad when he said it?" Sara asked her.

"Not really. Why, is it a sad thing?"

"It can be. I mean, it might feel sad at first. But sometimes it means that someone can be happier than they were before a divorce. Do you know who he was talking to?"

"I'm not sure. I didn't answer the phone. But Mom, what IS a divorce?"

Sara sighed. She took Lily out of the tub, lifting her wet body onto the towel across her lap and then wrapping her up in it.

"Divorce is when two people who were married decide not to be married anymore," Sara said, hugging Lily close to her and looking Megan in the eyes, trying to look calm and reassuring.

"Are you getting a divorce, too? Like Daddy?" Lily asked in a sleepy voice, sedated from the warm bath water. Megan's eyes were already filled with tears.

"Of course, dummy." Megan's voice was sharp, matching her angry words. "Mommy and Daddy are married to each other. If Daddy's getting a divorce, then Mommy is too."

"Well, hold on Megan. First, don't call Lily a dummy. She's only four, she doesn't know. Second, I don't know if we're getting a divorce. Daddy and I haven't talked to each other about it."

"Then why isn't he here?" Megan demanded.

"Because Daddy and Mommy are taking a small break from being married to each other. It's not a forever break right now, just a vacation break," she said, realizing how lame that terminology sounded. Vacations were when you went somewhere fun. This was anything but fun.

"So when is he coming back from his vacation break?" Megan asked.

"I don't know," Sara said. "I'm not sure if he's coming back," she admitted.

"You won't let him come back, will you?" Megan accused her. "You got mad at Daddy and told him to leave."

"What are you talking about, Megan? I didn't force him to go," Sara defended herself.

"Yes you did! I heard you! You told him to leave that night, to not come back." Sara realized that her daughter had been awake the night they had fought and she told him to pack up his things. Megan had heard every word from their argument.

"Megan, it's not like that," Sara started to explain.

"I hate you! I hate you and I want to leave here too. I want to live with Daddy! He has a pool and tennis courts, and lives near a park. All you have is stupid stuff, and you make people go away." She ran from the bathroom and down the hall, slamming the door to her bedroom behind her.

"I don't hate you, Mommy," Lily said underneath the towel. Sara swiped at her eyes and smiled down at Lily. She ruffled her wet hair with the towel.

"I know, bug," she said.

"Is it okay if I miss Daddy, too?" she asked her mom. Sara smiled.

"Of course you can," she told her. "Want to know a secret?" Lily nodded with wide eyes. "I miss him too."

After Lily got dressed in her pajamas and crawled into bed, Sara kissed her goodnight on the forehead and then shut off the light. She kept the door open a crack and then crept down the hall. Megan's door was still closed, no light escaping from the bottom of the door. It appeared she had gone to sleep. Sara tapped on the door. When there was no answer, she eased the door open and peered in. Megan's sleeping body rose and fell with each shuddering breath, the kind that happened after a good, hard cry. She hoped her daughter had escaped to happier dreams, a place that was free of moms and dads who divorce.

Sara closed the door without making a sound. She went around the house and turned off all the lights, did a quick clean-up of the bathroom, and then retired to her bedroom where she took a long, hot shower. She lathered up her hair, but paused in the midst of it. John had told her she smelled like me. She inhaled, taking in the mango scent of the shampoo we both had fallen in love with as teens.

Sara had discovered it first, a more expensive brand that she bought with her own money to avoid using the cheaper brand our mom bought for the household. She often had to fight me about using her shampoo, too, until she learned it was best just to take it out of the shower when she was done to keep me from using it. I soon gave in and bought my own whenever I thought to save enough money instead of spending it on books or music.

Sara put two and two together and realized that John smelled me in her hair. She sped through the rest of her shower, rinsing out the shampoo and then wrapping her hair in a large towel. Grabbing the bottles of both shampoo and conditioner, she started to toss them into the waste basket, but thought better of it. *Such a waste to throw them away,* she thought of the half-full bottles. Instead she placed them under the cabinet of her sink, promising herself she'd find a new brand in the morning.

When she came out of the bathroom, she could see a lump under the covers of her bed across the room, a mass of dark hair peeking out from under the blankets. She smiled, pulling on a nightshirt and slipping into bed beside Megan.

"I don't really hate you," Megan mumbled against her pillow.

"I know you don't, sweetie," Sara said, kissing her on the cheek before turning out the light. "Goodnight, darling," she whispered, using the same endearment we both had heard often growing up, a nickname her daughters had now inherited. Sara closed her eyes in the dark, pushing against the thoughts that kept swimming at her, focusing instead on this moment when her daughter didn't hate her, and relishing the closeness they still shared while she was still the biggest part of her daughters' young lives.

Twenty-one

John spent the next few days trying to forget Sara, forgetting to mourn my absence as well in the process, at least for a time. He had too much to do anyway. The last of his things were in the moving van, and Sam helped him out of the apartment, erasing all proof of our life there to ensure at least a partial return of the deposit. Sam was staying with him for the next week, using part of his summer break to help him with the move, but also to escape his mom and all of her rules. He didn't share that last reason with his dad, but John wasn't oblivious to this fact, either.

The two worked hard, their words few and far between, only speaking when they needed to give or take direction. John was amazed at how much Sam had grown in the time he'd been gone. In the year since he'd lived with his mom, he had gained a quiet wisdom that leaned more toward the man he was becoming and further away from the boy he once was. He'd been driving for a few months, a concept that John could still couldn't believe. As if seeing him behind the wheel weren't enough of a clue that his kid was growing up, Sam stood half-a-head taller than John, towering over him whenever they stood side by side. The angry teenager he'd once been was now replaced by a quieter, reserved young man who wasn't afraid to roll up his sleeves and get some work done.

"I'm proud of you, son," John said out of the blue, producing the hint of a smile on Sam's face. The apartment was done, and they were surveying each room to make sure they hadn't forgotten anything.

"Why is that?" Sam asked. His dad never said anything like this when they lived together. Even after he moved in with his mom, his dad appeared distant and unavailable. But ever since the heart attack, it seemed like his dad was reaching out to him more. It still wasn't as often as he wanted, and Sam sometimes resented him for that. But in the times they were together, Sam forgot to hold a grudge, amazed that he enjoyed hanging with his old man.

"I just am, I guess. Nothing specific. Or maybe it's because of everything," John said. "I'm just really proud of the man you're becoming. I love the person you are."

"Uh, thanks," Sam said, unsure how to respond. I could see him smiling on the inside, though, soaking up his dad's words to take the place of at least one of the hurts he'd carried from his youth.

John dropped the keys off with the apartment manager, and then drove the moving van across the bridge to the house in San Anselmo. Sam followed in John's car and helped him carry the boxes into the house, placing each one in the room they'd be unpacked in. His own room, the one he would stay in on the days he would spend with his father, held little more than a bed. Sam still hadn't brought any of his things over from his mom's, but was pleased to have a place to call his own in his dad's new house.

That evening they hung out in the living room surrounded by boxes as they attacked a hot platter of just-delivered pizza. In five minutes, half of it was already missing.

"So, are you seeing anyone?" John asked him. Sam groaned.

"Jeez Dad, is that all you ever wonder about? You ask that every time I see you."

"So you *are* seeing someone," John said, laughing out loud when Sam confirmed it with a smile he failed to hide. "What's her name?"

"Alana," he admitted, realizing any attempts at secrecy would be worn down by his persistent father. Truth was, he was head-over-heels in love with Alana. It had only been a few months, and even his mom didn't know she existed. But he had finally lost his virginity to her, making himself a man in the middle of his mom's living room next to the throw pillows and two dozen picture frames she kept around the room for appearance's sake. If she knew how he had soiled the innocence of that room, it was a good bet she'd have it redecorated.

"Is she nice?" John asked.

"One of the nicest," Sam said, unmasking the sincerity of his smile. "And the prettiest."

"Ah, the pretty ones. They'll get you in trouble by stealing your heart," John teased. "I'm happy for you, son. Maybe one of these days you can bring her over to meet your old dad.

"Maybe," Sam said without committing. "So, are you seeing anyone?" John took his time chewing, mulling over the question and how he should answer.

"Not exactly," John said.

"Not exactly, meaning you're not seeing someone or you are?" Sam asked, possessing a sudden interest in whatever his dad had to say.

"Not exactly, meaning I am not seeing someone, but that I did have a brief moment when I thought I might," John said.

"You're not making any sense," Sam said.

"Exactly."

"Dad…"

"Let's just say," John began, swallowing the last of his pizza in one final gulp, "that love is way more complicated than I thought it was, and dating sucks." Sam seemed to take this as an acceptable answer, though I could see the thoughts rolling around in his head. I was surprised to see my face pop into his mind. It didn't happen that much anymore, except when he was with John. So when it did, I perked up and listened with intent.

"Do you ever think of her anymore?" Sam asked. He didn't even need to specify who "her" was; John knew who he was talking about.

"All the time," John replied. "Do you?"

"Sometimes," Sam answered. "And of Joey, too. It's weird. I didn't think I even cared that much when they were around. But when they died, it was like something had been taken away from me that I wanted to keep holding onto. They were cool. I mean, it was cool having a little brother around. And Rachel would have been a great stepmom."

"I think she would have, too," John said. He felt good talking about me out loud, and I glowed with happiness as I was remembered by the two of them.

"Is that what makes it so hard for you to move on?" Sam asked.

"Probably. I mean, it just feels weird. It's almost like I'm cheating on her by even thinking of dating someone else," John admitted. Sam digested his words with a thoughtful nod.

"That makes sense," he told his father. "Still, it's been almost two years. I bet she would understand if you found someone else. She would probably want that for you."

I sat with bated breath in the corner. In the beginning months of my death, I would have disagreed. Even now, I couldn't claim that thought as my own. But I also knew it was best for him if he could move past me and find another who was lucky enough to be loved by him.

"Seems that everyone is moving into a new season," Aunt Rose said beside me, appearing next to me out of nowhere. I was no longer surprised when she appeared out of thin air, and I welcomed her regular visits. I knew she had been listening for a while before appearing, knowing she witnessed a lot of the same lives I watched over. I nodded at her sentiment, not even hiding the wistfulness attached to the reality. "Oh, don't be sad, Rachel," she said, smoothing my hair and leaning my head against her chest like a child. I let myself be babied by her, needing someone to feel sorry for me.

"They don't need me anymore," I lamented.

"No, but they'll always love you," Aunt Rose told me.

"Not if John finds someone else," I glowered. Aunt Rose made soothing noises, continuing to brush my hair.

"I have a feeling you will always hold a special place in John's heart," Aunt Rose said.

I hoped she was right.

Even still, it troubled me that it was Sara's face on John's mind as he drifted off to sleep in his new bed, and not mine.

Back in the city, Sara's mind was also on John and the night they shared. She tried to block it out, but it kept coming back to haunt her. Even the next day, as she prepared for her lunch with Kevin, she couldn't help wishing she were getting ready to meet with John instead.

"Knock it off, Sara," she said aloud to herself, shaking the images that haunted her from her mind. Megan was already at school when she walked Lily over to the neighbor's house to be watched for a few hours. Sara caught a taxi on the corner and directed him to the restaurant Kevin had texted her mid-morning. He was already there and seated, and he waved at her from their table. Even though he looked confident and handsome in his usual suit and tie, Sara could note a sense of nervousness beneath his demeanor.

"Hey!" he said, his enthusiasm evident as he jumped up to pull her chair out for her before taking his seat next to her. "Thank you for meeting me here." Sara thought he seemed...kind. "Do you want something to drink?"

"Something tells me I might want something strong," Sara said, only half-joking. He chuckled at this.

Looking around, he caught the eye of their server, who came to the table. "Two Old-Fashioneds, please." They

248

made small talk while they waited for their drinks, discussing the kids and how fast they were growing, and chatting about the flower shop and some office gossip at his job. When the drinks were placed in front of them, Kevin still didn't get to the point, and say what this was about. The pit in Sara's stomach was getting bigger and deeper by the moment and she had the sudden urge to beat him to the punch, forcing him to lay it all out on the table. Taking a deep sip of her drink, she prayed for a bit of liquid courage and began.

"Megan said you were talking about divorce at your house," she blurted out. The look on Kevin's face was more shock than confirmation.

"Are you finding out information about me through the girls?" he asked her. Sara shook her head, her eyes widening at the prospect.

"No! Not at all! But she was asking me about it. She didn't know what it meant when she heard you talking about it, and wanted to know what it was. When I explained it to her, she got mad. And Lily wanted to know if we were getting one."

"What did you tell her?" Kevin asked.

"I told her I didn't know," Sara said. "Because I don't."

Kevin was silent after this, leaving an uncomfortable pause lying on the table right next to the fragrant appetizers and bourbon drinks. Sara squirmed under the crushing weight of the silence.

"Kevin, why *did* you ask me to meet you today?" she asked, unable to avoid the elephant in the room any longer. Her eyes flashed, begging him to just rip the band-aid off the unanswered questions holding their marriage together by a thread. He took in a deep breath before letting it out.

"I *was* talking about divorce this weekend," he began. "I didn't think Megan could hear me when I was on the phone. Did she tell you anything else?" he asked.

"No," Sara said. "Were you talking to your mother?" For just a moment, Sara was hopeful. He shook his head. Sara held very still. "Was it a woman?" He nodded. His confirmation was a punch to her gut, and she let out the breath she hadn't realized she was holding. She wanted to leave, picking up her purse to get ready to flee. But when he reached for her hand to stop her from going, she didn't fight him. "Do you love her?" she asked him.

"I barely know her," he said. She could see the truth in his face, and understood there would be no lies at this table. "Sara, she asked me if I was going to divorce you. I had just started seeing her. I wanted to know what it was like to be with someone else, and she wanted to know if I was serious about her."

"What did you tell her?" Sara asked.

"I told her I didn't know if I was going to divorce you," he said. The words lingered between the two of them.

"You don't know?" Sara asked. He shook his head with a small smile. "So what about her?"

"Well, that's about when she told me not to call her until I had signed divorce papers."

Sara stared at his face, studying the emotions there. It had been a long time since she'd known what he was thinking. Her eyes began to fill with tears. "Is that why we're here? You want me to sign them so we can move on?"

"Sara!" Kevin was incredulous. "Are you even listening to a word I'm saying?" He heaved a huge sigh and threw caution to the wind. "Honey, I miss you. I miss us. I miss us being a whole family. I want to come home. That is…if you'll have me." Sara was dumbfounded.

"But you said you didn't love me anymore."

"I didn't know what I wanted, Sara. My mind was so muddy from being overworked that I couldn't see what I was throwing away. All this time I was blaming you for not giving me the attention I wanted that I couldn't see how much you were doing already." He chuckled in embarrassment. "Taking care of those girls is really hard work!"

"Right? They'll suck the life right out of you," she laughed. Sara's heart warmed at the acknowledgement.

"But they're so dang smart, and fun! I realized I had been letting all the parenting fall on your shoulders, and I was actually missing out on them growing up. These past few months I've been forced to stop focusing on all my stuff when they're around, and it's been really eye-opening." He took Sara's hand in his. "Sara, if you'll have me back, I promise to be around more. And not just physically. When I'm at the house, I promise to be your partner in life, and not just someone who lives there."

She couldn't believe what she was hearing. Of all the scenarios that had played through her head, this was one she never thought of. She'd been so sure he was going to start making arrangements for the divorce, to discuss lawyers and paperwork, to rip her heart out of her chest and crush it with the bottom of his shoe. And here he was, wanting her back, wanting to be a family. A brief glimpse of the other night with John burst into her mind.

"Oh god," she said, pulling her hand away from Kevin's grasp.

"What is it?" he asked in alarm. "Is it me? Are you saying no?"

"No," she said. She saw Kevin's face fall, and she rushed to correct herself. "No, I mean I'm not saying 'no.' Oh Kevin, I did something. I did something really awful."

"Did you sleep with someone?" he asked her, guessing on the very first try. She nodded, fearful tears filling her eyes.

"But it was just once, and it wasn't planned," she swore.

He thought for a moment. "Do you care for him?"

"No. I mean, not like that. It was a total accident, and we decided it wasn't ever going to happen again," she insisted.

I caught just a flash of Kevin's thoughts in that moment. John's face appeared in his head, and he brushed it away as soon as it came. He knew it was him. He was the only man Sara was even close enough to become intimate with. Kevin knew she wasn't like him. She wouldn't have been able to sleep with just anyone – unlike he had with the first person who showed interest in him.

He took her hand back in his.

"I don't want to know anymore. It doesn't matter. None of it matters. The only thing that's important is if you'll take me back." Sara didn't say anything, afraid to answer, afraid of what he was asking, afraid that it could mean she would be trapped in a passionless marriage, afraid that he would walk out of the restaurant and never come back. "Sara, do I need to get on my knees and beg you? Because I will if I have to," he promised. He started to get up.

"No, stop!" she said, laughing. "You've just caught me off guard."

"Does that mean you need time to decide? Or is your mind already made up?" he asked her.

"I'm just afraid," she admitted. "What if it doesn't work? What if we're fooling ourselves into being trapped in a miserable situation?"

"Thing is, Sara, being miserable without you is way worse than being miserable with you," he told her.

"Well, that's reassuring," she laughed. "I'm being serious."

"I am too. And if things get rocky, we fix it before it gets worse. We go to counseling. We read all those self-help books by your bed. We talk it out. Hell, I'll even go to church if I have to. I just don't want to be without you," he pleaded. When she still didn't answer right away, he slid off his chair onto one knee before she realized what he was doing.

"Sara Marie Ashby Ferguson. Will you do me the immense honor of being my wife?" he said, his voice carrying through the whole restaurant. Sara reddened as she felt hundreds of eyes turning to look in her direction.

"Oh my goodness, he's proposing!" she heard a woman gush at a table behind her.

"We're already married," Sara said to the woman. "We're already married, Kevin," she repeated to him. "Get up off the ground, you're embarrassing yourself."

"I'm not embarrassed," Kevin said with a grin. "In fact, I'm quite enjoying this."

"Then you're embarrassing me," she hissed.

"Will you?" he asked. "I'm not getting up until you give me an answer."

The rest of the restaurant was quiet as they all waited for Sara to say something, the only sound being the occasional whisper and the clink of a fork on porcelain. She glared down at him as he continued to hold her hand tight. He smiled in encouragement when a little smile crept onto her face. She thought about how absurd the situation was, Kevin bent on one knee and both of them the center of attention. At last, she nodded. The whole restaurant erupted in applause as he got up and pulled her up in a huge embrace.

"You won't regret this, Sara," he whispered in her ear. "I'll spend my whole life making sure of it."

Twenty-two

It had been several months since John had last seen Sara, and he still couldn't get her out of his mind. He had tried, putting all of his energy into unpacking the house and making it a home, as well as diving headfirst into work. With the summer weather extending into fall, work had been steady enough that he was always busy. His contractor had secured a project for a new subdivision in South San Francisco, taking one of the rare rural areas and building high-priced homes on it. Many days he didn't see his own home except in the glow of streetlights, spending all his daylight hours working on someone else's house under the October sun.

Days were easy; his only focus a job that demanded all his attention. But at night, when he lay within the quiet of his empty house, it was Sara's face that haunted him in the moments it took him to fall asleep, and who greeted him when he woke from a dreamless slumber. It was easier for John to focus on Sara than it had been to be so consumed by me. I tried to remind myself of this every time I started to get hurt that he no longer seemed to need me. It helped that he still thought of me from time to time. But whenever he did, he traded my face for Sara's, giving his attention to someone more attainable than a dead fiancée.

He had only called Sara a handful of times in the past three months. The first time, he hung up after her voice gave instructions on how to leave a message, before the beep obligated him to say something back. The second time, he tried to act casual, giving an unbelievable performance of someone who was just checking in to see what was new in her world. By the third phone call, he was aware that she was avoiding his calls, and he called her out on it in the phone message. But it was the fourth call he left that he regretted the most, one that he replayed over and over in his head and wished he could take back.

"Sara, it's John. You might not want to see me, but your girls might. After all, I was a part of their lives too. I was almost their uncle. So… Shit. Okay, this isn't going how I planned. Leave it to me to try and get you to call me back by reminding you that I was once going to be married to your sister. But I'm going crazy here. Look, will you just talk to me? Damn, I probably should just re-record this-" Beep.

The phone cut him off before he could do anything, holding his jumbled up message hostage in her voicemail box until she listened to him make an ass of himself. He almost called back, but decided the damage was done. Calling her repeatedly wasn't going to make any of it look less crazy. So he left it as it was, and never called again.

But her non-communication was eating away at him. And on his next Sunday off from work, he knew he needed to see her in person and at least plead his case.

Most flower shops in town were closed on Sundays and Mondays. Knowing this in the beginning days of opening our shop, Sara and I had decided we would place the odds in our favor by keeping limited hours on Sunday mornings to fill the needs of those in a bind. At first, staying open for four hours on a Sunday morning didn't make much sense. We only saw one or two customers on the first dozen Sundays, making the expense of staying open cost more than closing one day a week and losing the small amount of business. But soon word got out that we were available on Sundays, and we began to see the church altar guild buying replacement lilies for the ones that had wilted too soon, funeral directors who needed a last-minute arrangement, and apologetic husbands who had strayed into the excitement of the city, afraid to go home empty-handed to their waiting wives. This was one of the reasons our shop didn't fold when many new businesses were affected by the economy. It seemed that even in the poorest of times, people still needed flowers to say what they couldn't with words.

With the limited time Sara would be at the shop, John knew he needed to move fast. His conscience told him just to let her go. Or perhaps it was my voice he heard somewhere within the thoughts that scrambled up his mind, pleading with him to forget her as I tried to protect him from breaking his heart any more than it already was. But he wouldn't listen. He knew he wouldn't be able to rest until he had seen her face to face, pled his case, convinced her that he was the answer to everything she needed and she was his answer as well.

He took a quick shower, pulling on the cleanest pair of jeans he could find in a pile of laundry that had been building up for weeks. He then grabbed a granola bar for breakfast and hopped into his truck, taking the drive over the Golden Gate Bridge to reach the small shop Sara and I had set up so many years before. As he drove, he went over what he was going to say to her. In truth, he didn't have a clue. All attempts to formulate a plan failed, fluttering away like the leaves on his windshield.

There were no customers when John walked in the door. Not even Sara was in sight, leaving John alone in a room of flowers. He paused in his mission and looked around. It occurred to him that this was where he had first laid eyes on me, when he had fallen in love with me but wouldn't know it for a few more months. The room seemed smaller than he remembered, encased by flowers on the walls and in buckets around the shop. The claustrophobia set in before he even knew what was hitting him. I was everywhere he turned - my eyes, my smile, the mango smell in my hair.

"What am I doing?" John said out loud, his hands shaking. He couldn't breathe, the air swallowed by the fragrance of flowers, suffocating him with their sweet aroma.

"John?" Sara asked, emerging from the back room. "What are you doing here?" She saw how pale his face was, and changed from curiosity to concern. "Are you okay?"

"I need to get out of here," John said, rushing back through the doors he came in from. Sara grabbed a bottle of water from beside the register and followed him out.

"Here," she said, handing him the bottle. "Drink this." He took it with an embarrassed smile, and drank half of it without pausing. Wiping his mouth, he sank to the ground, squeezing the area between his eyes in efforts to get his mind to shut up. "Feel better?" Sara asked him. He nodded, though his hands were still shaky.

"I'm sorry, I shouldn't have come here," he said.

"Why *are* you here, John?" Sara asked. I could tell she already knew why, having listened to each of John's messages with a guilty heart, afraid to answer the phone or even call him back for fear of rocking the boat with Kevin. Things were good at home. She didn't want anything to interfere with that. Seeing John here, she knew it was because she had cut off all communication. She remembered how it had felt, months earlier, when she had been the one on the other line, searching for some kind of connection since her husband was unable to give it to her. But she found it easier to pretend innocence than to admit she knew what John was going through.

"You won't talk to me, won't even answer your phone. Look, I know what happened that night was sudden. But we were friends before that. And now you won't even give me that," John said.

"I can't, John."

"Why not? I mean, I know it's totally weird. It will be hard to explain to everyone around us. But... Shit. I'm not good at this anymore. I haven't dated since before your sister." Just mentioning me flooded his brain with my face once again, and he took a deep breath in and out. "What the hell is wrong with me, Rachel? Why am I having such a hard time even talking to you?" he asked.

"I'm not Rachel," Sara murmured.

"What do you mean?" John asked. "I know you're not Rachel. You're Sara."

"No, you called me Rachel."

"I did?" He racked his brain over the past few minutes, and realized it was a huge possibility that he had slipped up, using my name instead of hers. "Sara, I'm sorry. I know you're not Rachel. I think just being here is making me think of her more than ever."

"But don't you see? That's exactly why that night was a mistake. You don't love me, you love the idea of me – the one that is mixed up with thoughts of my sister."

"That's not true," John protested. But just the mention of it made him question what was going on.

"What happened in there?" Sara asked. "I know that wasn't from me. What were you thinking of when you entered the store and suddenly needed to leave?"

"I was thinking of her," John admitted. He sighed, rubbing his temples at the realization he wasn't over me yet, that he had transferred all of his pain over losing me into obsessing over Sara. "This was where we first met. It was an accident, really. But it was one that was meant to happen." He relayed the story, telling her about how the forgetfulness of his friend brought him to this shop. "From the moment I saw her, she took my breath away. She didn't know it, of course. She was adorably flustered as she tried to help me with some last minute flower needs. But it gave me the in to be able to ask her out." He smiled at the memory, taking in the details of the dress I wore that day, the way my hair escaped from the loose bun I wore at the nape of my neck, the rich coffee of my eyes.

"You know, you were the first guy she really let get close to her, I mean, since Joey's dad took off. She had a hard time trusting anyone. But something about you let her believe that even she could fall in love. I never saw her as happy as she was when she was around you." Sara paused, her eyes twinkling at a memory only she and I shared. "If she were here, she'd kill me for telling you this. But she called me the day that she met you. She actually told me she had met the man she was going to marry."

"You're kidding."

"No!" Sara insisted. "I remember thinking that was so unlike her. The few dates she had gone on before she met you, she saw as dead-ends. Eventually she just gave up dating altogether, finding it easier to take care of Joey and focus on the shop than, in her words, 'deluding herself that any man could be anything more than disappointing.' So to hear her tell me that you were the one, after only having just met you... Let's just say I was both delighted by her hopefulness and fearful that she was about to get her heart totally ripped to shreds." She smiled at the memory of her sister in those early days of love. "I don't believe in soul mates, John. But when I was witness to the beginning of my sister's relationship with you, seeing how it grew so purely out of just a chance meeting, even I had to re-evaluate how I perceived the idea of love at first sight. You two were meant for each other, and you made her final years on earth the happiest she ever had."

"I guess everything happens for a reason," John mused. "If it hadn't been for a forgetful friend, I never would have met her." He paused at the thought, remembering how that meeting had led to a night of dancing at the wedding, the first of many consecutive days and nights we spent talking to each other, getting to know each other, and when we weren't together, thinking about each other. But his thoughts darkened at the loss that followed a life that had promised so much happiness. "Or maybe it was a mistake. If I hadn't been in here that day, I never would have known what it feels like to lose her."

"And you never would have known what it felt like to love her, either," Sara pointed out. The tears he had worked so hard to keep at bay broke free and ran down his cheeks in sheltered sobs. He tried not to let it all go, but when the first sob shuddered through him, the rest barreled down and bowled him over in unbridled sorrow.

I watched with compassion as everything he had kept so close to his chest was now pouring out of him. He held no power to stop it either. He was healing as he mourned, enveloping the whole section of the world where we were with the strength of his emotion. They couldn't feel it, of course, but I experienced every teardrop as a tiny ocean of hope, the breaking of his heart allowing the past to break free and make room for whatever the future held.

And I was suffocating him.

By indulging my selfish need to be close to him even as he grieved, I was making it impossible for him to let me go. I hadn't thought I would ever be able to walk away, that if I did it would mean I didn't love him enough. But I was beginning to believe I was ready to leave, that I could move on and leave behind all I loved in this world. John was taking the first real steps toward doing the same. I also saw, for the first time, that leaving him was an act of love in its own way.

"I'm sorry I came here," John whispered when the tears allowed words to form once more.

"I'm not," Sara said. "I think you needed this more than you know." He nodded in quiet agreement, raw from allowing himself permission to break. He turned to her with a sad smile.

"And you, are you going to be okay?" he asked her. "I mean, I know you've been the strong one here by being firm that this...thing...won't work. But raising the girls all by yourself and everything..." he trailed off. "Will you be okay?" She smiled at him, breaking into a grin of happiness she couldn't contain.

"Actually, Kevin has come back home. We're starting to put our marriage back together. And so far, it's working," she told him, her eyes filled with hope.

"Oh god," John stammered. "But we... Does he know about us?"

"Yes," Sara confirmed. John's eyes widened at the complications that presented, but Sara waved her hand as she finished the thought. "I mean, no. He knows that I had an indiscretion while we were apart, but not that it was you. We both made our fair share of mistakes during our time apart from each other, and all we can do is forgive them, understanding we didn't know what the future held."

"And are things better?" John asked her.

"They've never been so good," Sara breathed with relief.

In the past few months, she was introduced to a part of her husband she never knew. He was proactive in being a parent to the girls, which she assumed was a result of his months as a single father with no other parent to lean on. He helped out around the house, even surprising Sara that he knew how to cook a meal or two. And he was more attentive to Sara and her needs, reading her like a book and keeping himself open to communication. She was falling love with Kevin all over again.

"How about you?" she asked. "Are you going to be okay? Do I need to call someone, or anything?" He gave a light chuckle in response, staring at the street in quiet reflection. The city never slept, but it was beginning to rouse from its sedated state of morning peace – the cars starting to pass by with more frequency, as was the increasing number of people pounding the pavement. Not one of them noticed Sara and John huddled off to the side.

Sometimes it is good to be invisible.

John took in the details of the green grass that poked through the cracks in the sidewalk, the black of the tar on the wooden light post in front of them, the contrast of the colors in a small square flyer boasting of the carnival that was coming in a couple months. And he breathed in the smell of San Francisco, a mixture of the foggy air with a slight hint of fish from their close proximity to the wharf. He turned to Sara and smiled.

"I'm going to be just fine," he said. And for the first time, he believed it.

Twenty-three

I spent the last few moments of my time on earth memorizing everything and everyone I ever loved in life, taking a full six months of human time to say my goodbyes before I was gone forever. I danced on the cables of the Golden Gate Bridge, running up the rusty orange rails toward the top of the towers and taking a long look at the expanse of the bay. I climbed into the trees on Telegraph Hill, letting the parrots that lived within the branches project their colorful thoughts back and forth from their head to mine and back again. I ran the bases at AT&T Park at the same time as Chewy Mendez, this year's favorite San Francisco baseball player. I even pretended the crowd was cheering for me as we both rounded third base and slid into home. I visited old clients I adored, my son's former third grade teacher, and the young gal who made my latte every morning at the coffee shop. Even my mailman received a momentary sojourn, a brief glimpse into his house while he served dinner to his family, just because I could.

I asked Aunt Rose to accompany me on all of these visits, in part so that I had someone with me on this side of the world, but also to keep me from changing my mind. These were my goodbyes. I wanted to make sure that I was clear on my intent, that nothing in this world altered my resolve to find peace in closure and leave it all behind. But I also wanted to make sure that I had one last memory of every part of the world I cherished, something I could hold onto once I had crossed over from this world to the next.

If Aunt Rose disagreed with what I was doing, she never let on. Instead, she hid in the corners of every place I visited, and melted into the shadows of every person I bid farewell. She didn't speak to me, only offering comfort through her presence.

And I found the exercise cathartic. I started out easy, breezing through parts of my life that were once forgotten, coming to terms with loose ends and people who had slipped from my life. I checked in on old high school friends I had lost touch with, saw each of them in a different phase of life. Some had kids, some were divorced, and at least one of them made it big by becoming a rock star just as he swore he would in high school. I discovered my cat, who had escaped from our apartment a few months before my death, living in the apartment of Mrs. Rhodes down the hall. I laughed when he saw me, floating near him as a light in the air. And he knew it was me.

"Damn Mrs. Rhodes," I laughed, remembering how she had seemed so concerned when I came to her door with a photo of him, swearing she hadn't seen him but would keep her eye out for him. All that time, Pepper had been in her house. "Good for you, Pepper," I told him, glad that he was at least well-loved in his new home even if he had betrayed me in his abandonment.

I traveled to Sebastopol to visit Sam in his mother's town. I watched him as he moved with ease among his friends, an air of confidence unmistakable around him as he joked with those who looked up to him. He was different than I once knew him. We were so unfamiliar with each other in life, our defenses still strong as we became accustomed to living under the same roof. There was so much I didn't know about him in life that I now knew about him in death. My regret with Sam was that I never got to experience the other side of being his stepmom, moving beyond our initial awkwardness to a place where we showed how much we cared. I sent him a silent farewell from my world to his, taking comfort from knowing he really had cared.

I visited Joey's dad, Tony, exploring a part of my life I thought I'd never want to see again. My heart softened for him when I found him, living in a drug-induced stupor that seemed to be a permanent thing these days. He was the only one who lived in his home, the place trashed with beer cans and a sink full of dishes. The whole place smelled of old booze and cigarettes. He didn't have much, but what he did have was worn out and old. However, one thing shone out among the piles of dirt and junk, and that was a photo of all three of us on his shelf. Tony had his arm around me in the picture, holding me up as I held Joey in my arms. My face was unsure, a hint of hope flushed in my cheeks. It was when Joey was only a few weeks old, when Tony had reappeared for just a moment to check in and see how we were doing, and, in an out-of-character move, hand me a wad of cash to help out with some expenses. He'd only stuck around for a few days, more than I had expected of him even then. I had forgotten about the photo until now, which he had asked a random guy on the street to take as if we were tourists instead of a local broken-up family. The moment was captured forever, now sitting on his bookshelf that held no books, us as a family for the last time in our lives with a backdrop of pork buns in a store window in Chinatown.

And next to the photo was our obituary.

The visit to my parents' house in Sonoma was the one that worried me the most, and I begged Aunt Rose to stay close to ensure I wouldn't fold. She nodded, holding my hand in silent support as we manifested to the home where I had grown up.

My mother was in the garden when I arrived, her hands deep in the dirt as she took advantage of the late afternoon sun. She was planting bulbs, a pile of them near her as she took her time digging six inch holes and placing a bulb in each one, covering them over with dirt and patting it down so they could sleep through the winter. Nearby, a Japanese maple I'd never seen before shone in red and gold. She glanced over at it when the last bulb was planted, offering a silent prayer.

"I miss you, sweet Rachel."

It was all she said, but it spoke volumes. I understood that this was her way of keeping me close, that the tree was her offering to me and a beacon of hope for her. I had only visited her a handful of times in my death, but somehow she never looked as lovely or as young as she did in this moment. I memorized how the sun shone through her hair, casting a golden glow through the silver that now stood as the prominent hue. I traveled along her laugh lines, creases that made up an older version of my own face when I was human, and proof of a life filled with laughter. I captured the blue of her eyes, painting my dress the exact same shade so that I couldn't forget the warmth of indigo that had smiled upon me at every stage of my life. I watched her hands as she worked, noticing the signs of age both in weathered skin and in age spots that hid among patches of dirt. I held onto Aunt Rose as I watched my mother's hands, feeling cautious as I longed for the time when I was once cared for by those hands.

"It's okay to feel," Aunt Rose said, giving me permission in my goodbye to grieve. "I've got you." And I cried as the memories of a really wonderful childhood flashed in front of me like slides to a moving picture show, scenes of my life passing me by. There was the time my father took Sara and me to the dump in his truck, all the windows rolled down and the radio turned up as we enjoyed being my father's honorary sons for the day. There were all the times my mom rolled up her sleeves to teach us the art of baking bread, or how to outline the pictures we were coloring before filling them in with a lighter shade. The hills behind our house became the road of connection with our father, the hikes he took us on as teenagers serving as magical bridges when we couldn't see eye to eye.

On this late afternoon, my father came out to join my mother, handing her a cup of ice water and inviting her to take a break. And the four of us stayed out there until the sun went down and cast a shadow over their bit of land in Sonoma. My father held my mom's hand, a gesture I had taken for granted in all my years of life. I never took the time to notice how in love they were, even after years of marriage. I may have never been able to experience that kind of love in a marriage to John, but I got to be a part of it through my parents – two people who had served as an example of what a true partnership looked like.

The sky took on a purplish hue, the moon appearing over the ridge in magnified brilliance. It was why our hometown of Sonoma was referred to as the Valley of the Moon, the magical way the moon appeared larger than life when it first rose, before shrinking to a more demure orb. My parents stood up to go inside. But I stayed where I was, watching them walk away for the very last time. When they closed the door, Aunt Rose and I were already gone.

Sara's house was a tornado of happiness - a naked Lily running to avoid bath time with a fit of giggles while Kevin and Sara worked to corner her, and Megan, in hysterics, who was doing her best to help her fleeing sister. When Kevin was able to capture the wriggling four-year-old, she squealed and twisted in his arms, not ready for the game to be over. To her delight and her parents' dismay, it continued in a flurry of tidal waves and bubbles once she entered the bathtub. I left with this memory, the four of them as a family, only Sara and I aware that the number would grow by one more in nine months' time. But I was the only one who knew that this one would be a boy.

I saved John for last. I wanted his to be the last human face I saw before I took off. It was only fitting that he was at the carnival in Santa Cruz with Sam. It seemed like ages since Jane and I were here, not just the two and a half years that had passed. I felt like I was a different person back then, amazed that the effects of time were still able to touch those of us in the afterlife.

Jane was there, and she ran to me, surrounded and followed by a storm of balloons.

"You're doing it, aren't you?" she accused me with a smile. "You're leaving all this behind for something better. Am I right?"

"How did you know?"

"Honey, it couldn't be clearer if you hired a plane to write it in the sky," she laughed. "Yee! I'm so excited for you!" she squealed.

"You could come with me, you know," I pointed out. She shrugged with a grin.

"Maybe one day. Hold me a seat when you get there. I'll join you when I'm ready. But for now, I think I'm okay being right here in my own little Heaven."

We sat together and people-watched. Or rather, Jane watched the random faces passing us by while I kept my eyes locked on John. I didn't want to forget a thing. But there was something different about him, a lightness in his step and a permanent pull at the corner of his mouth. He and Sam looked more at ease than I'd ever seen them before, even in life. Sam held just a hint of being a boy, wisdom in his eyes from experience and growing up. And the two of them joked with each other, an easy camaraderie between them as they spent a silly evening at the carnival among the lights and balloons, men walking on stilts, and music enveloping the whole scene.

I saw her at the same time John did, a girl with strawberry blonde hair. She was sitting with friends several yards away from where he stood, and it was as if the crowd parted to create a path that led straight to her. She got up to leave with her friends, leaving her purse behind on the bench where she had been sitting.

"Hold on, I'll be right back," John said, rushing forward to grab the purse before someone else took off with it. "Miss!" he called out, and she turned. "You left this behind." Her eyes widened when she saw her bag in his hands. She thanked him, taking the purse from his hand and brushing her fingers against his in the motion.

It was as if time turned sideways and broke open, spilling all the contents of the future out in front of me. Time skipped, and she was there in front of him, kissing him while dressed in white as they stood in front of all their friends and family. Time jumped again and it was Sam's college graduation, the two of them cheering a few rows down from Wendy and her husband. Each jump brought them further along in life, the lines showing on their faces from years of laughter. I waited for the jealousy, the painful feelings that he had forgotten me in the eyes of another woman. But it never came. Instead I felt elation, the magnitude of happiness growing as they fell deeper in love. I experienced joy through their joy. I lived in the fast-forward of their lives until the final scene, John now an old man at the edge of her grave, smiling as he thanked her for a life well-lived. And then it all wound back up and we were at the carnival, music surrounding us as John handed her the purse.

"I'm John," he said. She smiled at him then, letting her fingers remain on his just a little too long before pulling away.

"My name's Hannah."

John wouldn't find out until after they were married that she worked for a month at a flower shop, filling in when the owner's sister died.

Twenty-four

I was coming to the end of my time here on earth. It seemed like so long ago that I had entered this divide between Heaven and Earth, and it made me think back to that very first day when I had been knocked from my body and found myself lost and alone in a forest filled with both wonder and fright. And to think, I'd had no idea before it happened that I was taking my last breaths among the living.

When a moment is so tremendous it knocks the familiar part of the world off balance, you'd think there would be some sort of clue before it happened. Maybe just a hint, or even a premonition that would have allowed me to at least hold my breath until the moment had passed and I could find my footing once again.

But life doesn't work that way.

Life is often unfair. Sometimes things have to hurt, sometimes they're even unbearable, and sometimes the pain is necessary.

I learned this lesson the hard way. But I learned much more than just that.

Bad things can happen to anyone. Or rather, things happened that I wouldn't have chosen for myself. When it came down to it, any notion that I'd had absolute control during the course of my life was but a comforting thought covering a cloud of absurdity. I was merely a miniscule blip on a very large course of time that had only just begun.

Sure, I'd been able to mold my path in the general direction of my choice. I took half-blind leaps of faith, and conjured up my very best intentions in a five-year plan in which I'd banked all my hopes and dreams. But as it was, even my most fervent efforts at success were thrown off-course by someone else who had the same freedom of choice that I did. Because of this, I was cast into the Bermuda Triangle of Life After Death, leaving me in uncharted seas where my only chance of survival was to tread water until I became familiar with my surroundings.

But perhaps that was supposed to be the plan all along.

I'd learned so much about myself since the day I had died, and I'd learned so much about life and love. Once I finally stopped fighting the current and trusted in the mercy of the waves, the tempests, and the creatures that lurked at my feet, the storm began to calm and revealed a really beautiful ocean. It was only when I abandoned control that I was able to discover pure freedom.

In my death, I discovered what it was like to truly live.

Twenty-five

"I think I'm ready," I told Aunt Rose. She stepped forward to take my hand.

"Are you sure?" she asked. I glanced one last time at John who was now in deep conversation with Hannah, Sam at his side as they chatted as casual as long-time friends among the bright lights and loud music. I smiled.

"I really am," I told her. I could hear the songs of Heaven flirting with the sounds of the carnival. I was being overwhelmed with a sense that this world was no longer mine, that I didn't belong here, that I didn't even want to belong here. It was like all of the past was one sweet memory of a more naïve time, and I was about to go home.

Before I could take one last look, say a final goodbye, or even breathe in a final whiff of the world around me, Aunt Rose and I were whisked through the air at a speed I had never experienced. We broke through the atmosphere of earth, plummeted through space like shooting stars, and whipped by the silent planet giants in the sky like passing mile markers on a highway. The air around me tasted like a copper penny, though sweet in the strangest way. And I kept my eyes open so I wouldn't miss anything.

We reached the barrier in what felt like moments, slowing to a stop right in front of the glowing wall. I could see the swirling wind storming on the outside of the border of our galaxy, and I reached forward to touch the wall and feel the vibration of its movement. The wall glowed brighter under my touch, and then moved aside to create a vacant doorway of space that created a safe passage through the swirling tornado to the other side of our galaxy. I peered through and could see a whole universe of beauty, lands farther than the eye could see or imagine, showing all the parts of earth I had loved in my life that now existed in Heaven. Streams flowed into lakes, the fields of lush green expanded to the horizon, and deer grazed on leafy bushes. A mountain towered over a lake, a waterfall streaming down its side and creating a luscious fog that misted over a garden holding every flower I had ever seen in my life.

And this was just what I could see from where we hovered on our side of the galaxy.

I wanted to see more. Still clutching Aunt Rose's hand, I moved forward. She began to loosen her grip, startling me from continuing through. Confused, I looked back at her.

"This is as far as I go," she apologized. She smiled at me with kind eyes, her comfortable beauty radiating in the glow of barrier. I embraced her, though I felt no sadness. I pulled back and looked into her eyes, the silky blue I alone hadn't inherited. If I looked deep enough, I could catch glimpses of her thoughts, her life, and the very parts of her that made her who she was. And within it all, I felt her yearning to join me and leave the sadness and heartache behind.

"Come with me," I said to her, but she pulled back at the suggestion. She looked back in Earth's direction, even though it was far too distant to see.

"I can't," she said, but her tone was unconvincing.

"Yes, you can," I assured her. "Leave all that behind. Let's move on together. Let me be your final traveler to Heaven."

"But what about Sara?" Aunt Rose asked. "Who will guide her when it's her time?"

"Sara will be fine," I promised her. "There is always someone for those who cross over. You told me that. But it's your time now to move beyond this divide. Let's cross over together." I took her hand in mine. She hesitated for only a moment, taking a deep breath and letting it out as she weighed the decision. She looked through the doorway, peering at the worlds that were waiting for us to explore. The look in her eyes went from fearful and unsure to longing and determined anticipation.

"Let's go," she whispered, her hushed voice filled with giddiness, her smile that of a child, and we walked through. And the songs of the angels cascaded over us, reminiscent of the cicadas' song in a forest a long, long time ago.

The end.

A SYMPHONY OF CICADAS

Acknowledgements

This book was born from a bad dream I had while planning my own wedding. With my wedding so close, I kept worrying that the worst would happen before I married my best friend. The dream was so haunting, I knew I needed to get it down in a book. And while the story is a work of fiction, I was able to draw from the experience of being a stepmom and starting a new family.

This was the very first book I ever had the courage to follow through and publish, and there are many people I want to thank who supported me in this journey.

First and foremost is my wonderful editor, Carol Weber, who took the story and made my words sing. Carol, you saw my vision for this book and made sure everyone else could, too. And I'd like to thank the wonderful people at NaNoWriMo.org, who told me I could write a whole book every November.

I want to thank my kids – Summer, Lucas, and Andrew – who tried not to need me too much while I typed away at the novel, and who I hope will forgive me when being a writer and a good mom and stepmom didn't go hand in hand. I'd like to thank my mother, Nancy McLerran, who took the first stab at editing my book and couldn't quite look me in the eye for weeks after reading Chapter 19, and who also didn't shy away from telling me when certain facts didn't match up.

And for all my friends and family who have encouraged me along the way, I couldn't have done it without your support! My sisters Melissa Moreno and Heather McLerran, my dad Gary McLerran, my Grandma Elsie Chretien, my fabulous in-laws Joan and Dave O'Connor, my honorary brother Brian Moreno, my sisters in crime Anne Schmidbauer and Pam Enquist, and my friends Wendy Dunnagan, Kristin Meyer, Alberto Melendez, Katie Talbot, the homegroup homies, the Girl Talk gals (your support means the world to me!), my friends and family at New Life, and everyone who stood behind me at The Press Democrat.

And I couldn't have done this without my husband, Shawn Langwell. Darling, you encouraged me from day one, read my horrible, awful first draft and still believed in me. Now if that isn't love, I don't know what is! Thank you for your patience when I chose to go to bed with the computer much to your dismay. With this book, I give you back your wife. I love you!

About the Author

Crissi Langwell is a writer in Northern California. When not writing fiction, Crissi writes for her local newspaper, The Press Democrat, and maintains several of the newspaper's websites. She lives with her husband, three children, and a couple of very needy cats. This is her first novel.

Please visit her website at CrissiLangwell.com.

A Symphony of Cicadas
Discussion Guide

Chapters 1-6

1.   *"I know you're awake," the muffled voice called from the hallway. "I'm trying to sleep, and between your racket and Joey talking in his headset, it's kind of hard."* (pg. 6)

Rachel and John are in the beginning of a passionate romance, and raising their blended family of teenage sons. How might this combination make things difficult? How might it make things easier? Have you ever had one of your kids interrupt an intimate moment?

2.   *Tony had stepped out on me when I was still pregnant, visiting just a few times after Joey was born before disappearing altogether. It seems he decided that fatherhood just wasn't for him, something he stated in a letter he sent me weeks after his last visit, explaining that he couldn't handle the responsibility of parenting.* (pg. 9)

Rachel spent more than a decade being a single parent to Joey. How do you think this affected how she parented Joey? How might her experience with Tony have changed her views on men in general?

3.   *"When you're inside the world, you can only see what's right in front of you. But on the edge of the world, you can see everything that's going on in it,"* he explained. (pg. 12)

Joey is describing his videogame, but this sentiment also becomes the theme of the story. Has there ever been a time when you were too close to something to see the whole picture, only to realize this when you were able to take a step back?

4.   *I felt my head grow even heavier against the car seat, the pain in my body evaporating with the sounds. When the last bird had sung, the whole world became quiet. And I was cast into a sea of nothing. (pg. 29)*
What were your thoughts as Chapter Two came to a close?

5.   *To keep from unraveling, I focused on his halcyon expression, willing him to open his eyes and see me, too. Instead, a small spark of light, the same light that had been sent to me earlier, emerged from his forehead and hovered just above him. (pg. 38)*
What do you think the light is? Where do you think Joey is?

6.   *"Oh, my dear," Rose crooned. "There, there. It's all going to be okay." She pet my hair as I shook, her compassion opening the floodgates. Free to let my guard down, I stopped fighting against my fear and sadness, and allowed myself a good, ugly cry on her shoulder. (p. 46)*
Rachel is at her most vulnerable when Aunt Rose shows up. She represents the link to her family when she thinks she's separate from everyone else, and becomes Rachel's anchor to hold onto just when she thinks she's lost. In your life, who is the one person that makes you feel comforted, even just by thinking of them?

2

7.   *And that's when it hit me. Aunt Rose had said the way to be close to someone or a certain time, we were to feel it in every fiber of our being. While Rose had wanted to move on and be free, she was unable to because she loved me too much. I looked at her in alarm, my eyes burning as they searched over her panicked face.*

"I'm so sorry, Rachel. I didn't mean for this to happen," she pleaded. "I didn't know!"

"You killed me?" I whispered. "You killed me, and you killed my son?" (pg. 54-55)

Did this part of the story surprise you? Did it make you think differently about Aunt Rose than before?

8.   *"But Rachel always described Sam as a kid she had difficulty getting to know," Sara noted, curiosity in her eyes.*

It was as if she were mirroring my thoughts. When I had first moved in, Sam spent most of his days shut off in his room. Despite the fact that John and I had been dating for three years before I died, I didn't know the kid very well. It took some time and lots of patience before he began opening his door and joining in on the conversation with us. (Pg. 70-71)

Not only were Rachel and John getting married, they were also blending their family. How is a stepparent's relationship with their stepchild different from the one they share with their own child? Before the accident, how do you think Sam felt about Rachel and Joey living with him and his dad?

Chapters 7-12

9.   *"Don't listen to him," I shouted at them. "There is no Heaven or Hell, there is no God welcoming us home or devil trying to snare our souls! When you die, you just exist forever in this nothing of a hellhole. There is no reason, no purpose, nothing!" (pg. 92)*
Have you ever questioned the religion you are, or the religion you were raised on?

10.   *"A carnival?" I squealed. "That's your distraction?"*
"Can you think of anything better?" she asked. (pg. 99)
Jane's happiest place in the afterlife is at a carnival. Where would your happiest place be?

11.   *I was beginning to understand even more what Aunt Rose had described to me, the addiction that takes place when surrounded with those we loved in life, and how much heavier it became with time. I knew that on this Ferris wheel I was being presented with a choice – to walk away or to run back into the addiction. I knew that I was making the wrong choice. But I didn't care. I realized that no heaven was truly perfect unless I could see John's face every moment of the day. (pg. 105)*

Do you think Rachel is making the right choice? Would you be tempted to stay near your loved ones after life if you had the choice?

12.   *This sudden act of waking up from wherever he had disappeared to confused the hell out of Sam. He didn't know whether to be angry or grateful to have this glimpse of his old dad. He wanted to confront him on it, ask him who the hell his father thought he was, say everything he wanted to say in the past six months about his dad having been a vacant vessel. But instead, he grabbed a towel off the counter and began drying the wet dishes John had placed into the rack. (pg. 115)*
Discuss how you think John and Sam's relationship has changed since Rachel died. What should they do differently? How has grief changed the way you handled parts of your life in the past?

13.   *And in one swift movement, he lifted his arm and flung the rest of the rocks out into the water with all of his force, hearing the satisfying sounds they made as they disturbed the smooth surface. Except, not one of those rocks took away the pain he was carrying. (pg. 135)*
In Chapter 10, we get to know Sam a lot better, particularly all the things he keeps hidden from those close to him. What are your thoughts on Sam? Have you ever felt the same way as he does?

14.   *It had been so long since she had been held with such care, making the distance that had been growing between her and Kevin that much wider. She pushed away*

the feelings of comfort the hug gave her, giving a vague smile to John as she picked up her purse. (pg. 140)
This is the first hint that something is going wrong at Sara and Kevin's house. What are your thoughts about this scene?

15.   *"What are you saying, Sam?" John asked, his body rigid as he waited for what they both knew was coming.*
"I'm moving in with Mom." (pg. 148)
How is John feeling about Sam moving out? How would you feel if your child wanted to live with their other parent?

16.   *Despite my disbelief in Heaven in those early days of my death, I had grown to believe that there really was something out there. I could sense a stirring within me at the faint trembling notes that existed in the corners of space, and I felt its pull whenever I let go of my hold on the living long enough to exist in the world of the dead. And I believed Joey was there. (pg. 154)*
What else do you think may have contributed to Rachel's change of mind about whether Heaven existed or not?

Chapters 13-17

17.   *"If you don't stop wishing him with you, he's going to die, Rachel." Her eyes flashed with determination as she tried to get me to see what I was refusing to see.*
I had caused this. (pg. 164)
Rachel was almost guilty of killing John simply by wishing they could be together again. It was the exact way she died when Aunt Rose wished she could be near Rachel again. Do you think it helped Rachel to better understand her Aunt Rose's mistake?

18.   *Every one of the kids kept a safe distance from the boy, as if his paralyzed body and mind of marbles were catching; only glancing over their shoulders when a baritone laugh would escape from his lungs. (pg. 170)*
When Rachel and Aunt Rose visit the hospital, Rachel can't help but notice the children who are staying there are avoiding one severely handicapped child – even though they are all sick, as well. What do you think makes others afraid of those who are different from them?

19.   *Jacob kissed her on the cheek, smiling at his mother with love, and then ran back to his aunt. Together*

they evaporated from the room as his mother collapsed in a shaking and silent cry with her head on his lifeless chest. (pg. 178)

Jacob is able to leave his mother, even though it's apparent he loves her very much. Why do you think it's easier for him than it is for Rachel or Aunt Rose?

20.   *Without thinking, John inhaled, catching once again the familiar scent of my hair in my sister's blonde locks. It stirred something inside him, just as it had before. Except this time, instead of seeing my face in front of him, he saw Sara's. The feeling caught him off guard, but he managed to tuck it away. Sara didn't see it, but the newness of this emotion inside him felt like a slap in my face. (pg. 190)*

All this time, John has been mourning the loss of Rachel. This is the first time Rachel has ever witnessed him thinking of another woman – a woman who happens to be her sister. How do you think it must be for Rachel to see the man she loves turn his attention towards her sister?

21.   *When we reached the house, I prayed that my sister had already left for one of her many friends' houses. But there she was, swaying back and forth on the swing that hung from the tree outside our house. I groaned and held Eric's hand tighter.*

"Who's that?" he asked.

"That's Sara," I said. "She's my older sister." I tried to ignore the way he looked at her, seeing something in her that I thought he had seen in me. (pg. 204)

Why do you think Rachel is so competitive with her older sister? Have you ever felt this way with one of your siblings or close friends?

22.   *"Who is that?" I asked Frank.*
"That's her second husband, Oscar," he told me, smiling with kindness in the direction of the man who now held fast to his wife.
"You're not jealous," I stated with surprise. "Doesn't it hurt to see someone else looking at your wife that way?" (pg. 213)
Why isn't Frank jealous of the man who is now married to his wife? How do you think it affects Rachel to meet someone who views love the way Frank does?

23.   *"What would happen if I walked out upon the fog, Daddy?" I had asked my father that day driving above the covered valley.*
"You'd pass right through and fall to the ground," my father had told me, stripping away all the magic my five year old self still held when it came to science and life.
The fog touched the edge of Mauna Kea, inviting me to test my father's theory and prove him wrong. (pg. 216)
Why do you think it's so important for Rachel to prove her father wrong?

Chapters 18-20

24.   *Still, Sara called every now and then just to check in on him. He had let her calls go straight to voicemail each time. Then he listened to them as soon as his phone signaled a message, hearing my voice within hers as she let him know she was thinking of him and hoped everything was going okay. (pg. 220)*
Why was John ignoring Sara? If he didn't want to talk with her, why was he so eager to hear her message?

25.   *I crouched in the corner, frozen by the scene unfolding in front of me. I was afraid to stay, but more afraid to leave. I could feel everything – the way it felt to be touched after countless nights alone, the elation of being in each other's arms, the confusion that went alongside it, and the sadness that each of them stuffed down as they pretended in the moment that this was something   it   wasn't.   (pg.   226)*
How do you think Rachel is feeling as she watches things heat up between her sister and her fiancé? Scared? Jealous? Understanding? How would you feel in this situation?

26.   *"You smell like her," he whispered, his movements slowing as he voiced his thought. She tightened her hold on him.*

"Please, just go with it," she said. She didn't elaborate, afraid that too many words would take away from the moment. She knew he missed me, even as his body molded against hers. He needed this to be able to move past me, but also to feel close to me. She needed this for a different reason - just to feel wanted once again. (pg. 228-229)

Why do you think Sara and John are together? Could they be falling for each other? Or are they merely using each other for what they aren't getting from the one they really love?

27.   *"I don't love you anymore!" Kevin blurted out. Sara gasped, the words slicing right through her. They both stared at each other, neither one able to believe the words had been spoken. Her hands trembled as she lifted them to her mouth, her eyes filling with tears. The regret was evident in Kevin's eyes, but it was too late. "I'm sorry, Sara. I didn't mean that. I—," but she waved him off with a flip of her hand as the tears broke over the barrier of her eyes, spilling down her cheeks.*

"Don't. Don't even try to take it away. You said it. You finally said what I knew was true." (pg. 233)

Why do you think Sara and Kevin's marriage is falling apart? What could they have been doing differently to make things work?

28.   *John was confused by her reaction. The Sara he knew wouldn't be this casual about a night of passion. Or*

11

would she? He'd never been intimate with her before, so how would he know how she'd react? John realized he might not know her as well as he thought. (pg. 239)

How does John feel about Sara? How does Sara feel about John? Why do you think Sara is reacting this way to John?

29.   *"...I don't know if we're getting a divorce. Daddy and I haven't talked to each other about it."*

"Then why isn't he here?" Megan demanded.

"Because Daddy and Mommy are taking a small break from being married to each other. It's not a forever break right now, just a vacation break," she said, realizing how lame that terminology sounded. Vacations were when you went somewhere fun. This was anything but fun. (pg. 247-248)

Sara is trying to explain divorce to her kids, and what's going on between her and their father....and it's not going as well as she wanted it to. Could she have done it any differently?

Chapter 20-25

30.   *"Seems that everyone is moving into a new season," Aunt Rose said beside me, appearing next to me out of nowhere. I was no longer surprised when she appeared out of thin air, and I welcomed her regular visits. I knew she had been listening for a while before appearing, knowing she witnessed a lot of the same lives I watched over. I nodded at her sentiment, not even hiding the wistfulness attached to the reality. (pg. 255)*

How have the characters changed from the beginning of the story to where they are now?

31.   *She couldn't believe what she was hearing. Of all the scenarios that had played through her head, this was one she never thought of. She'd been so sure he was going to start making arrangements for the divorce, to discuss lawyers and paperwork, to rip her heart out of her chest and crush it with the bottom of his shoe. And here he was, wanting her back, wanting to be a family. A brief glimpse of the other night with John burst into her mind.*
"Oh god," she said, pulling her hand away from Kevin's grasp. (pg. 260)

Do you think Sara and John's romantic evening might complicate things for her and Kevin?

32.   *"But don't you see? That's exactly why that night was a mistake. You don't love me, you love the idea of me*

– the one that is mixed up with thoughts of my sister." (pg. 268)

Do you agree with what Sara is saying to John? Why?

33. *"I danced on the cables of the Golden Gate Bridge, running up the rusty orange rails toward the top of the towers and taking a long look at the expanse of the bay. I climbed into the trees on Telegraph Hill, letting the parrots that lived within the branches project their colorful thoughts back and forth from their head to mine and back again. I ran the bases at AT&T Park..." (pg. 274)*

What if you knew your time on earth was coming to an end? Where would go? Who would you visit? What would you want to experience before it was all over?

34. *It was as if time turned sideways and broke open, spilling all the contents of the future out in front of me. Time skipped, and she was there in front of him, kissing him while dressed in white as they stood in front of all their friends and family.... (pg. 281)*

In the beginning of the story, Rachel felt as if she could never let go of John. Here, she is at peace with him finding his forever mate...someone who isn't her. What happened throughout her journey to help her come full circle with her feelings?

35. *"Life is often unfair. Sometimes things have to hurt, sometimes they're even unbearable, and sometimes the pain is necessary.*

I learned this lesson the hard way. But I learned much more than just that. (pg. 283)

This passage is repeated from the prologue at the beginning of the book, but it goes on to reflect how Rachel is a new person. How would you describe her at the beginning of the story? How about now?

36.   *"Let's go," she whispered, her hushed voice filled with giddiness, her smile that of a child, and we walked through. And the songs of the angels cascaded over us, reminiscent of the cicadas' song in a forest a long, long time ago. (pg. 287)*

What do you think happens after this final scene?

37.   After reading the book, what message do you think the author is trying to tell through this story?

Bonus: Email the answer to #37, and any other thoughts you have on the book to crissi@crissilangwell.com.

Thank you for reading!

Preview of

Forever Thirteen

Coming Spring of 2014

Prelude

Thirteen is supposed to be an unlucky number, but everyone I've ever known has decided it's actually the luckiest. It's almost like a joke, staring superstition in the face and laughing at it while choosing thirteen donuts to make a Baker's Dozen, reserving a room on the thirteenth floor, or running 13.1 miles to complete a half-marathon. It's even one of the numbers my mother used on her lottery tickets, and wasn't even considered unlucky when she never won.

I guess I never viewed thirteen as unlucky, either. To me, thirteen was always a magic number – the age when a child crosses the threshold and enters the teenage years. Thirteen is supposed to be the first step on the way to first love and the very first kiss. It's when the toys are packed away to make room for books, music, a computer, and whatever else can put distance between you and childhood. It's an age when bedtimes are done away with, rules are amended, and finally, *finally* you're not seen as some dumb kid, but an almost-adult with an opinion that matters.

For as long as I could remember, I longed for the day when I would turn thirteen. I was sure that everything would change when that happened. Maybe my mom would stop babying me. Maybe I wouldn't be so fat or so lame. Maybe girls would find me attractive. Each day closer to thirteen, I added to my list of things that would happen once I became a teenager. I would get a job. I'd stop playing so many video games and start exercising to lose weight. I'd ask out Becky Johnson, that girl who never seemed to give me a second glance. I'd do something huge to be remembered forever.

Thirteen candles came and went, and not much changed. No girl ever liked me more than a friend. I was still fat and lame. And my mom continued to treat me like a child. I never crossed anything off that list. However, I did accomplish one milestone without even trying. I did something huge, something that would forever be linked to my name whenever I was thought of by those who knew me.

I died when I was thirteen.

My name is Joey, Josiah if you hate me. I am no longer alive, but a spirit in the afterlife. And I am frozen in time – stuck just on the cusp of childhood and teenager – forever young, forever short, forever awkward...

...forever thirteen.

Chapter One

Death happened without any warning at all. One moment I was in the car with my mom. In the next, a truck on the country road headed straight for us. Even when we left the roadway, headed for the trees that lined the steep hillside we had been traveling along, I never figured we'd actually die. I mean, I knew things wouldn't be good. I braced myself for the pain, the broken limbs, the shattering glass puncturing my skin. But none of it happened – rather, I don't remember the experience. Instead I recognized the fear in my mom's eyes while she reached for my hand.

"I'm sorry," she mouthed to me in that moment. *I love you,* I thought back to her, the silent words piercing through me while I squeezed her hand, holding on to it with all my strength as if her mere grasp could save us both. *I wish I could have had more time to tell you,* I screamed in my head, losing myself in her face while the world streamed by us. *You were a great mom, and I'm sorry for all I put you through,* I pleaded with her through the connection of my hand in hers. But I was so afraid of what we were about to experience, all I could do was nod without ever saying a word.

And then I was ripped from her grasp and thrown from my body.

I never felt the crash, though I knew it had happened. There was no mistake that we'd been through something terrible because in one moment our fragile car had been hurtling through the trees, and in the next I was lying on the ground, staring into the vacant face of my body. I couldn't stop looking at myself – or rather, what used to be me underneath a series of wounds that littered my pale skin. It wasn't like peering into the mirror, moving my head from side to side to see my expression from all points of view. Instead, it was like seeing an old friend, a familiar face that I never wanted to leave despite the ghastly condition the body – my body! – was in. But it was the only recognizable thing in this strange forest. I lay there next to my body, both of us on the forest floor for hours while I memorized the faded freckles that were scattered across my nose and the dimness in my amber eyes staring back at me.

In the distance I could hear the soft singing of birds and an eery buzzing of insects that hid within the trees. It all served as background noise while I studied every part of me I'd once seen with hypercritical eyes. Too chubby, too ugly, too stupid. It had been my mantra whenever I peered at my reflection in the mirror, pointing out every imperfection and ignoring everything else. Every blemish had been a red flag to me, waving with wild abandon to announce the hopelessness inside of me that I would never be enough in this world. And now, I embraced these imperfections one by one, wishing more than anything I could reclaim them as my own, just to be alive again.

I knew I needed to find it in me to leave this forest, or at least separate myself from my body. But I was afraid to venture away. Where would I go? What was I supposed to do? It occurred to me just how alone I was. My mom was nowhere in sight, and I wondered if she had died, too.

"Mom," I whispered into the thick air, my voice breaking the strange muted noises of the forest without even an echo to give it life. "Mom!" I called out, willing my voice to venture out beyond the trees that surrounded my spirit and my broken body. But my voice remained stagnant in the air just before me. And I never heard my mom respond back.

I stood up, stepping around my body as if it and I were of the same world. And I craned my neck to see the tops of the trees. It only surprised me a little when I rose from the ground, floating to the canopy of the forest without any effort at all. While aware that this motion was anything but simple in my former life, it was as natural as breathing in this new spiritual existence. Nonetheless, when I reached the tip of the tallest tree, I held onto the slender branches as if holding on for dear life. From there, I scanned the confines of the forest. However, it was like the entire shelter of trees was encased in a glass terrarium. I could hear the soft singing of birds, but they sounded so far away. The song of the insects could only be heard when I strained to listen for their buzzing harmony. If I didn't concentrate on the sounds of the forest, I was encased in silence. My ears seemed clogged with water, and I shook my head to rid myself of the clouded feeling.

Nothing helped. But I did have the distinct feeling I was being watched.

5

I spun around from the top branches of the redwood I was gripping, and saw a young girl around the age of six. She felt familiar, though I couldn't quite place why I knew her. Even so, the slight recognition gave me the same comfort I felt when I was close to my body. Here was someone I knew, even if I didn't know how. If nothing else, she represented something safe in a world where I knew no one and didn't know which direction to turn.

"Hello," I said to her, the sound of my voice hanging in front of me. Frustrated, I shook my head once again. I needed to be clear of the fog that separated me from the rest of the world, and from this young girl. In the strangeness of my new reality, I yearned for a connection with anything. The fact that I still couldn't reach her, despite our close proximity, left me feeling lost. To my relief, she smiled. She could hear me.

She drifted closer until she was hovering in front of me. Up close I could almost count the freckles that crossed her nose. Her face was young, the softness of her features like that of an infant. But it was her eyes that were the most mesmerizing. I had a hard time drawing away from them, the blue-green kaleidoscope of color, and the whole world reflected in her irises. While her face was that of a six-year-old child, her eyes held thousands of years.

She reached her hands towards me. I didn't flinch, trusting her even though I didn't know what she was going to do. With a flutter of her hands, the world broke open, the figurative glass shattering while the life that surrounded the two of us thrust itself within my senses. I was now aware of every movement, every sound, every musing inside the crowded forest of towering redwoods. I absorbed the flurry of images bouncing through the minds of wildlife that called this wooded haven their home – from the squirrels foraging on the ground to the cicadas hiding in the leaves of the trees. I observed the thoughts of the emergency crew that had now reached my body and were preparing to take it away; I heard their unvoiced dismay that a child of my age would have died in such a way. And I searched for my mom, scanning every inch of the forest floor through the curtain of trees. With heightened senses, I found I could see past the thick branches and flourishing pine needles, receiving a telescopic view of anything I wished to perceive. But my mother was nowhere to be found.

I turned to the young girl, and she smiled once again while she took my hand. *She's not here,* the girl said. But she didn't say it with her mouth. Instead, she placed the words in my head from her thoughts to mine.

"Then where –" I stopped talking, surprised by the sound of my voice ringing through the air. Free from the invisible shield that had encased me, my tone resounded all around us, the echo of my voice bouncing off the trees and back to my ears. I laughed at the amused expression dancing in the little girl's eyes, knowing that the newness I was experiencing was like watching a puppy discover small parts of the world a piece at a time. "Where is she?" I murmured, my voice still echoing across the tops of the trees, but this time much quieter.

I'm not quite sure, she projected to me. *She could be here, but in another dimension of our existence. Or she could be somewhere else in the afterlife.*

"But she died, too?" I asked her, already certain that the answer was yes. But the girl just shrugged her shoulders.

I'm not here for her. I'm here for you.

Her answer confused me. Here for me? Who was this girl? I wanted to ask her, but the smell of smoke interrupted my curiosities. A flock of birds flew from the woods, covering the sky like a dark cloud before scattering in all directions. Flames appeared out of nowhere, licking at my feet as they crept up the tree I clung to. While I was certain the fire couldn't burn me, I could still feel the intense heat of the wild blaze, the flames threatening to consume the large redwoods that had once served as the canopy sheltering my lifeless body.

All around us was chaos while the habitants of the forest scrambled to safety. I could sense the panic in the wilderness, and it echoed in my own thoughts despite the fact that this fire couldn't kill what was already dead.

Come with me, the girl projected to me, taking my hand. My last vision of the forest was the first drops of rain falling from the darkened sky, landing on the fire with a sizzle. The black smoke mingled with delicate strands of white, and the whole world lost color and faded away. With a lurch in the pit of my belly, the forest disappeared and everything turned black. I could feel our surroundings race past us, though I couldn't see a thing. But the speed with which we were traveling left me with an uneasy queasiness inside. I shut my eyes and held her hand tight, wishing it were over.

Open your eyes, she instructed, loosening her hand from my grip. Frantic, I reached for her again, afraid to lose her in our plummet through the nothingness, and in terror peered through a slit in my eyes. I was amazed to see we were no longer surrounded by darkness, but by a vast ocean that surrounded us on all sides. I was perched on a rock that sat in the middle of the calm waters, and the waves lapped at my toes under a flawless sky. Hovering next to me, the girl descended to a seat on the rock and rested her hand on mine. We sat in silence for hours, taking in the view of the setting sun mirrored in the dark waters. The colors of the sky deepened from light cerulean blues to deep rosy hues, shifting to plum tones before settling into an opaque onyx sky littered with millions of sparkling stars. The papaya crescent of the moon emerged from the waters at our side. It appeared so close I felt like I could reach out my hand and touch the textured valleys of the lunar surface.

"Everything is so beautiful," I told her, managing to keep my voice quiet, and absorbing the world with new eyes while the ocean shimmered around us. I could hear the songs of the whales deep under our feet in the darkness of the waters. The sound of the waves danced through the air like bells chiming in the wind. I felt warm inside, happier than I had never felt before, at peace in this strange new existence. I wished my mom could be there with me, experiencing all the wonders of the planet we resided in with senses never before exercised.

The thought of my mom brought on a hint of sadness. It burrowed itself within the warmth bubbling inside me, unfurling into a feeling of intense anguish. I realized I might never see her again. The beauty of our surroundings

9

was forgotten, and the first teardrops filled my eyes and spilled down my cheeks.

The young girl held my hand while my tears erupted into a downpour of emotion. I'd been holding my emotions at bay since I first came upon my body and realized that my life was over. There were so many things I still wanted to do, things I wanted to be. I had only been thirteen. I hadn't even received my first kiss, or known what it was like to fall in love. I'd never know what it was like to be taller than I was now. I was stuck at awkward forever.

****

"It's just a stupid party," I said to my best friend, Cameron, peering over his shoulder at the flier he held. Abby, one of the more popular girls at school, smiled back at us from the piece of paper. Her face was surrounded by exclamations, "Celebrate my 13th birthday!" "Bash of the year!" and the one that petrified me the most, "Come in your favorite jammies!" If we were being honest with ourselves, this invitation was never meant for us. Cameron had discovered it at the base of his locker, leaning up against the metal door. To him, it was a clear attempt to get the invite into his hands. Watching our classmates gab about the party on their way to their next class, I couldn't help but pretend we'd been invited for real.

But being invited and going were two different things.

"Cameron, we can't really go to this party." I was never more aware of how chubby he was, fatter than me, or how he breathed through his mouth when he was excited about something. Most of the time these things didn't matter. Neither one of us was even close to making it onto the list of most popular guys. Still, we were geeks together, and that made all of our downfalls disappear. But when it came to being surrounded by a bunch of kids way cooler than we could ever hope to be, all of the things that kept us from reaching the status of the social elite was painfully obvious. "I mean, what do you think they're going to do if we show up?"

"I don't know, give us cake?" he said. I groaned. That was just the thing we needed, more cake to add to our flabby midsections. "Besides," Cameron continued, "it looks like Becky is going."

I glanced in the direction he was gesturing and held my breath while Becky made her way down the hall, surrounded by a group of friends. Our eyes met, and everyone in the hall disappeared except for us. It was just for a moment, and when she looked away the hall was filled with our classmates once again. But in that second, I was sure my heart had stopped beating. She passed us by, leaving a scented trail of her shampoo and the lingering smell of her lotion behind her. I couldn't miss the flier she held in her hands.

I should have listened to my initial instincts. But two nights later, I was standing in the center of Abby's backyard basketball court wearing blue flannel pajama bottoms and a sweatshirt, clutching a red cup of punch like my life depended on it. Cameron stood next to me, taking in the party in his Batman pajamas as if we weren't out of place. And all around us were our classmates, everyone wearing t-shirts and sweat pants instead of actual pajamas like we were.

"What are *they* doing here?" Todd Sanders sneered at us, saying it loud enough to Abby so we were sure to hear him. Abby laughed and pushed Todd in the arm.

"Stop it!" she giggled. "They're fine." I had always liked her, even if we had never spoken a word together before. She grabbed two plates with cake and headed over to us, holding them out to us as if she were giving us the world. She may as well have been. I hadn't planned on eating anything there, certain that a missed piece of cake might help me lose a few pounds in one night. But there was no way I could refuse the plate of green and blue frosting that she offered. Soon, small bites of sweetness were exploding into my mouth, even while I felt my stomach growing larger.

"Cool pajamas," Abby said to Cameron. His mouth was too full to properly respond, but his muffled words sounded like he was thanking her. "No one took it seriously that this was a pajama party, so it's cool that you guys actually wore pajamas." She didn't wait for a reply before turning around and going back to her friends.

I decided to accept the fact that we were here, even as out of place as we were. My mom wouldn't be picking us up for another two hours, anyway. Cameron had already sat down in the middle of the court, so I lowered myself to the ground next to him and rested my cake on my knee. All around us, groups of friends were split up into their separate cliques. While Cameron and I stared out at everyone at the party, they were engrossed with each other, talking and laughing and oblivious to us.

I scanned the crowd of guests, none of them catching my interest. There was only one face I wished to see, and that was Becky Johnson's. I didn't rest from seeking her out until I found her. To my dismay, so had Todd. He leaned close to her, his mouth whispering something in her ear while she listened with intent to whatever he was telling her. She giggled, her dark hair swinging behind her, her chin tucked down in laughter. My heart sank when I saw Todd reach for her hand, both devastated and in awe of how simple he made the action seem. I could never be that smooth.

From that point on, it was like watching a horror movie. I couldn't turn away, no matter how terrifying the images were. I watched them snuggle closer together to keep warm against the dropping temperature. They shared private glances, their fingers laced together. My eyes followed them when they migrated away from the group and formed their own private twosome. And when Todd leaned over and kissed Becky on the mouth, my stomach did a slow somersault. I groaned in discomfort, regretting the piece of cake I'd inhaled.

"I think I'm going to be sick," I whispered to Cameron. Before he could react, I scrambled to my feet and ran to the darkest part of the yard and started heaving.

"Gross!" one girl squealed. My head pounded and the sharp pains in my stomach cut me in two, and I couldn't help but feel grateful when everyone scattered from where I was throwing up. The nauseating smell of sweet frosting made sour by stomach acids mingled with the scent of earth, and it overwhelmed my runny nose. If ever there was a time to give up cake forever, this was it.

"Are you okay?" Cameron asked behind me. He placed his hand on my back, unfazed by the contents of my stomach in a puddle below me. I wanted to tell him to go away, that he was making things worse by comforting me. But my stomach was still churning, the motion setting off a chain reaction of vomit until nothing was left inside me. Even then, I couldn't stop lurching forward, my insides twisting in anguish. And as much as I didn't want to admit it, Cameron's hand on my back made me feel less alone while everyone else stood far away and watched me retch into the dirt. His hand was the only thing anchoring me down. And he stayed near me until my mom came early to pick us up.

To be continued…

To be notified of the release of
Forever Thirteen
sign up at
crissilangwell.com/mailing-list